**"Can we ever stop being agents?"
Jack asked suddenly. "Truly?"**

Lark froze, her lips millimeters from his. "Why not?"

"I never know what's real with you."

Slowly, Lark tipped her chin to see his face. Jack's expression—or what she could see of it—was thoughtful. The shades had to go. Sliding upward, she pulled off his sunglasses and kissed him.

The effect was instant. His fingers tangled in her hair, drawing her close. Lark's pulse began to pound, a giddy pleasure tingling through her body. The warm electricity coursing in her veins found a home low in her belly at the same time his fingers slid beneath her shirt, seeking out the lacy edges of her bra. Her fingers curled in the soft cotton of his sweater, gathering bunches of the fabric as she leaned in, savoring his flavor.

"Does it feel like I'm seducing you for nefarious reasons?" Jack asked.

"You've done it before."

Sharon Ashwood is a novelist, desk jockey and enthusiast for the weird and spooky. She has an English literature degree but works as a finance geek. Interests include growing her to-be-read pile and playing with the toy graveyard on her desk. Sharon is the winner of the 2011 RITA® Award for Paranormal Romance. She lives in the Pacific Northwest and is owned by the Demon Lord of Kitty Badness.

Books by Sharon Ashwood

HARLEQUIN NOCTURNE

Possessed by a Warrior
Possessed by an Immortal
Possessed by a Wolf
Possessed by the Fallen

HARLEQUIN NOCTURNE CRAVINGS

Lord Dragon's Conquest
Valkyrie's Conquest

POSSESSED
BY THE FALLEN

—

SHARON ASHWOOD

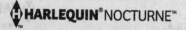

Recycling programs
for this product may
not exist in your area.

ISBN-13: 978-0-373-00949-7

Possessed by the Fallen

Copyright © 2015 by Naomi Lester

Printed in U.S.A.

www.Harlequin.com

Dear Reader,

To say Lark and Jack have baggage is the biggest understatement since the Crusades. He's a vampire and she's a fairy double agent, but that's only half the problem. Their previous breakup occurred at knifepoint, she got badly burned in a fire and he perished in a high-speed chase—but what's a love story without a few setbacks?

There's nothing like a common enemy—an evil fairy queen, no less—to bring sparring ex-lovers back together again. Both Jack and Lark are determined to guard a royal wedding, but the Dark Fey are about to break out of prison and destroy the happy day—not to mention everything else in their path. Our hero and heroine have to boldly venture into treacherous fairy-tale lands to put things right.

It doesn't take long for desire to spark between Jack and Lark, and that only complicates things. There are trolls and dragons to battle, but inner demons—literal and metaphorical—pose the greatest challenge. Love heals, but love also demands revealing our personal monsters. To put it mildly, that's just messy.

Romance is seen as the discovery of another. But what do you do when you find out your beloved is the enemy?

Best wishes and happy reading,

Sharon Ashwood

This is for those readers
who have followed the Horsemen along with me.
I hope you've enjoyed the ride as much as I have!

Alone we can do so little.
Together we can do so much.

—Helen Keller

Prologue

Fairy tales often begin with humans making foolish choices, and this is no exception.

Long ago, three princes lived in a kingdom on the north shore of the Mediterranean Sea: Vidon, Marcari and their youngest brother, known as Silverhand. The best of the three, Silverhand became a knight and went to the Holy Land during the first war of the Crusades.

In time, he returned with a fortune in gems, planning to share it with his brothers. Unexpectedly—or perhaps not—Silverhand was murdered as he slept and the treasure was stolen. Vidon and Marcari quickly accused one another of the crime and so began a war between brothers that split the country in two.

It was not just a war of humans—the brothers dragged the Night World into their affairs. The Dark Fey fought for Vidon, the Light Fey for Marcari. Vampires and were-wolves also did battle for one side or the other, and the slaughter was epic.

Vidon blamed the carnage on the supernatural creatures, even though he had himself enlisted their aid. He demanded his knights swear vengeance upon them, and so Vidon's realm became a nation of slayers.

However, Marcari took responsibility for his all-too-human greed. Recognizing his sense of honor, the vampires pledged him their service. They became *La Compagnie des Morts*, or the Company of the Dead. So it was that the Kingdom of Marcari became a refuge for the supernatural, who were forever hunted by their enemies, the Knights of Vidon.

But the one thing everyone could agree on was that the Dark Fey had to go. Under the leadership of their queen, they had committed crimes of war that sickened even the werewolves. A spell was cast to lock the Dark Queen and her people behind magical gates, and they were banished from the mortal realms forevermore.

Or not. You never know with fairies.

Fast forward to the present day when Crown Prince Kyle of Vidon proposed marriage to Princess Amelie, the only child of the reigning king of Marcari. Here, nine centuries and many, many generations later, was a chance for peace between the two nations.

Needless to say, the Dark Queen and her exiled clan were not invited to the wedding. In fact, most had forgotten she still lived.

That was not wise.

Chapter 1

"Enemy agents are coming to kill you," Jack Anderson said, sarcasm leaking into his tone. "Do you think you might want some help with that?"

"Don't exaggerate. It's nothing I can't handle." Jessica Lark sat behind her desk. At the moment she was glad to have the heavy piece of furniture between her and Jack. If she touched him or smelled the clean, spicy scent of his skin, she would surely lose her nerve. Whether as a lover or as an operative, Jack was a formidable presence.

He was darkly handsome in a way that made women stop and turn, the blue of his eyes like an arctic sky, pure and wild. With wings and a flaming sword, he might have been the archangel Michael—but Jack would have mocked the comparison. He was a vampire of the Company of the Dead, a covert agent and pure sin between the sheets.

And Lark was about to betray him. She was afraid, but beneath the trepidation a hot ball of grief hovered in her chest. She missed Jack already. She'd made the basic mistake of falling in love with her mark.

Her expression must have betrayed her nerves. Jack leaned forward, his hands on the desk. Those eyes of his, so icy cool with everyone else, were warm with concern. "Are you sure you don't want my help? You're the lead on this. It's your call, but if you think they're coming here to-night, you need backup."

"This is only a burglary, so no big deal. I have an alarm system," she said lightly.

"Alarms don't help if you're here alone and the thieves have weapons. I know you're tough, but you're only one agent."

She shrugged. "I don't know if my information is good. You're worrying over something that probably won't happen."

His grimace said she was an idiot, and he was right. She was absolutely certain she was about to get a visit from the bad guys, but bringing them down single-handedly would be a redemption of sorts. An apology for what she was about to do, and maybe proof that Lark of the Light Fey wasn't altogether a traitor.

She pushed back from her desk, crossing to an armoire against the wall. Her Manhattan design atelier was huge—wood floors, cutting tables and bare brick walls with high arched windows to let in the light. Now those windows looked out on the glamour of the New York nightscape that sparkled like a fantasy through the darkness. This was Lark's kingdom, and she was its queen of fashion and beauty. Any one of her clothing designs fetched a ransom. Starlets and royalty came knocking at her door.

And so did creatures from the Night World. Jack was by far the most civilized among them, but there were others. She'd warded her private office so that no one could see or hear anything extraordinary, not even her assistant right outside the door. Lark was well prepared for sudden upsets.

"Lark, listen." Jack shoved his hands into his pockets. He was wearing a gray flannel suit, the artful cut of his jacket hiding his many weapons. "Let me stay tonight."

"You'll spook them if they come, and waste your time if they don't."

"I'll do surveillance from a safe distance. If nothing happens, we'll go for a drink and call it a night."

Lark paused, tempted. She fingered the handle of the armoire, wishing she could change her mind. It would be so easy to agree and let everything stay the same. She'd be safe, Jack would remain her lover and she'd keep this glamorous life a little longer. Her masters in the Light Court, the ones who'd sent her to spy on Jack, would be none the wiser. Sometimes orders could be dodged, at least for a while.

But she was a double agent. Behind the masks of fashion queen and playboy, she and Jack worked for the Company. And behind *that* mask, she worked for her own people. She was weaving a very tangled web—but then she was a fey. Tangled webs were their favorite thing.

She opened the armoire door, sticking to her plan. If she failed now, she condemned her entire race. What was a single love affair weighed against that? *Selfishness. Weakness. Cowardice.* Lark swallowed down burning regret.

"I'll be fine. I have something I need you to do." She pulled a dress box from the armoire and walked it over to her desk.

"What's this?" Jack asked.

Lark lifted the lid. Inside was a nest of blue tissue paper, and beneath it a glittering confection of white satin and lace. It was the masterpiece of the collection she'd been commissioned to create for the royal wedding, and as a designer it was her personal best. She touched the garment lightly, feeling a surge of pride. "It's Princess Amelie's wedding dress, sewn with the Marcari diamonds. This is what the enemy agents are after. Between the gems and the dress itself, it's worth a fortune."

A fortune the enemy would use for much worse crimes than theft. Every diamond would fund countless deaths. Lark put a hand on Jack's sleeve. "I need you to get it away from here. Make sure Amelie wears it on her wedding day."

Jack gave her an incredulous look. "So you want me to save the dress and leave you here to face the thieves?"

Lark slipped the lid back on the box, feeling a flush of dismay creeping up her cheeks. *It would be so much easier if he didn't care.* "Yes. You save the dress. They can't steal what's not here."

Jack slipped an arm around her waist. "Forget the gown. Amelie has a palace full of dresses. I've got only you."

She turned, bracing her palms against his chest, putting a few inches between them. "I'm not covered with a significant portion of the crown jewels."

Undeterred, he bent forward, his lips brushing her cheek. "I'd like to see that," he said, voice intimate and teasing. "Just the diamonds. Nothing else but skin."

"Promise me you'll take the dress. Give me your word." *Don't kiss me. I can't bear it if you kiss me.*

His brows furrowed. "I'll take it, if it's that important to you."

"It is. It's Princess Amelie's wedding. Whatever else happens, she deserves a perfect dress for it."

That was absolutely true, as was the fact someone would try to steal the gown and its jewels tonight. Preventing the theft—and the crimes that would flow from the stolen fortune—was her last act as a Company agent, and one she had to complete. Hopefully it would salve the guilt to come.

"I give you my word," Jack said, obviously confused.

"Good." If he gave his word, he would do it, regardless of whatever horrible thing she did next. There was something to be said for the old, proud vampires and their sense of honor.

Jack took her arms, turning her to face him. "You're shivering. What's gotten into you?"

She froze, her head bowed, not able to answer right away. She was desperately trying to keep her mission front and center in her mind. Her people were weak, at a time when their darkest enemy threatened to return. The Light Fey needed a weapon—and Jack was the most powerful vampire walking the earth. Lark's mission was to find and harness that source of strength.

But whatever made Jack unique was a secret he guarded closely. Two years in his bed had given her only the smallest of clues, and she'd run out of time and options.

He was looking at her as if she was the most precious creature on the planet.

"You're different from anyone I've ever known," she finally said. "You're different from other vampires."

"I don't know about that," he said quickly. But it was true.

Lark looked up into his face. His brows were drawn together. Tension was creeping into his expression—an awareness something was seriously wrong. Regret plunged through her, stiletto sharp. Beneath Jack's power and courage, beneath the physical beauty and astonishing strength, was the kindest heart she knew. *I love you, but my people are dying. Our children don't live to see their first name day, and I was the one chosen to help. Forgive me for this.*

She slid the spelled dagger from her sleeve, and with a quick, upward thrust she drove it into his abdomen. She was strong, but it took all her force to pierce the hard wall of his abdomen. Their cries mingled for a horrible moment—his filled with surprise, hers with grief.

It wasn't a fatal blow—not to a vampire—but the magic in the blade would rip away every secret he possessed. Lark looked into his eyes, and knew her mistake with mounting dread.

Secrets, once revealed, can't be unlearned.

Kingdom of Marcari
February, nine months later

"It's time you came in, Jack."

Jack Anderson gripped the cell phone, but he didn't respond to the gritty voice telling him to give up almost a year of surveillance work. He'd wait a beat before disobeying orders, even if he'd already made up his mind. Somehow, it seemed more polite.

Silence only made the narrow backstreet that much lonelier despite the quitting-time rush on the neighboring roads. Sunset had flamed out, and now the February dusk seeped into the stone and wrought iron of Marcari's ancient capital. Jack welcomed the growing darkness, his vampire's mind sharpening as the night breezes rose. "I'm close to figuring out exactly what the Dark Fey are plotting. Crashing the royal wedding is just their opening number."

"Maybe," said the commander of *La Compagnie des Morts*, "but I need you here. Now. Tonight. We've got intelligence you're going to want to look at."

Jack grunted. "Is there a connection to my investigation?"

"What else? I don't call in undercover agents just to spoil their fun."

Jack leaned against the wall, a shadow melting into shadows. The moment he set foot into Headquarters' compound, everyone would know he was still walking the earth. "There's a difference between having a look and coming in off a case. I've spent too long on this. Besides, everyone believes I'm dead."

"So? They'll be pleasantly surprised."

"I'm tired of surprises."

Last spring had been bad for Jack. First his lover had stabbed him, and a week later he'd nearly burned to death in a fiery car crash arranged by extremely determined assassins. He'd used the opportunity—and some skills he liked to keep to himself—to drop off the grid and start hunting the hunters. But that had meant cutting himself off from anyone who mattered, and there was no way he was letting that sacrifice swirl down the drain.

The commander seemed to read his thoughts. "I'm not asking this lightly. This is about the Company."

Jack wanted details. "Is there anything you can tell me?"

"Yes, come straight to my office. My counterparts in administration have called a general meeting and everyone else will be in the auditorium talking policy. That will give you and me a chance to meet undisturbed and undetected. You'll be gone before anyone knows you're here."

"And?" Jack prodded.

The commander's voice dropped low. "There's a threat close to home and it needs your expertise. Fast and silent. Even you'll agree that what I've got trumps your mission."

"There are other qualified agents. Get Sam Ralston on it."

"Stop arguing and get your undead arse in here tonight. You're pushing your luck with me." The line went dead.

A blinding flash of anger surged through Jack. He swore, stuffing the phone into his pocket and struggling for calm. A fit of temper might as well have been a spark among gunpowder. Strong emotion made Jack's self-control falter.

Without warning, his body burned with tingling waves of raw power. It climbed as his mood darkened, seeming to feed off wounded pride and rage. Jack sucked in a breath of cold air and leaned his head against the bricks, reasserting mastery. In the deepening shadows, he could see arcs of blue static crawling over the bare skin of his palms. It was the mark of the curse that bound him to demonkind. He curled his fingers, hiding the web of light. Hiding the evidence of what he really was—and the destructive power that implied.

Jack's head pounded as he reeled the power back into his core. It felt like dragging barbed wire through his flesh. The raw force of his abilities was as brutal as a keg of explosives—and about as useless, unless he intended mass destruction. *But that's why they call it a curse, and not a bonus gift from the superpower catalog.*

The blue fire finally winked out, and Jack slumped against the bricks, his muscles rubbery as they unclenched.

The pain receded slowly, leaving a faint nausea in its wake. He'd won. His control was still stronger. A flicker of pride stirred, soon drowned in plain old relief. His secret was safe for another night.

After nine centuries, he wondered if the iron control he relied on was all that remained of his humanity. When that went, the taint of the Fallen would take him over—an unthinkable end. Demons made the worst vampires look as cuddly as shar-pei puppies.

Jack's symptoms were getting worse.

With that happy thought, Jack started walking, his footfalls silent. The winding road between the buildings was typical of Marcari's old quarter, hardly wide enough for two cars to pass without locking side mirrors. Light spilled from a café ahead, and he instinctively moved out of the glow. After spending so long as a spy, invisibility had become a habit. And yet, he felt the telltale tug on his consciousness that said someone had seen him and was interested.

Jack slowed. There was no sound or scent, nor did a casual glance reveal movement in the darkness. That meant his shadow belonged to the fey. Only they could touch another's mind with such delicacy.

Tired of being stalked, he stopped and spun on his heel. The psychic touch withdrew as suddenly as a hand snatched away. "What do you want?" he snapped.

His words hung in the darkness. Dusk had deepened to night, and a faint drizzle made the cobbled street glisten. The pungent smoke of French cigarettes wafted from the crowd at the café door, along with bursts of jazz from the sound system. For a long moment, Jack waited for a reply.

And then a piece of the shadows seemed to grow more solid, separating itself into a denser blackness. It wasn't exactly movement, but was enough to catch Jack's eye. His tail was using a glamour, one of the fey spells that tricked the senses. Such magic could make a person look, sound or smell like someone else or disappear altogether. "And people wonder why I don't trust your kind," he growled.

The darkness shifted until he saw a slender figure on the opposite side of the narrow road. Even without the benefit of detail, there was no doubt it was female. The curves were just right by Jack's standard, full despite her lithe frame. Memory tugged, aching to color in features the shadows erased—but the person he wanted to see was lost to him forever.

"Trust is a slippery creature," the woman's voice said. There was something achingly familiar in that silvery, feminine softness—like a dream that lingered on waking.

The voice came again. "Will your friends trust you when they find out you're still alive, Jack?"

It can't be her. But vampire hearing didn't lie, and ghosts didn't haunt the undead.

Chapter 2

Jack's first reaction was shock, a sheer incredulity that Jessica Lark was alive. He staggered forward a step as if jerked on a leash. He wasn't a creature given to emotion, but his heart ached as if it had suffered a terrible blow. And then a second reaction slammed home—anger. "You tried to kill me."

"No, I didn't. You're a vampire. A knife to the gut would never kill you." She stirred, the darkness still washing out detail, but Jack could see enough now to be sure it was Lark. "But everyone believes you died when you wrecked your Porsche. Or rather, when a gunman helped you wreck it." She added the last bit more softly, as if she actually cared.

"I survived." His words came automatically, almost devoid of feeling. Seeing Lark, hearing her, was too much. Every possible emotion was making a log jam in his gut. As if he was going to overload, Jack's fingers began to shake. "I survived, but not all the shooters did. The body they found was one of theirs."

"And no one noticed they had the wrong vampire?"

"My servant identified the remains and immediately went into witness protection. I owe him a big favor."

She made a noise that sounded suspiciously like a whispered curse. The scent of her fear found Jack, giving him a twinge of satisfaction. She'd seen his demon side, and she knew she'd crossed him. She had every reason to tremble.

But vengeance wasn't all he hungered for. What he felt was infinitely more complex, and simple revenge wasn't going to satisfy him. He took two more steps, shock robbing his movements of grace.

"Jack?" she said cautiously, pulling her trench coat closer.

He raised his arms, his first instinct to touch her. She swayed forward, but the moment dissolved once her gaze flickered across his face. Whatever she saw there stopped her cold.

Jack let his arms fall. "How do I know it's really you?"

Her full lips twitched. "Do you think I'm a warty goblin out to trick you into kissing me?"

"Your design studio burned the night you stabbed me," he said, keeping his voice even. "I thought you died."

She moved a step deeper into the shadows, keeping distance between them. "I almost did. It's taken me until now to recover. Whoever tried to kill you got to me first. There was more than a simple robbery that night." She lifted her chin as if daring him to doubt her. "Go ahead and say it. I should have let you stay."

"Instead of sticking a knife in me?" This time, he let his anger show. "Don't bother asking forgiveness for that one."

Her head bowed, as graceful as a flower. "I won't."

"Good. It'll save us both time."

Silence fell. Jack could hear his own breathing, harsh with emotion, but Lark remained immobile as a mouse beneath a hawk's shadow. After a long time, Jack found composure enough to go on. "But you survived."

"I like to defy expectations," she said, lifting her gaze. Her eyes held a trace of rebellion. It was a look he knew too well.

"Why didn't I know you were still alive?" he demanded softly.

They were within a few paces of each other now. He could see the mass of her hair falling past her shoulders. Old memories prompted him to touch it, to feel the soft mahogany waves spring beneath his fingers. His hand reached out to her almost of its own accord.

She held up a hand, palm out. "Stop, Jack. Stop where you are."

"Why?" He reluctantly obeyed, his fingers closing on nothing. He could smell her anxiety, sharp and tantalizing, but he could also sense her desire. Her clash of emotions resonated through him, at once delicious and heartbreaking.

"You know why." Her voice was barely more than a whisper.

Because you're afraid of me. Because you know I don't trust you. He clenched his jaw, rejecting everything but the urge to touch her. He'd loved her, loathed her, thought her dead, and now she was inches away. Faster than thought, his hand cupped her cheek. It was like silk, cool from the night air, but beneath that perfect surface, life beat hot and red.

He felt her flinch, but pretended he hadn't. Right then, denying logic or even a decent sense of self-preservation, he needed her the way mortals needed breath. "Just this once, tell me the truth."

But he didn't give her a chance to speak. For a delirious instant, desire trumped his wrath. His free hand closed on her shoulder, pinning her against the rough stone of the wall. Although she was strong enough, he moved too quickly for her to struggle. Her sigh came out in a warm rush, fanning his face. She was so alive.

Almost against his will, his mouth closed over hers. Now that he had her in his hands, Jack knew beyond a doubt she was Lark and no fey trick upon his senses. His body knew her—the exotic scent, the rhythm of her breath, the feel of her skin under his. No glamour was that precise. Jack remembered every intoxicating detail, even if he'd tried to scour her out of his soul. "I mourned for you."

"And I for you."

But her voice cracked on the words. He could feel her

pulse, speeding with the rush of her panic. She'd seen the demon in him, and it terrified her. The sensation of it went straight to his sex, making him press closer. She struggled a moment, but it was barely for the span of one racing heartbeat. And then she surrendered—or stood her ground—fitting herself to him as if they'd never been apart. Her kiss told him everything he longed for.

As a human, Jack had thirsted in the desert, and she was sweeter than the taste of life-giving water. But poetry wasn't uppermost in his thoughts. Lust and hunger uncoiled inside him, bringing out his fangs. He braced his arms on either side of her, his fingers digging into the wall. Stone and mortar crumbled in a shower of dust.

Her body arched under his, the movement showing her smooth, white throat. His tongue found the spot where her skin was warm and fragrant, tasting the beat of her heart through the thinnest veil of flesh. He pressed his mouth there, teasing with the points of his teeth. Her skin held the tang of fear, though still she refused to show it completely.

At the sharp intake of her breath, he broke away. His head was starting to spin with the need for blood, and he didn't trust his self-control. There was too much anger in him to be completely safe.

Slowly, Lark's eyes met his, the low light turning their rich brown color to black. Her voice was hoarse with lust and regret. "I disappeared after the fire because I was hiding from the men who tried to kill me. And you were dead, or so I thought. Fiery deaths were trending last season, in case you don't remember."

Jack drew back with a noise of disgust, sanity crawling back like a whipped dog. "It was nice of you to grieve, after the knife and all. Although you obviously knew I was walking the earth, or you wouldn't be following me."

The sudden widening of her eyes said he'd caught her out. "There were rumors in the Light Court that you were in Marcari, but I didn't let my heart believe it until I saw you on the street a few days ago. I don't know what to think about you anymore, Jack. Not after our last conversation."

"Conversation," he mocked. "That's a polite description for stabbing your lover."

She was shivering, but he knew better than to think it was just the cold. *Our last conversation.* The magic in the knife had ripped away his self-control, and Jack had let his demon side show. It was the only slip he'd ever made in his long life, but she'd learned his secret that night.

That discovery had been her mission, the game between them, and she'd won. He'd loved Lark as he'd never loved anyone in all his long centuries, but she had been nothing more than a spy in his bed.

What she'd learned was a danger to him. In purely practical terms, her death that same night had solved his problem, even as it left a world of unresolved pain. Now he had to decide what to do about her sudden resurrection.

He cupped her face again—none too gently—his thumb stroking her cheekbone. "Who did you tell about me?" he asked.

"No one." She pulled away.

"I find that hard to believe. You don't go to such lengths and not follow through."

"I was hospitalized. I couldn't talk, just think. I decided I wouldn't tell unless…"

"Unless?"

Her eyes narrowed. "Unless I needed to."

That meant she had leverage over him. Anger sparked, and his fingers curled into a fist. "That covers a lot of circumstances and a lot of convenient excuses."

She shot him a sour look. "Believe what you like."

"What about your orders from the Light Court?" A single spark of blue energy snaked across his hand.

"They were too busy healing my burns to ask questions."

"So you stabbed me for no reason."

"It's not that simple, Jack. They were curious about the

source of your strength and whether it was something they could replicate. Now I know it isn't. I can afford to say nothing."

Jack didn't answer, but closed his hand over the spark. If she was telling the truth, she was picking and choosing the bits that suited her.

She slowly shook her head. "You're changing."

"What's that got to do with anything?"

She put up both hands. Her back was against the wall, a whisper of space between them, but her expression wasn't giving an inch. "You don't see it, but there's something going on with you. I overheard your conversation with the commander."

Jack didn't doubt she had. Fey ears were almost as good as a vampire's. "So?"

"You've always been the perfect soldier, and right now you're sailing close to the edge of subordination. Plus, you're sparking like a faulty coffeemaker. You're losing ground to what's inside you."

He walked away a few steps. She was right, but putting distance between them was easier than framing a reply—especially when he had no good answers.

"How can I help you, Jack?" she asked, her voice suddenly soft with concern.

"You can't," he said, barely giving it a thought. Even if he wanted her help, a fey didn't stand a chance against a demon. "No one can."

"So I can't help you and you can't forgive me."

"That's about the size of it." He kept moving, his eyes fixed on the glow from the café window. The gabble of music and voices seemed unnaturally loud in the darkness.

A long silence followed before Lark spoke again. "That doesn't leave us anywhere to go."

"No."

"Like you said—why waste our time?"

It was a goodbye. The realization hit him like an electric charge. He spun on his heel, turning toward the spot where she'd stood. There was nothing but empty wall and fresh gouges where he'd clawed the bricks like a feral beast.

She was gone.

The emptiness that followed hit Jack like a boot to the gut. The sound that came from Jack's throat was a snarl of anger and need tangled together. He hadn't found Lark just to lose her again like this.

Damn the commander's orders. He had to look for her.

Chapter 3

"I can't believe Jessica Lark is still alive." Faran Kenyon's voice crackled over the bad cell phone connection. He was a werewolf and the only one of Jack's team aware that Jack was undercover. "But if Lark disappeared without a trace like that, are you sure she was real? She wasn't a fey trick or hallucination meant to throw you off guard?"

Two hours had passed since Jack had seen Lark. He'd scoured the area around the café, looking for her in every nook, cranny and dive in the surrounding streets, but he was only one vampire. When reason finally began seeping through his wall of snarled emotions, he realized the Company was his best resource in terms of manpower to find her. They'd have an intense interest in what an AWOL fey agent—previously presumed dead—was doing in Marcari, a few hours' drive from their headquarters. And since the commander wanted to chat anyway, why not ask for his help?

"She was real," Jack said. "There was no question about that, at least." Her touch, her smell had been achingly familiar. His body knew her flesh and blood. No spell could duplicate the way her lips moved under his. *And what are you going to do about it? Kill her? Punish her? Admit that you're insane enough to still want her more than any other woman?*

The one thing he could never do was love her again. Her treachery had destroyed every chance of that.

"It's bizarre. What are the chances of the famous designer of Amelie's bridal dress reappearing now? I blame everything on the royal wedding," Kenyon added. "That's what made every magic-happy villain in all the realms start planning their own version of the bridal apocalypse."

"Yeah, well, that's one way of putting it." Jack Anderson glanced at the dashboard of the Escalade, where his cell phone was set on hands-free. The display screen was bright in the darkness, showing the reception this far out in the Marcari foothills was down to one bar and bursts of static. "Anyone planning to sabotage the ceremony has less than two weeks to do it, and I'm not ruling out the Light Court. They were our allies in the past, but they've kept to themselves for a long time. We don't know their priorities."

"So what do you need?"

"Help."

"What kind?"

"I need the Horsemen."

Named after the riders of the Apocalypse, the team was as close-knit as the fabled Musketeers but far darker and even more deadly. Jack, code-named Death, had been their leader. Plague and War—Mark Winspear and Sam Ralston—were also vampires. Kenyon, the only werewolf, was Famine. They were the best operatives *La Compagnie des Morts* had, and Jack needed them at his back.

"You've all been working this case from the start," Jack said. "And by case I mean ensuring the wedding goes ahead without interference from the Dark Fey. Like you said— bridal apocalypse."

The wedding would be on Valentine's Day and would turn Marcari's capital city into one huge party zone. The rich, famous and royal—not to mention the international media—were arriving in droves to add to the security nightmare. And then there were the supernatural implications of the event. Weddings made powerful magic, and a joining of royal houses conjured more than most—and this marriage had the power to seal the gates to the Dark Queen's prison forever.

"Our earlier cases are connected," Kenyon agreed. "I mean, first we had the wedding gown disappear."

"Lark designed the dress," Jack pointed out, pushing away the memories of Lark back in New York, holding the diamond-encrusted gown like a sacred treasure. Jack had never married, but he'd been about to fall to one knee at the sight of it. What a fool he'd been.

"Yeah, well, it was a dress to die for," Kenyon complained. "As in, we all nearly died in the process of getting it back, and it wasn't even my size. And then, after months on the run, Lark's assistant shows up with that enchanted book. We nearly lost Winspear over that one."

Lark again, Jack thought. Her presence was like a glittering thread running through events and binding them together. *And yet everything points to the Dark Fey. So why is the Light involved?*

Kenyon continued, his tone growing deeper and more growly as his disgust increased, "And then the Dark Queen's flunkies stole the wedding ring and tried to use it to open the gates to her prison."

"If you hadn't gotten it back, the carnage would've been staggering," Jack said. "But they'll try again. The wedding ceremony has enough magical juice to seal the gates forever. It's now or never for them."

"Tick-tock," Kenyon replied. "If I were Prince Kyle, I'd be packing up my princess and skipping town for Vegas."

"I wish."

"Elvis chapel. European royalty. Vampires and werewolves. I dig it."

It had been way too long since Jack had laughed, and it felt wonderful.

"I'm coming out from undercover, but only on a need-to-know basis," Jack said as the cell signal crackled again. "Tell Ralston and Winspear. I need them on board ASAP."

"They still think you're dead. Deader. Whatever. They're both out of town anyway. It'll take some time." Kenyon fell silent and Jack heard the rattle of dishes. By the sound of it, the werewolf was at a restaurant.

Kenyon's next words were cool. "Don't think they won't kick your ass for holding out on them. I've said this before, but it bears repeating. Friends don't let friends think they got barbecued in a fiery car wreck when they didn't. You should have trusted them. You barely trusted me, and that's only because I found out you were lurking around the palace."

Jack flinched. The werewolf was as much of a son to Jack as a vampire would ever have. Lark's words came back to him: *Will your friends trust you when they find out you're still alive, Jack?*

"It's not about trust."

"Are you sure? What aren't you telling me, Jack?" Kenyon asked, all business now.

That I'm a demon. That it's getting harder to hide. "Everything I've learned undercover. I haven't been spending my time knitting. I'll fill you all in as soon as we're together."

"Give me a summary I can take to the others. They deserve to know what's coming around the corner."

Jack opened his mouth to answer, but the cell signal vanished. Odd. Reception was bad along the route, but it had never disappeared altogether before.

And yet one more bit of bad luck was par for the course tonight. Jack cursed and stepped on the gas, taking his temper out on the accelerator. The Escalade barreled up a rise.

He'd barely reached the crest when a warning ripped through him with razor claws. It was primitive instinct, straight from his lizard brain, but as clear as a siren.

Jack slammed on the brakes. The Escalade slewed on the loose gravel, sending up a spray of dust and stones. Tension corded his muscles, and he gripped the wheel hard enough to make it creak. An eternity passed before the vehicle finally stopped—although that eternity lasted but a human heartbeat.

The next moment passed in perfect stillness. Jack listened past the thrum of the motor, searching for whatever it was that had triggered his instincts. The phone was still dead. He could pick out the night sounds of the forest—an owl's screech, the rustle of small creatures among the leaves and grass. Vampire hearing was preternaturally acute, allowing him to detect even the distant rush of the Mediterranean Sea, but there was nothing that spoke of danger. It all looked peaceful.

But if he couldn't hear or see trouble, Jack could smell it. A choking, acid stink clung to the air. There had been a fire—and not just of trees. This was the scent of manufactured things—buildings, fuels and plastics. And ruined flesh. There was the oily scent of death on the wind.

Cautious now, Jack drove the Escalade to the side of the lane and killed the motor. He got out, hand reaching for the grip of the Walther pistol beneath his jacket. But the road to the Company's main compound was deserted, even though the facility was just a mile up the road. He was the only living—or undead—thing in sight. Slowly his hand slipped away from the gun, fingers twitching as if they wanted to return to the familiar handgrip. Dread crept out of the darkness and into his bones.

If there was a fire, someone from the Company should be here. Cleanup crews. Vehicles. Construction. He knew the routine. He'd spent years working on those very teams. Come to think of it, he should already see the lights from the buildings bright against the inky-black sky. But no glow shone above the canopy of trees.

Jack cursed softly, refusing to follow that logic one inch further. He would approach his old home silently—and that meant on foot. With his insides slowly turning to ice, he changed his mind and drew the gun, advancing toward the

Company's main gates in perfect silence. The ashy stink grew stronger with every step, as did the gut-churning smell of charred flesh—human, vampire and other. Nausea worked its way up Jack's throat. The path made another turn, angling down to the left where the Company's compound nestled, almost hidden in a shallow valley.

A white piece of paper had drifted to the base of a tree, the page so bright it had to be new. Jack snatched it up. It was the printed copy of an email about a meeting that night, all agents to attend. It was from a general administrative account, just like the commander had said. Such meetings were far from unusual—the Company had its share of bureaucracy. Still, the email made Jack uneasy.

Jack rounded the final corner—and stopped. Where once-thick foliage had concealed the view, he had an unobstructed line of sight between charred and splintered trunks. Clearly there had been an explosion and then a blaze. Forgetting all caution, he abandoned the path, rushing to the lip of the valley with vampire speed. He crouched on the ash-covered loam, looking down on the devastation. At that moment, he hated his long experience with war and violence because he could read what he saw like a book.

Whatever had happened, the Company hadn't stood a chance.

Chapter 4

The compound had been reduced to dust, as if a giant fist had smashed it. Blackened rubble sketched the outline of buildings. Where there had been gardens, nothing but scorched earth remained. Heat still rose from the devastation, telling him the damage was fresh.

Of course it was. He'd spoken to the commander just that night. Whatever had happened had struck hard and fast, burning out almost at once and leaving nothing but ash behind.

Jack closed his eyes, fighting against the reek of death that rose up like a curse. The email slipped from his fingers, fluttering down the slope and into the ash. *All agents to attend.* Anyone who'd survived the initial blast had been trapped in a ring of fire. None of them—his friends, his mentors, the young ones he'd nurtured like sons and daughters—could have escaped. Jack's fists clenched as rage welled in his blood, effervescent in its intensity.

If Lark hadn't held me up, I would have been here. So why had she picked that moment to show up? *Because she's involved up to her slender, perfect neck.* Her presence boded nothing good. Had she betrayed him and the Company again?

A roar of frustration ripped from his throat. Pale blue fire crackled along his fingers, arcing and snapping like something from a Frankenstein film. The urge to destroy rose up like strong liquor in his blood, ballooning inside his skull. Delirium made him feel suddenly weightless, as if he could dissolve into a formless cloud of death and retribution. He rode the sensation, letting it numb the wild pain in his heart.

Revenge would be better than sorrow. Revenge would taste as sweet as living blood on his tongue—and be every bit as addictive. But then Jack clenched his fists, exerting iron control. Once more he dragged the searing energy back into his flesh. The demon wasn't going to win. Not today of all days. He drew in a shaking breath, more to steady himself than because he needed air.

"What happened here?" Lark asked from behind him.

Her timing couldn't be worse. Jack whirled, gun at the ready and demon rage fresh in his heart. His senses quested, searching out his prey.

There was no one in sight. "Where are you?"

"Will you shoot me?"

"Probably." His lips curled back to show fangs. "But my hands around your throat would be more satisfying."

He'd been too distracted to notice Lark's approach, but now could sense her. How could he not? His entire being was flooded with desire and rage, and she was at the core of it all. Her presence was like a magnet, drawing him as inexorably as iron—and yet her glamour was good enough to disguise exactly where she stood.

"Put away your gun, Jack." That soft voice had an edge now. Whatever uncertainty she'd shown in the alley was gone.

"You're in no position to make demands." Fresh anger rose, warring with incredulity. He lowered the gun, but didn't holster it.

Apparently that was good enough. Lark stepped out of the dark forest without warning. Here the moonlight was bright enough to catch her features, showing more than the shadowy murk near the café. For the second time that night, Jack's dead heart nearly stopped all over again.

"Why did you disappear like that? Where did you go?" he demanded, but the words lacked force. It was hard to growl when he'd lost his breath. And then for a blessed instant he forgot the horror where the compound had been. He forgot everything but her.

Lark was beautiful, like all the fey—tall and slender with pale skin and delicate features. But her coloring, all creamy skin and mahogany hair, radiated warmth and life. It had been that vibrancy that had attracted him, her fey light to his profound darkness.

"I meant to leave," she said. "But I got curious about what the commander wanted with you. I couldn't figure out what was so important."

"And so you kept on following me?"

She didn't answer, but scanned the devastation below. The night vision of the fey was almost as good as a vampire's and her eyes widened, her expression mirroring his horror. She crossed to his left, keeping distance between them, and peered down at the ruin. Slowly, she sank down to a crouch, one hand gripping the thin trunk of a sapling. She looked as if she might faint.

"By Oberon," she gasped. "It's all gone."

"And everyone in it. There was an email calling a general meeting tonight. It came from administration. No way to know who actually sent it." No way to know who had lured all the agents into the trap.

She turned to look up at him, her eyes wide and bright with tears, but her lips clamped in a grim line. "Did the commander have some hint of this?" Her voice was barely above a whisper. "Is that why he called you?"

"He knew something was up and that it was urgent, but obviously he didn't know enough. He asked for my help." Jack kept his voice steady, but his heart raged at the admission. "I should have come straight here."

"But then you'd be ash, just like them." Tears slid from her eyes, glittering as they fell. She wiped her cheeks with her fingers. There was no fuss or drama. Lark rarely wept, but when she did it was as graceful as everything else she did. Jack wanted—needed—to hold her, but logic stopped him from dropping his guard. She'd deceived him, abandoned him and spied on him.

And yet here she was again, sharing his tragedy in a way no one else could. The look on her face was identical to the emotion slashed into his soul. At a fundamental level, beneath the deception and anger, they'd always understood one another like twin spirits.

So Jack stood there in fury, cycling through love, desire, distrust and anger one more time. He had no idea what to do with her. He had to trust his head, because his heart was spinning out of control.

"Who did this?" Lark asked.

Fey. But he needed hard evidence, or at least more information. "I don't know. But I do know you're a wild card standing next to a crater where my home used to be."

Lark's head jerked up. She looked genuinely shocked as she rose to her feet. "I didn't have any hand in that." She gestured toward the scene of devastation below. "I swear."

Jack holstered the gun, if not his suspicions. "The fey lie as easily as they breathe."

The spark died from her eyes, replaced by anger. Without a word, she took three steps to close the distance between them, her long coat swinging with her strides.

"Don't," he warned.

But she kept coming. One moment she was out of reach, and the next her coat was brushing his knees—and he'd let her get so dangerously close because some mad part of him wanted her there.

Her fingers curled into fists and she raised them, poised to strike. He knew from experience she was a more than capable fighter. Quick as lightning, Jack grabbed her wrists. He felt her tense, her fierce fey strength straining against his.

"Don't what?" she growled, her voice husky with anger.

"Don't lie to me. Don't do that to me again. Not now." For an instant, her very nearness put him off guard. Yearning froze him where he stood and softened the iron strength of his grip.

"I didn't do this!" She gulped a shattered sob, her anger sliding suddenly back to grief. "You have to trust me that much!"

"No, I don't. I have no reason to." Nevertheless, relenting, he released her wrists.

"No." She shook her head, her eyes tightly closed. Tears stained her cheeks again. "You know me better than that."

"No, I—"

"Remember this." Lark slid one warm hand on either side of his face, pulling him down so that her mouth was on his. Jack took a breath to protest, but then she was stealing the air from his lungs and filling him with a painful longing that burned down to his core.

In that scene of death, she tasted like something hot and sweet and golden, and his emotions rocked with the contrast. Desire clawed through him, merciless as a tiger. It had been like this whenever they touched, as if madness could be transmitted by skin-to-skin contact. He jerked her close so roughly her feet left the ground. There was no need to hold back—the fey were almost as indestructible as the undead.

But the undead could be destroyed. They were standing next to their cold ashes. Reason slammed down like a sheet of ice, forcing Jack back to his senses. He released her almost as quickly as they had joined. His sudden move made her skitter back, panting from their kiss.

She opened her eyes, her dark gaze searching his face. Her expression was full of guilt, but there was anger sparking through her sadness, too. "What's the matter, Jack? Didn't you like that? You were the one pushing me against a wall just hours ago."

Heat rose to his face, proving that once in a while vampires could blush. Of course he wanted her. The truth ached in his groin, but that wasn't his smartest asset. "Don't ask me to remember what we had. The ending's not to your advantage."

Her mouth flattened into a line.

He pushed on. "Now explain what you're doing in Marcari. Did the Light Court send you? Why did you talk to me tonight of all nights?"

"I wanted to." She smoothed the front of her coat, her look resentful. He saw the slight guilty tell—a downward shift of the eyes.

"I don't have time for your games," he snarled. "Not after *that*." He jerked his head toward the ruins.

Slowly, Lark nodded. "Whoever did that needs to be caught. No question."

"Who did it?"

She gave a slight shrug. Her lip was trembling, as if holding back another bout of tears. He prayed she didn't start to cry, because as the first shock faded, howling grief was setting up shop in his gut and planning to stay for a good long while.

"It changes everything," she said. "A move like this has got to be a part of something larger."

She was right, but it wasn't enough of an answer to satisfy Jack. Gruffly, he grabbed her by the elbow and began marching her toward the Escalade.

She tried to jerk her arm free without success. "Where are you taking me?"

"Away from this grave. It's not safe to linger."

"I can help you."

"Do you really think so?" He quickened his pace, his long legs making her run. "No, sweetheart, helpful people don't spy on me. They don't lie and they don't stab and they don't disappear without a trace. How deeply are you involved in all this? Did you help burn down Headquarters, or are you one of the ones out to destroy the bride and groom?"

Lark made a furious hissing noise, much like a scalded cat. It was a fey warning that raised the hair along Jack's neck.

"Don't be a fool!" she spat. "Whatever else you may think, you know we have the same enemies. They did their best to kill us both, and now they're here, killing our friends."

Jack didn't answer. He just forced her along the road.

Finally, she dug her heels in, forcing him to stop. "The wedding is almost here. Wake up, Jack. We have to work together."

Work together. The notion held promise—of time in her company, of an excuse to bury their differences for days on end, of accidental intimacy. He'd been down that treacherous path before, and he'd lived the wreckage. Worst of all, he'd fallen in love with her.

But he knew better now. The past was over and done. "Do you think I'm stupid?"

Lark opened her mouth, but didn't utter a word. He could see the memory of his demon written all over her finely boned face. Terror just made her more lovely—and the fact that he noticed it sickened him. She was right. He was slipping.

Impatient, he shoved her forward. He was almost back to the car. He could see a sports coupe parked farther down the road—no doubt the vehicle she'd followed him in, complete with spells to hide the tail. More fey deceptions.

"Jack, I…"

"Save it." There were few things that could burn a vampire, but Jessica Lark was as deadly and beautiful as the sun.

He pushed her against the Escalade, spreading her feet apart as if she were any suspect. She suddenly seemed to lose heart, and stood quietly as he frisked her for weapons, taking the Smith & Wesson under her coat and the smaller backup in her thigh holster. His mood had gone icy, and it was possibly the first time he'd touched her without pleasure foremost in his mind. Then he grabbed her wrists, hooking them together with handcuffs that seemed huge around her slender bones.

It was the click of steel that finally got a reaction from her. She struggled free of his grip and wheeled around, her eyes wide with panic. In a painful throb, he realized that despite an instinctive fear of his demon side, she hadn't predicted that he'd take her prisoner. She'd trusted him more than he'd trusted her.

"Jack, you have to listen to me!" she cried.

There were a lot of things he could have said, but it was better not to give the fey words they could turn against you.

So he kept it to one. "No."

Chapter 5

Jack got Lark into the car and got the car back on the road. He was *not* going to let the woman he'd loved and lost in a thousand different ways make him crazy.

No, no, hell no. Denial ran like a chant inside his head as he drove the Escalade back toward the capital city, bumping over back roads to stay out of sight. But try as he might, Lark was irrefutably there, growing increasingly angry with every passing minute. He could tell by the set of her lips.

Jack mentally drew the blinds. He watched for headlights instead, but they were alone on the path that snaked down from the forested hills toward the resorts and beaches at the edge of town. Above the esplanade, he could see the gleaming domes and spires of the palace. His goal was to get to a safe distance from the blast just in case the attackers were picking off survivors, but there was an almost preternatural quiet.

"Jack," Lark began for the third time, venturing into the chill silence that was all but frosting up the windshield.

"Don't speak." He held up a hand. "I don't want to hear it."

But of course she didn't listen. That wasn't Lark's way. "I know what the Company means to you. It's more your home than any of those fancy houses you own."

"Stop there." He put steel into the words. "Don't talk about my feelings. I'm not even human."

"Jack." His name was barely a whisper. "That doesn't matter."

Her words slid under his guard, wrenching raw places he hadn't even acknowledged yet. He'd just lost friends whom he'd known for centuries, and after so many years it got harder and harder to share any part of one's soul. True friends became rare and precious things.

"Jack?"

He didn't answer. His brain was roiling, too much crashing through it. Destruction. Demons. Loss. But Lark's presence cut through it all like a bolt of sorrow.

I loved you.

It had been the first green, fresh thing he'd felt for so long. Before she'd come along, he was sure he'd turned to stone—but Lark had taught him how his heart could still rejoice. And bleed.

"What do you want, Jack?" She sounded impatient now.

Jack gripped the steering wheel, glaring at the narrow strip of road. "I want revenge. I want whoever destroyed my…home."

Lark turned away, speaking to the window of the Escalade. When her voice reached his ears, it was strained. "Then, you should listen to what I have to say. I can help. Whatever else you think, you know I'm as good an agent as any member of your team."

He almost laughed. "There's a lot I could say to that. You still count yourself a member of the Company? Then, how about this—good agents don't go AWOL."

"I was caught in the fire when my atelier burned down," she said. "It was bad. Fey heal well, but it takes time. We're not like vampires or shifters."

"You could have sent word to the Company that you were still alive."

He finally looked at her, and she narrowed her eyes. For all its focus, the look was almost sleepy, reminding him of too many bedroom scenes for comfort. Especially with the handcuffs. "I had my reasons. You can believe that or not."

"Duty doesn't care about excuses."

"You're a fortunate man if you can believe in absolutes."

He couldn't read her tone well enough to guess if it was sincere or mocking. He decided to play it straight. "I would have liked to know you were alive."

"So you could silence me?" She was looking out the window, avoiding his gaze. "Besides, I thought you were dead, remember?"

He pulled the Escalade off the road and killed the engine, but it was a long moment before he could force himself to look at her. They were a few miles from the palace gates, still in the country, and it was dark. For a long moment Lark remained still, the lush fall of her hair a wave of shadow in the surrounding darkness. She looked as she always had in his mind's eye: lovely and serene. He wanted to stay like that, with only the wind rustling outside the car. But then she turned, moving slowly as if facing him was painful. Moonlight traced the edge of her cheek, turning that thin strip of blood-warmed skin to silver.

"The hospital called my family to come get me from New York," she said. "I thought you were dead and I didn't know who'd compromised my cover. The attack was real, Jack, and it was brutal. I just wanted to go home and heal."

He said nothing, hating the thought of her hurt and alone. And then hating the fact it bothered him so much.

"I missed you, Jack. That was the worst, but there were other things. I missed our friends. The life we had. It was hard, you know, losing the fashion-design business," she said, her voice oddly brittle. "It was supposed to be just a cover but I liked it. I had a knack."

Jack sat back, his leather jacket rustling in the silence. "People pay fortunes for a Jessica Lark original, especially now that you're dead."

She gave a stifled, bitter laugh. Her features remained

in darkness, as if he was gazing at the ghost of his memories. Lark in her jeans and bare feet, sitting cross-legged on the floor of her studio; Lark walking into a room and turning every male head; Lark lying in his arms. In every image, she was bursting with life. He was—not. He was the hollow grave. A vampire, and worse. He swallowed hard, suddenly ravenous.

She saw the look. He caught the surge of adrenaline wafting from her skin. Jack jerked his head away, reining himself in.

"Listen. Very few things can destroy a site that quickly. With any normal blast, there would still be fire and smoke for hours. That's not what we've got here. By all indications, a spell blew up HQ, and it left a stink," Lark said suddenly, pulling them back to safer ground.

The abrupt change of subject caught him off guard. "A stink?"

"On the magical plane. Whoever wove that spell was Dark Fey."

Dead leaves swirled across the road. The tick-tick of the cooling motor sounded like an old-fashioned time bomb. "Explain."

Her voice was brisk, every inch the agent now. "An explosion that big would have rocked the city, and it would've been loud and bright. It wasn't, so it was magic."

"And the magical, uh, smell?"

"Fresh. Barely hours old."

"That fits," Jack agreed. "It's been long enough for the attackers to get away, but not so long that the shutdown has been detected. Otherwise someone would have noticed HQ was offline. That still doesn't explain why you think it's a Dark Fey spell. They're not the only magic users around."

She angled her chin away, her expression stubborn. "I know the reek of the Dark."

"How? The gates to their kingdom have been locked for nine hundred years," Jack said, his voice gruff with dread she was right. "I was there when the gates were closed, but you weren't even born."

"Believe what you like, Jack." Her voice grew sharp. "The Light Court elders kept artifacts of the Dark spells. An entire library. They made us learn the signs of their magic, and one of those signs is stink. And this is worse than anything I've ever encountered."

With that, she got out of the car, slamming the door behind her. For an astonished second, Jack watched her stalk away. She was rubbing one wrist while the other was still circled by the dangling bracelets. Of course, any agent worth their salt knew how to get out of cuffs. Whatever else had happened to her, Lark hadn't lost her touch with a well-concealed lock pick.

"By the devil." Jack scrambled out of the car. He caught up to her in three strides, catching her arm. "What else do you know?"

The force of his grip made her slender body collide with his. She shot him a look, temper mixed with wariness. "I thought you didn't believe me."

Jack hesitated, measuring out how much he should say. "Dark Fey operatives made an attempt to open the gates less than a month ago, so I buy that they're active. We barely stopped the ritual, and only because they couldn't get all the ingredients to the spell."

Lark's mouth turned down. "I know. Word has it you dropped off the grid a year ago to find out who is working on behalf of the Dark Queen."

"How do you know that?"

"The Light Court has its sources. They sent me to find you because they want to know what you've found out. Who is helping her?"

Jack was barely listening. Their argument had stirred his hunger—but then Lark aroused him like no one else he'd ever met in his long existence. She was so close he could feel the warmth of her flesh seeping through her coat. Saliva filled his mouth, reminding him it had been a long time since he'd fed. Vampires his age didn't need a constant flow of blood, but the desire to drink never entirely faded—and fey were a particularly delicious vintage.

This wasn't good—especially when the disaster he'd just seen had stirred his most primitive survival instincts. Summoning the last dregs of his will, he forced his fingers to uncurl from her arm.

"The Light have stood on the sidelines until now. Why get involved?" His voice had gone rough with more than one kind of hunger.

Lark studied his face, no doubt seeing the flare of appetite in his eyes. She backed out of his reach. "We're on the same side. The Dark Queen has always been our enemy. You'll need us now that the Company is…is in trouble."

"The Company is not defeated. Not as long as I'm still standing." Jack looked down the sloping road toward the city. The palace stood on the hill at the center of town, the huge gates outlined in shimmering lights. It was a vision from a child's picture book, made of fireflies and dreams, and it was the Company's mission to keep it safe.

And that mission came first. Not every agent could have been in the building, and those who were left had work to do. Jack would find those survivors—his friends—but as much as he wanted to start making calls, there was a protocol to follow. The first order of business was to maintain silence until he reported what had happened to the king of Marcari, the ultimate ruler of the Company and all its agents. King Renault had to be the first to know what had happened here.

"You're coming with me to speak to the king," he said evenly.

"Am I?" Lark asked with a hint of defiance. "Thank you for informing me."

Without even looking her way, Jack gripped her arm again. There was no way he was letting her out of his sight. "We need to warn him. You need to explain why you're in town."

Lark squirmed in his grasp. "Aren't you undercover? If there are spies in the palace, there's no point in letting the enemy know you're around."

"King Renault knows I'm here. I get around without anyone else seeing my face."

And there was his next problem. He knew plenty of secret passages in and around the palace, but he didn't want to reveal them to Lark. If she was going with him, he needed another way in.

Jack licked dry lips, hating his next words. "If we leave the car here, we can walk in under a cloak of invisibility."

A beat of silence followed. Then she gave a short, sharp laugh. "You, inveterate hater of fey magic, need me to cast a glamour for you?"

He clenched his teeth. "I'll like your magic better if it's working for my side."

Lark dropped her chin to her chest, feeling the sting of his words. "I'm on your side."

"I doubt that," Jack said, pain and anger radiating from him like heat.

Lark tried to ignore the jab, but her vision blurred with tears. She was devoted to her people, but she'd also worked with the Company. The agents were her friends, and someone had struck deep at their heart. The image of the blast site burned like a coal of fury in her chest, fueling the hot prickling behind her eyes. If she wavered for one instant, let that grief inside her unfold, she would start howling like a banshee.

"I want revenge as much as you do," she said. "If getting into the palace will help you, I'll do it. But first, I need something from you."

His mouth twitched with some unspoken protest, but his voice was even. "What?"

Lark sighed, regretting her words before she spoke them. "Kiss me."

He cocked an eyebrow. "Haven't we done that already?"

"I know it's not the time… It's all wrong, but if I'm going to share magic…" She trailed off awkwardly, then cleared her throat.

She realized she was looking at Jack's feet like some awkward teenager, and slowly dragged her gaze upward to look at him squarely. It was a fascinating visual journey. He stood tall and hard with muscle, forged at a time when men fought with broadsword and ax. Once she'd claimed every inch of that flesh. She knew for a fact that his skin was only slightly cool to the touch, and it would warm with encouragement. The truth was, Jack had conquered her the night they'd met. She hadn't stood a chance. Talk about going for the bad boys.

Except now his pale blue eyes, haunted and a little terrifying, froze her where she stood. She tried an apologetic smile. "I need to feel your energy. This is the fastest way."

She could see him resisting the idea, but there was nothing else she could do. They had kissed earlier, but that had been more a battle than a sharing. For the glamour to work, she had to merge their energies, and it had been too long since she'd let herself sink into the essence of him. That lapse could cost them, for even the subtlest error could cause the glamour to fail. "I know you're angry with me, but I have to kiss you for your own good."

A corner of his mouth twitched—a hint of humor. "Men have wept for less."

Lark drew closer, resting her fingertips on his chest. Despite the low light, she could see the lines of tension in his face—no surprise given the devastation they'd just seen. Like so many of the warriors she knew, he let such things in a bit at a time, measuring it out so that he could keep on fighting. Such self-control demanded a price. She knew that Jack had nightmares—and a vampire's night terrors must be terrors indeed.

She ran her hand up the swell of his chest, her thumb brushing the collar of his jacket. He swayed slightly under her touch, but it was she who stretched up to take his mouth. His mouth was hard on hers—stiff for a moment but then greedy with a hunger that made her reel. Lark gasped, her senses overwhelmed as Jack's strong arms pulled her close once more, her feet barely skimming the ground.

It would have been so good to bury her face in his shoulder and weep for everything—for them, for the Company, for all the friends she'd lost and the secrets she kept. But he wasn't there to give her comfort, even though his mouth was on hers again, brushing over her eyes, her brow, her lips and throat as his hands studied her form as carefully as if he meant to sculpt it. Desire rushed through her, and with it vivid remembrance of the times they'd shared. He was angry and despised her and was—*let's face it*—at least partially a *demon*, but she also knew the beauty of his heart.

Ironically, he had been the one who made her believe in her work as an agent. He was the one who had argued that a fey could be trusted in the field. That was the Jack she would always believe in. Tears leaked beneath her lids. There was so much regret between them.

She reached out with her sixth sense, searching for the pattern of Jack's essence. It wasn't easy to find, muddled with her own yearning and the raging hunger of the vampire. But he was there, that unique core of power that each being possessed.

Blood pounded in Lark's ears. After so long apart they were close, too close. She could feel the brush of his extended fangs against her skin, tantalizing with the promise of erotic pain. A shudder took Lark, her skin suddenly too sensitive as Jack's lips trailed beneath the arch of her jaw.

And as part of her surrendered to him, he yielded up the pattern of his essence to her. Gently, so gently, Lark pulled

away, wishing they were lovers again. But that wasn't the
bargain they'd made.

Lark would help Jack find the vile creatures who had
attacked the Company because that was the right thing to
do. But explanations were another matter. Secrets were
how the fey did business, and Lark's business was her own.

She kissed him again, just because she could, and just
because she might never get the chance again. A heady
rush made her head swim as her spell took them both. In
a blink, they disappeared from sight.

Chapter 6

"Don't let go," Lark whispered in Jack's ear, although there was no one there to see them. Their kiss had left her in an intimate mood she couldn't bear to break.

"Why not?" Jack's fingers traveled lightly down her arms, leaving a trail of gooseflesh in their wake.

It was oddly erotic, to be touched by invisible hands, to experience a man only by his voice and the heat of his flesh. Lark leaned into him, spinning out the moment a little longer. "The glamour will break if we are not skin to skin. It does not need to be much. Holding hands will do."

By way of reply, Jack gripped the handcuff that still dangled from her wrist. She heard a metallic snick. He'd chained his wrist to hers.

"Why did you do that?" she demanded, tugging on the cuff because the primal part of her demanded she struggle.

"Now we're bound together," he said with more than a tinge of sarcasm. "Just so we don't lose one another."

Invisible or not, she had a good enough sense of where he was to deliver a sharp kick to his shin. He grunted, but it didn't satisfy her as much as it should have.

"If you trust me so little, why am I helping you?" she said in a low, angry voice.

"I wish I knew." His fingers laced firmly through hers. "But given our history, I don't know what's real between us and what's just business."

There was nothing Lark could say to that. She wished it wasn't true.

Cursing silently, she followed him toward the distant palace. Visiting the king hadn't been in her plans, although they were heading in the right general direction for her next appointment. She would slip Jack's leash when the time came to finish tonight's mission. After all, she'd already proved she could get out of the cuffs.

The walk to the gates was a good half hour. It had been years since Lark had held a glamour on more than just herself for that long. By the time they approached the palace, she was starting to get a headache.

A silver limousine pulled up the moment before they arrived, and when the huge, wrought iron gates swung open, Lark and Jack followed the vehicle through. There were no wards in place against the supernatural, so Lark's magic tripped no alarms. That might have seemed a ridiculous gap in security, but the Night World was a secret known only to the royals and their trusted circle. Most humans had no idea magic was real, and the vampires and werewolves who guarded the king weren't about to install a security system against themselves.

Of course, getting past the gate was only the beginning. They had to make it across the grounds, where the overflow of wedding guests wandered the flower gardens and fountain plazas in search of a little fresh air. Dodging people who couldn't see her wasn't as simple as it sounded—not when she had to be utterly silent. Not with Jack's fingers wrapped around hers as if he'd never let her go.

As good at sneaking around as he was, Jack wasn't used to being invisible. He had an alpha male's way of owning the sidewalk, and she was forced to hip-check him off the path just as an elegantly dressed couple appeared from behind a hedge.

"Sorry," Jack whispered in her ear, sounding more annoyed than thankful.

"Pay attention," she muttered and then froze as one of the passersby turned around, looking curiously in their direction. Lark's heart beat double time—she recognized him as the son of the Italian ambassador. He was a bright young man, and the type to be suspicious. The moment passed, and the man turned around and walked away, his pretty companion leaning on his arm in a way that said their night was far from over.

They made it inside the palace doors without more trouble. "The king's suite is to the left," Jack said in a low voice, his lips close enough to tickle her ear.

"All right," she whispered back.

Anyone else's footsteps would have rung out loudly beneath the high, gilt ceilings and vast sweeping staircases, but they trod quietly as shadows, Jack's cool hand still enfolding hers. Lark's mouth ran dry, her blood tingling with memories of what those fingers could do against naked skin. The image of Jack, rumpled and naked, slid through her mind with the warm sweetness of melting syrup. Heat settled low in her core.

She almost groaned with relief when she saw the double doors to His Majesty's rooms. Soon she could put an end to this torturous closeness and attend to her mission.

As if reading her thoughts, Jack stopped, pulling her against the wall. Lark shivered, feeling the hard curves of his muscles against her side. His hand was still laced through hers in an unyielding grip.

"Don't get any ideas," he said.

She heard a scrape of metal and, in seconds, he had removed the invisible cuffs without breaking the glamour. "Impressive dexterity," she murmured, "but next time use the furry ones. Those chafe."

She heard the clink of metal as he put the cuffs away. His answer came soft and low. "If memory serves, you like a bit of chafing."

That sounded like the old Jack, her Jack. A bittersweet pang ached in her throat. "Only for a good cause."

The leather of his jacket rustled and his grip tightened. "Let's get going."

There were royal guardsmen outside the king's chambers, but Jack simply barged past, Lark in tow. By the time the sentries reacted to the doors opening by themselves, she and Jack were in the room. The large, high-ceilinged space was done in greens and yellows, gold leaf decorating every other surface. King Renault of Marcari was alone. He stood at the window, framed by a vista of city lights and the distant harbor. At the guards' cries, he turned with alarm flashing in his dark eyes.

Jack let go of Lark's hand, and the glamour vanished.

At the sight of them, the king gave a shout of astonishment. The air filled with the thunder of the guards' feet. Lark's hand twitched toward her Smith & Wesson before she remembered Jack had taken it.

But the twitch was enough to alarm the help. Hands grabbed her, forcing her to her knees. She went down hard, the carpet barely cushioning the impact. The guard wrenched her arm behind her. Lark gave an involuntary yelp as pain shot up her shoulder.

"Don't touch her!" Jack commanded.

Just as quickly, she was free again. Through the curtain of her hair, Lark saw Jack lifting her attacker—one hand hauling him into the air by the front of his jacket, the other wrapped around the man's throat. Lark gasped, relieved and afraid at once. The look in Jack's eyes was feral, the pale blue of the iris disappearing as his pupils enlarged. He snarled, lips drawing back. Predator eyes and predator fangs. Not quite the demon she'd seen that night she'd betrayed him, but close enough. Fear froze her lungs.

There was the unmistakable clatter of weapons getting ready to fire, but the king held up a hand. "Wait."

Time stopped, filled only with the rasping breath of the guards. Lark remained perfectly still, knowing better than to come between a beast and its prey. "Jack," she said softly. "Put down the human. He's only doing his job."

Jack let the guard go without ceremony. The man stumbled awkwardly, giving the vampire a filthy look. Jack turned his back, dismissing him, and immediately bent down to help Lark back to her feet. His eyes resumed their normal arctic shade.

"Are you hurt?" he asked. For a moment, concern softened his expression—and then it was gone, vanished like a trick of the light.

Her stomach twisted, wanting that softness for a moment more. "I'm fine."

He gave a slow blink and bent until his lips nearly brushed her cheek. "No one else handles you."

His words, the brush of his breath, raised the fine hairs along her neck. She wasn't sure if it was a threat or a promise. "How flattering."

Jack made a noise that might have been a laugh, and dropped her hand. Then he turned and bowed to the king, his manner instantly somber and respectful. "Your Majesty, I have dire news to report."

Catching his mood, the king's face darkened. He waved to his guards. "Leave us and say nothing of our visitors."

Obediently, the royal guardsmen bowed and withdrew without a word. As soon as the door was shut, King Renault folded his arms. "What is this, Jack? And who is your companion?"

Jack spread a hand toward Lark. "Your Majesty, this is Jessica Lark, an agent of the Company. She also designed Princess Amelie's wedding gown."

As introductions went, it could have been much more damning. Perhaps the double-agent part would come later. Counting her blessings, Lark sank into a deep curtsy.

"Ah, I thought you had perished in a fire, madam," the king said drily. "The agents of the Company seem to have a phoenix-like talent for resurrection."

Lark rose from her curtsy, reading curiosity in King Renault's expression. Though in his middle years, he was extremely handsome with his neatly trimmed beard streaked with gray.

"Your Majesty," she said. "Forgive the intrusion, but as Jack says, we have dire news."

"Then, speak," the king said. "Whatever worries both a fey and a vampire has my full attention." He gestured to a cluster of armchairs, inviting them to sit. It was a gesture of royal favor, and there was little they could do but obey.

Once settled, Jack related what they had seen in the woods. As he spoke, Lark felt her pulse begin to quicken, her body reliving the horror through Jack's words. She wasn't the only one affected. The color drained from Renault's face until he was ashen.

The king immediately rose and picked up the phone sitting on the desk in the corner. Although Lark only heard his side of the call, he was checking the duty roster. All of the Company guards who were scheduled to work at the palace had booked off that night to attend a meeting, leaving the human guardsmen in charge. That fit with the email Jack had found. The king set down the phone, even paler than before.

"We shall find the authors of this outrage," Renault said as he returned to his seat, rage snapping in his dark eyes. "I will inform the other Company leaders as soon as we are done here. Los Angeles, Paris, Bombay—they should be able to send reinforcements. My loyal agents will not go unavenged. But fine words are nothing without action, and action is useless without intelligence behind it. I have heard your account, Jack. What do you have to add, Ms. Lark?"

Lark's throat had clogged with aching grief, and she cleared it. "I saw what Jack saw, Your Majesty. There was nothing left of the compound."

The muscles of Jack's jaw twitched as he turned to her. "But there are things left to tell us, aren't there?"

"Such as?"

Lark braced herself, her stomach sinking. His mood had darkened as he'd told his tale, and whatever softness she'd seen in him minutes before was gone. All that remained was the Company agent who'd seen the grave of his friends. "What exactly brought you to Marcari?" he asked.

"I'm here on behalf of the Light Court. The Light is well aware of the attempt to steal Princess Amelie's ring and open the gates to the Dark Queen's prison. We also know that they are likely to try again. As I told you before, Jack, our aim is to keep the gates to the Dark Queen's prison firmly closed."

"Is that all?" Jack asked.

"We're also tracing one of our own." That much was true. Of course, there was more she hadn't said.

"Who are you seeking?" asked King Renault. "Is there some official assistance Marcari could offer?"

"Perhaps, Your Majesty," Lark replied.

The king gave a nod, his expression carefully neutral. "Go on."

"The spell that would release the Dark Queen requires very specific ingredients, including blood from the Haven clan of the Light Fey. My mission is to locate the two remaining members of that family and ensure their protection. After years of living under a false name, the last full-blooded member is on the move."

"Therrien Haven?" Jack asked, sitting back in his chair.

"Yes. A week ago he paid cash for a plane ticket from Prague to Marcari under a false name. It seems he has a half-human daughter living here whom he hasn't seen since she was a girl."

"Her name is Lexie." Jack frowned. "I had no idea Therrien was aware of Lexie's whereabouts."

"The photographer who is to shoot my daughter's wedding?" King Renault asked.

"Yes, Your Majesty. Haven has followed his daughter's

photography career," said Lark. "His apartment in Prague was filled with clippings from magazines that featured her work. He must know she will be at the wedding. He might have come hoping for a reunion with his daughter."

"Or to protect her," said Jack. "She's a potential target of the Dark Fey, too."

"A father would be likely to do either," Renault murmured, no doubt thinking of the princess.

"Haven booked a room but never checked in," said Lark. "As far as I can tell, he's vanished. My next step is to question his daughter."

Jack's eyes narrowed. "I can tell you right now, she doesn't know a thing."

Lark bridled at his tone. "That's something I'd like to figure out for myself. I'll tread softly."

Jack held her in his ice-blue gaze, his expression stubborn. It was clear he was protective of this woman, Lexie. Then his manner shifted as if he was mentally turning a page. "Are there other reasons that you're in Marcari?"

The angry suspicion in his tone made her pulse jump, but the king spoke before she could reply. "Why do you ask that, Jack?" He didn't sound pleased.

Jack leaned forward. "Ms. Lark suffers from complicated loyalties, sire, since she's both an agent of the Light Fey Council and the Company. Given what has just happened in the woods, I'm certain there is more that she's not telling us. I don't believe in coincidences. There is a connection between the attack and her arrival in Marcari, even if it is an innocent one—and I'm not easily convinced of innocence among the fey."

"Jack!" Lark protested, her already pounding heart now speeding with apprehension.

King Renault had clearly heard enough. "Unfounded suspicions are beneath us, but neither can we afford to be careless. Perhaps Ms. Lark should relax in a private room while you and I discuss what has become of the Company compound. Then I'm sure we'll have questions for her to answer, and she shall answer them."

Lark sprang to her feet, instinct screaming at her to flee from the king's stern presence—but it was Jack's eyes she sought. "No, you have this all wrong."

But his expression told her she'd run out of free passes. For an instant her old guilt robbed her of the will to fight, sapping her strength like a deadly fever. It was only for a heartbeat, but it was enough time for Jack's hand to close around her arm.

"That's an excellent idea, sire. I'll make sure Lark is comfortable."

His frown said she'd be anything but.

Chapter 7

The tiny room where Jack left Lark was mostly empty, with a chair and side table and not much else. Lark swore under her breath. The lock was electronic, operated by a keypad. In other words, she'd need more than a knack with handcuffs to get out of this mess. Lark prowled the few feet of floor, frustrated and longing for her guns. Blasting the guts out of the lock would have suited her frame of mind.

Finally, she slumped in the chair and buried her face in her hands. All at once the sheer awfulness of the past hours slammed into her like an avalanche. She leaned forward, folding her arms on her knees.

Disaster had struck. Even if, by some miracle, some of the local agents had survived the blast at the Company's headquarters, every sense she possessed told her the casualties had been high. No doubt Jack and the king were putting wheels in motion—securing the site, calling the other Company offices, preparing a cover story the human newshounds would believe. Then would come even more activity—forensics, notifications, burial arrangements. The Company had a protocol for every contingency, even one as dire as this.

But their orders only covered action, not emotion. Fine souls had been lost this night—good friends and brave hearts. The world was a poorer place now.

Face after face flashed through her mind, each one tearing away a piece of her. Tears slipped down her cheeks, the first signs of a coming flood. Alone and with nothing to distract her, Lark soon gave in to a storm of sobbing. *And Jack thought I played a role in that terrible destruction!*

She should have known her reunion with Jack would not go well. *I could have stayed in the shadows, but I approached you because you're slipping, Jack, and I'm the only one who knows why. You need someone who understands.* Helping him was the only way to make up for stealing his secret in the first place.

To make matters worse, what good had her betrayal of Jack done? He hadn't possessed the spell or formula or supernatural stardust that would restore the Light Fey to their former strength. His extraordinary power was a curse—not at all something they could or would want to duplicate for themselves. And now, with the Company in ruins and the Dark Queen on the brink of freedom, the stakes were getting steadily higher.

Lark rose and crossed to the window, fishing in her pocket for a tissue. She mopped her nose, her eyes feeling scratchy and raw. It was dark out, but there were lights enough to see the palace gardens below. They were clearly trimmed and manicured to human tastes—nothing like the half-wild gardens the Light Fey preferred.

She wondered how long those gardens—or the Light Fey—would last. What chance did her people have against the coming of the Dark Queen?

There was one last gamble, and that was why Lark was in Marcari—and why she had to get out from under lock and key.

Lark examined the windows. They were casements, opening out over a sheer drop to the rocky garden path below. Not her first choice of exit. She leaned her forehead against the glass. She was exhausted, and there was so much she had yet to do before the night was out.

She returned to the door with its keypad. Oddly, crying her heart out had seemed to clear her head, because inspiration struck. She placed her hand over the glowing panel, sensing the flow of energy from contact to wire to a central computer somewhere in a basement office. As her mind drifted along that energetic frequency, she detected magical residue thick in the air—probably fallout from the blast that had destroyed the Company's compound. It was causing static throughout the electrical grid, and anything wireless would be down. If there was one thing magic was good at, it was screwing up tech.

Sorry, Jack, but I can't afford to sit quietly like a good girl. Lark risked sending a pulse of power into the keypad. The buttons flashed spasmodically, and she heard the click of disconnection. She whisked through the door, pulling it shut before the system registered more than a negligible flicker of disruption like all the others. At the same time, she summoned her glamour, turning invisible in the space of a blink. She was free.

About time, too. She had to see a princess about a wedding. Lark walked swiftly and silently through the marble halls, feeling her spirits lift for the first time that night.

Once out of sight of King Renault's rooms, Lark pulled on a new glamour that made her visible but altered her appearance to a friendly but forgettable face. She glanced over her shoulder, catching a woman looking her way. For a moment Lark froze, but the woman's gaze skated past her. Lark frowned. Wasn't that the same woman who'd been outside with the son of the Italian ambassador? She couldn't be sure, but hurried on, mentally filing the incident.

Her path led past the apartment of Crown Prince Kyle, who was residing in Marcari these last few weeks before the wedding. Though the rest of his family had remained in Vidon, Kyle had chosen to be close to his bride. Beyond his apartment was a string of guest chambers and, finally, Amelie's rooms.

With a casual flick of a spell, Lark slipped past the guards and stopped at the entrance to the princess's sitting room.

Despite the best efforts of the staff, the princess's chambers looked like a bridal explosion. A swathe of sparkly white tulle sat mounded on a chair, and wedding magazines were scattered across every flat surface. A pair of long white gloves looked as if they had been dragged to the floor and mauled by a dog. Several servants in black-and-white uniforms hovered at the edge of the storm, tidying up as best they could.

Lark edged past the chaos to find an army of shoes marching from the princess's bedroom, as if Amelie had tried on every pair and abandoned them before she had made it all the way down the hall. Which, apparently, was exactly what had happened.

"They're all uncomfortable!" Princess Amelie complained to her attendant, a harried-looking woman who clearly had no fashion sense of her own. "I will be standing for hours and hours—on international television! The world will be watching and texting as I marry the man I love. It's all going to be hard enough without obsessing about the pain in my feet."

Amelie's attendant glanced around the drawing room, as if searching for answers among the litter of footwear. "Perhaps I can find something else for you to try, Your Highness."

"I think perhaps you should aim for something under a five-inch heel, Your Highness," Lark observed.

The attendant jumped and squeaked. "How did you get in here?"

"I'm sneaky."

The attendant looked alarmed, but a flash of amusement crossed Amelie's face. The princess knew Lark's many disguises, and waved an impatient hand. "I need all five inches. Prince Kyle is tall. We look like a comedy act unless I wear the heels."

She was right, so Lark changed the subject. "Please, may I have a word? There is something private that I must discuss."

Amelie nodded, and the attendant left, taking the other servants with her. As soon as they were alone, the latest pair of killer shoes were abandoned on the rich burgundy carpet. Lark let her glamour dissolve, resuming her own appearance. Then Lark chanted another spell, stirring the energy in the room enough to bind a cage of static around any listening devices.

Watching with rapt curiosity, the princess waved Lark to a couch. "You are always cloaked in such secrecy and mystery! What can I do for you tonight?"

"We have a problem, Your Highness," Lark said, feeling a wave of weariness as she sat.

"That is no way to begin a conversation." Amelie frowned, running a hand through the thick, dark mass of her hair. She sank onto the couch beside her. "What has happened?"

"I found Jack Anderson." The words opened the door to so much and so little. *I found him and...he will never forgive me for what I did to him.* "He's with your father now."

"Jack Anderson? The leader of the Four Horsemen?" Amelie sat back, her dark eyes wide. "But he was killed!"

"No more than I was. It seems he went undercover for a time."

Amelie brightened. "That is wonderful news! But how is this a problem?" A puff of white fur appeared over the arm of the couch. "Ah, Lancelot, isn't this good news?" Amelie picked up the little dog and cuddled it in her lap, stroking it as it wriggled happily.

Lark hesitated. She wanted to leave the princess as she was, not exactly an innocent, but at least less deeply involved in Marcari's Night World politics. Unfortunately, Lark had no choice. "We came here from the Company headquarters. Your Highness, there's nothing left of the place. The compound has been destroyed."

Silvery tears slipped down Amelie's cheeks. "Destroyed? My loyal vampires? What of the other Horsemen? Sam and Faran and Mark?"

"No doubt there are some who escaped," Lark said hastily as she felt her own eyes sting again. *By Puck's wings, this is hard!* Lark bit her lips to keep them from trembling.

"How did it happen?" the princess asked.

"Dark Fey magic."

"Dark Fey?" Amelie gasped. The little dog began to whine, sensing her dismay. "They are imprisoned! We stopped the ritual that would have let them out." Amelie grasped the ring that hung by a chain about her neck. The wedding ring bore the blood rubies of Vidon—a gift from her future husband, Crown Prince Kyle of Vidon, and key to the spell that could set the Dark Queen free.

Lark cleared her throat. "It seems someone's ready to try again."

"I thought we caught all the traitors. It seems we were fools." The princess fell silent, burying her face in the dog's fur. When Amelie finally spoke again, the words were muffled. "I thought the worst obstacle to marrying Kyle was the hostility between our countries, but now there is this threat."

Lark's heart went out to the young woman. "We will deal with the threat, my princess, and Kyle's people will come to know and love you."

"The Vidonese who know about the Night World have called Kyle a traitor for marrying me. They hate me just because Marcari welcomes the supernatural within its borders."

Lark reached across, cupping Amelie's face in her palm. "Kyle is true-hearted. He won't pay that any heed."

But Amelie gave voice to the thing Lark feared most.

"What if they knew the truth about me? About the fact my mother was half fey?"

It was true. Amelie's mother—who had died before becoming queen—had been the daughter of a Light Court noble. "That's exactly why I'm here. Your mother hid her fey heritage well, but we must be extremely careful."

Lark spoke softly. Despite her wards, she had to be sure that no one could overhear. There was much she couldn't explain even to Amelie—not yet. She didn't want to frighten the princess by telling her the fate of an entire race was in her hands.

The fey were beings made of magic as much as they were of flesh and blood. Very little bound them to a physical form in the earthly realm, especially after isolating themselves for centuries. Now they were dying before their time. Lark had held her own mother's hand, dry and lifeless as old paper and twigs, as she'd dwindled to nothing. Her eyes had grown dull as the magic within them had dimmed and guttered like a spent candle. Those had been the worst days and nights of Lark's life.

Only an anchor in the mortal realm would save the Light Fey from fading away, and that anchor would come through the power of royal blood. This was why the royal wedding and the coronation that followed mattered so very much.

The treaty surrounding Amelie's marriage to Kyle stipulated that within a year of the royal wedding, the kings of Marcari and Vidon would step down. Then Kyle and Amelie would ascend the thrones, unite the kingdoms and rule together in an equal partnership. Amelie would be a queen in her own right.

Like many coronation rituals, the oath of the Marcari monarch would symbolically tie her to the land in a wedding every bit as binding as her marriage to Kyle. Such unions worked in very concrete ways with the fey. Even though the princess had only a little of their blood, it was enough that Amelie's coronation would bind the Light Fey to the earthly realm and save them from extinction.

The fact that the prince and princess had a love match would make the magic that much stronger.

Amelie's face was grave. "If I marry Kyle, any children of ours will carry Light Fey blood. There are those among the Vidonese who would think nothing of harming them because of it."

"True, and that brings me to my business here tonight."

Lark reached into her coat pocket and withdrew a bottle containing a few ounces of clear liquid. It was small enough that Jack had missed it when he'd frisked her. "It took some time for our spell experts to find the right ingredients— some are incredibly difficult to obtain—but this was what your mother used to keep both her and you safe when you were very young. If you drink this, it hides every trace of fey characteristics in the blood."

Amelie took the bottle. "Why do I need this? I'm not having a blood test."

"Perhaps you should. Or perhaps you should cut your finger somewhere public enough to leave traces of your blood behind. Any enemies who suspect your bloodline will test the evidence only to find out their suspicions were unfounded."

"I would like to say that is an unnecessary precaution, but I know there are those who hate nonhumans enough to go to any lengths."

"Using the potion is a small price to pay for peace of mind. There are no side effects."

"Thank you," said Amelie. "Thank you for teaching me what my poor mother could not."

Lark felt a pang of sadness. The death of Amelie's mother had left her half-fey daughter without magical protection. Discreetly, without even the Company's knowledge, the Light Court had kept a watchful eye—which was why Lark had been given the task of visiting the princess as often as she could. During those secret visits, Lark had taught Amelie about her fey heritage. Bringing the rare potion was the final step, and now that her mission was accomplished, the Light Fey had only to keep the princess safe until the wedding and coronation were completed. That should have been easy, but Lark wasn't taking anything for granted.

"I'll look after you, Your Highness," she said. "I promise on my life."

No sooner had the words left her mouth than a shudder ran through the room, rattling the china and knickknacks. The abandoned shoes toppled off their high heels. A split second later, a roar pounded from outside, sending another convulsion through the palace. Startled, the little dog scrambled from Amelie's lap and bolted for the bedroom.

"That didn't sound like an earthquake," said the princess, her voice small and tight.

"That was an explosion." Lark jumped up, catching sight of the orange glow through the balcony doors. Instinct warred between terror and a reckless urge to rush to do battle. "There's a fire."

"What?" Instantly, Amelie was at her elbow. "Is anyone hurt? Can you tell?"

"Let me get a better look." Lark motioned to the princess to stay where she was. Cautiously, she opened the balcony doors, all of her magical senses on high alert. The sea breeze was cool, but held none of its usual sweetness. Instead, it reeked with the thick smoke hanging in the air—and with the now-familiar stink of Dark Fey spells. She stepped outside, keeping low. There was no point in tempting snipers.

Amelie was far less cautious. In seconds, she was crouching to Lark's left, craning her neck to see what was going on. Her stance was as urgent as a strung bow, every trace of the girlish bride abandoned like another pair of shoes.

"Your Highness, get back inside!" Lark exclaimed.

Amelie ignored her. "That's the memorial arch that's burning! How is that possible? It's made of marble."

Despite herself, Lark stared at the graceful monument that framed the entrance to the public garden. It was indeed on fire, eerie orange and blue flames streaming from its surface. The flagpoles beside it were burning, too, and the flags with the proud black hawk of Marcari were already all but consumed. "Marble doesn't burn, princess, but magic does."

Fear twined like an icy serpent up her back, and she barely gulped back the acid taste of panic. *Whatever happened at the Company headquarters is happening here.*

And after the fire that had burned her, flames were Lark's nightmare. She'd spent months healing from her injuries. Now the urge to bolt was so strong it made her shudder, and she gripped the balcony rail to steady her knees.

But this was no time for fear. Lark summoned her best voice of command. "Your Highness, get back inside. Now."

Amelie gave her an imperious look. She clearly didn't like giving in, but was smart enough to retreat indoors. Lark followed, latching the doors and drawing the curtains. Her hands trembled a moment before she let the lace panels go, then she took a steadying breath. She'd promised to protect Amelie, and the daughters of the Light Court kept their word.

"I'll be right back," said Lark. "Someone needs a lesson in manners."

Chapter 8

"I'm coming with you," Amelie said at once. "And don't tell me to stay here and twiddle my thumbs like a good little princess!"

Lark shot her a look. "I'm sorry, but that is precisely what I'm begging you to do."

"Lark!"

She tried for humor, hoping to soften her words. "I'm prepared to conjure a troll to sit on you if you try to follow."

Amelie's eyes went wide with annoyance. "I don't care if you're an agent of the Light Court or the Company, you have no authority over me!"

Lark had reached the door, but now she spun and regarded the princess squarely. Amelie's expression was a fierce blaze. Lark's heart went out to the brave young woman, and she blinked to hide the tears that blurred her vision. "My job is to keep you alive, Your Highness. I take that seriously."

With a sigh of frustration, Amelie subsided. Lark turned to go before the princess changed her mind.

As Lark opened the door, she saw palace security was reacting to the blast. Guards poured into the corridor to join the ones already on duty. Lark didn't like leaving Amelie, but at least there was no chance the princess would be left alone.

"Look after her," Lark said to the guard on duty, putting a tiny push of mental compulsion into the words, "and loan me your backup gun."

Lark didn't have a vampire's talent for mind control, but she had enough. The guard handed his weapon over, and it turned out to be a Smith & Wesson much like the one Jack had taken from her. It was the first stroke of luck she'd had all night.

With that, Lark sprinted down the corridor, her feet silent on the patterned runner. She had to get a closer look at the burning arch. Fey weren't exempt from the urge to view their handiwork, and there was every chance the culprit was lurking somewhere in the crowd and gearing up for his next move.

She dodged lightly around the guardsmen hurrying toward the stairs, but speed wasn't possible once she got to the main passageway. People were dithering in the stairwell like a herd of nervous sheep. She settled for using her elbows to force her way through the crowd. Once she reached the entrance hall, she dashed out the doors and across the lawn. Police, firefighters and throngs of onlookers were already there.

From the ground, the flaming arch was terrifying. Orange light painted the sky a ghastly hue and turned the tree branches into twisted claws. By then, three fire hoses were dousing the gardens, the spray a shower of gold in the reflected firelight. Although it seemed to be saving the neighboring oaks, the water was doing nothing to douse the monument. Lark slowed to a halt, swearing under her breath. Slowly, she made a complete turn, looking for someone out of place.

Gawkers stood in clumps around the edges of the scene, almost eerily transfixed by the roaring flames. The villain would be with the looky-loos. Lark fell back, her senses tuned to detect the scent or even the telltale tingle she felt near Dark Fey magic. It tended to cling to the user like static electricity—if she worked her way through the crowd, hopefully she'd pick up a trace of the culprit.

The bystanders spread all the way back to the trees, faces limned by touches of firelight. She deliberately pushed through where the throng was thickest, catching the scent of aftershave and cigarettes but not magic. These folks were all human. But then just as she neared the edge of the crowd, Lark's scalp prickled, as if a thousand ants swept over her—far more than just residue.

There wasn't enough time to do more than flinch. An oak tree exploded a dozen yards away. It didn't burst into flame; it fountained up in a cold blast of power that reduced the ancient wood to a hail of toothpicks. The noise was like a thunderclap, barely ending when the woman next to Lark screamed as a shard of wood buried itself in her cheek. It was too late to duck. The tiny pieces flew with such force that they burrowed right through clothing into flesh. The only reason Lark escaped injury was the number of bodies in her way.

Lark turned and suddenly she had a clear view of the path by the ornamental pond. There, barely visible in the shadows, a figure sprinted away. Immediately, Lark bolted after, using superhuman speed to close the distance between them.

Within seconds, she'd drawn close enough to see the figure. Despite the bulky coat he wore, it was plain her quarry was tall but slight, a shapeless hat pulled low over his brow. He ran across a small footbridge that arced over one of the ornamental ponds, heading toward the maze. *Oh, no, you don't*, thought Lark. Chasing someone around the palace's huge maze would be hopeless.

Lark cut to the right, intent on heading him off. As she ran, she drew her Smith & Wesson. Fey might have a thousand tricks, but a well-aimed bullet would still kill them. She leaped lightly over a bed of spring bulbs just starting to bloom and skirted a low rhododendron, startling a cat that streaked away with a yowl.

Her quarry heard the sound and glanced her way, his pale face a flash in the darkness. With a curse, he changed course. Gritting her teeth, Lark strained for more speed. Her breath was already ragged. Her burns might have healed, but a long convalescence had sapped her reserves. Her stamina wasn't what it should be for a chase like this.

A moment later, the figure glanced back again. He wasn't gaining ground, and the high wall of a yew hedge loomed in his path. Without warning, he stopped and spun, planting his feet as if bracing for a fight. Lark stopped a dozen feet away, the gun at her side. She sucked in air, letting it out slowly to quiet her rasping lungs. Behind them, flames still tore at the sky, fading the waxing moon to insignificance. The rushing sound of the fire drowned Lark's thoughts for a moment before training took over and she gripped the gun with both hands.

"What do you hope to gain by this?" she demanded.

"That will become clear enough in time." The voice surprised Lark. It was low, but it belonged to a woman. The shapeless clothes were an effective disguise.

"Who are you?" Lark demanded.

"That depends on who is asking."

Lark jerked the gun, reminding the woman she had the advantage. "Tell me something useful unless you enjoy getting shot full of iron."

The woman shrank back. Iron was to the fey what silver was to werewolves. Even if the wound was slight, it would poison the blood.

"Hurry up," Lark prompted.

"That fire will burn for several more hours before it goes out on its own. No amount of water or chemicals is going to smother it."

Okay, that was useful, but not the kind of intel Lark had in mind. "Are you working for the Dark Queen?"

"Naturally." The voice held scorn. "And whether you like it or not, so are you. For those first few days after you healed, your flirtation with the Dark made you incredibly easy to follow."

"What?" Lark didn't understand that at all. "I've never worked for your side!"

The attack came so fast, Lark barely had time to pull the trigger. She never even felt the recoil. A pale blue fireball slammed into Lark, sending her tumbling backward. Reflex conjured a shield against the worst of the impact, but she still felt her bones rattle. She rolled to her feet, shaking her hair out of her eyes.

The woman was clutching her shoulder, so Lark's shot had struck home. Quickly, Lark summoned a burst of power, weaving it small, precise and strong enough to punch the door off a tank. The woman batted it away as if it were a pebble. Lark gripped her gun, suddenly appalled. Who was this chick?

"Stop," the woman said as Lark took aim again.

Lark froze as the spell swamped her. When she suddenly remembered to move—she couldn't. For a horrifying moment, Lark remained still, gun pointed and feet spread apart like an action figure posed on a shelf. The smoke-scented breeze fanned her hair and brought tears to her eyes, but she couldn't even blink. Her brain and her muscles weren't connecting.

The woman took a step forward, then another. Her features were still obscured by shadow, but Lark could make out the sneer of her mouth.

"I should drop you where you stand," the woman said softly. "What business does the Light Court have working with the bloodsuckers?"

Horrified, trapped, Lark barely heard her. She'd never encountered any creature with this much power before, and the woman was drawing closer and closer. Lark's limbs began to tremble, agonized by the strain of trying to move.

Her chest, barely able to breathe, was pulling in tiny, panting gasps. Gradually, the world was starting to swirl as Lark starved for oxygen.

You've got to focus! She's strong, but you're tougher. The gun was growing slippery with sweat and Lark feared dropping it from numbed fingers. She willed herself to grip it tighter even as she strained to make out her approaching tormenter's face.

When Lark finally did, she wished she hadn't. It was the pretty young woman she'd seen watching her in the hall, but she looked different now. Her hair was pulled severely back, showing features freshly scrubbed of makeup—and now Lark knew her from surveillance photos. *Drusella Blackthorn.*

No wonder Lark was no match for her. She was a Dark Fey sorcerer of immense power.

Drusella gave a humorless chuckle. "I could send your dead body as a message to the Company to stay out of this, but I think we've got that one covered. They're nothing but a hole in the ground now."

In the depths of her panicking mind, Lark murmured an invocation to the Light, and tried with all her will to squeeze the trigger.

Her finger wouldn't move.

Drusella grinned.

Chapter 9

Jack had barely finished his conversation with the king when the blast hit. One moment they were organizing the next steps to respond to the attack on the Company. The next, he saw Lark bolting across the lawn right toward the conflagration, long mahogany hair flying like a banner behind her. Fear struck him like an electric charge. She was either doing her best to prevent disaster, or she had created it. With Lark, you never knew.

He didn't stop to ponder why she wasn't still locked up. That would come later. Without another word of explanation to his monarch, Jack charged from the room.

He didn't bother with the palace steps, but leaped from the porch to the ground, landing in a feline crouch. Springing up, he sprinted toward the burning arch. The magic of the flames rasped against his nerves, telling him that it came from the Dark Fey. No wonder Lark was on the move.

He reached the edge of the crowd and stopped, searching every face. Worry tore at him. This was magic on a scale he hadn't seen in centuries. He pushed through the mass of people, opening all his senses in hopes of catching some sign of Lark. She would have zeroed in on the source of the Dark Fey power more efficiently than he ever could—if he found her, he found whoever was behind the blaze.

His concentration shattered when something thumped into his knees. His temper flared, but then he looked down to see a boy of about five, red faced with tears and clearly frightened. The child was trying to worm past him, obviously preparing to hurtle onward. Jack went to one knee, catching the child before he could get away. "Where is your mother?" he asked gently.

The boy sucked in a jagged breath, readying a fresh batch of tears, when he looked squarely into Jack's face. His brown eyes flew wide, and a knot hardened in Jack's gut. Sometimes children and animals could see his true nature—darker than even a vampire's should be. He braced for a bout of hysterical screams, but instead the boy chewed his lip quizzically, as if he couldn't figure Jack out.

"Pierre!" A young woman burst from the crowd and snatched the boy's hand. Her expression wavered between panic and exasperation. "I told you to stay with me!"

Jack rose. "He's not hurt, but he's frightened. He needs to go home."

The woman opened her mouth, about to speak—maybe to tell him to mind his own business—but then an oak tree shattered into a rain of splintering wood. Immediately, Jack grabbed Pierre and his mother, sheltering them from the rain of spear-like shards. It was undoubtedly a dumb move for a vampire, but women and children came first.

He got lucky, but many didn't. Cries of pain ripped from the throng and Jack smelled the warm richness of blood. Hunger leaped to his throat like a viper, as his fangs descended.

"Go!" he ordered, giving his charges a shove in the direction of the palace, and then turned away before they saw his face.

Pierre's mother didn't hesitate, but grabbed her son and ran, joining a mass of fleeing humans. With a sense of relief, Jack risked a glance back just as Pierre looked over his shoulder. The look on the boy's face was filled with radiant awe, as if he'd seen an angel instead of a demon. Disconcerted, Jack plunged back into the fray.

At the edge of the crowd, he finally picked up Lark's

scent. It drew him like a beacon, unmistakably hers. Possessive hunger flared. He could feel her like a bright pulse somewhere beyond the throng of humans. He traced the scent away from the milling humanity, from the roar of the flames and engines, and found himself among the trees.

The relative quiet eased his nerves. Even so, she was still blocked from his sight. A wave of impatience surged through him, begging him to rip out every oak and ash in his way.

"Lark?" he called, straining to hear an answer.

No sound came back to him. He plunged forward into the trees, the familiar, peaceful garden transformed by the grotesque light of the fire. Danger hung in the air, almost a scent of its own among the smoke and blood and trampled earth. He scanned the scene, alert to the slightest motion, but nothing was there. *What if she found the source of the magic and it went horribly wrong?*

Eventually, unwillingly, he began to hunt among the low bushes for her fallen form. Success came just when Jack was fending off despair. No shadows could hide the familiar curve of Lark's body as it lay on the ground.

He froze, checking the area. He could smell blood, but heard nothing that said enemies were close—and that was all the discipline he could muster. He dashed forward, falling to his knees so fast that he skidded on the lawn. Panic lurched in his gut. She was curled on her side, long hair strewn against the grass. Instantly, he put a hand to her pulse and felt the knot in his chest ease. The beat was strong despite a wound to her scalp that said she'd been hit from behind. That, more than anything else, surprised him. No one got the drop on Lark. Instinctively, he looked around one more time, but still nothing stirred.

Of course, scalp wounds bled, and the luxurious aroma of fey blood nearly made him light-headed. He forced the goading hunger away and forced his attention elsewhere. A Smith & Wesson lay a few inches from her hand and

Jack took it, emptying the ammunition before sliding the weapon into his own belt. By the scent, it had been recently fired. Where had she gotten another gun? And did that mean there had been more than one opponent—one she'd shot at, and one who had crept up from behind? *Who dared to threaten her?*

With that thought, his fangs descended fully. Lark had been surrounded, and he hadn't been there to protect her. A growl ripped from deep in his chest, and he felt the demon stir. It understood protecting what belonged to Jack. It wanted to crush the enemy, too.

"Lark," he said softly, pushing the soft mass of her hair from her face. All the anger and suspicion he'd felt earlier that night collapsed beneath a surge of alarm. "Jessica. Wake up."

When she didn't stir, Jack ran his hands over her limbs, checking for other injuries, but there were none. Her warmth, her softness, and the silk of her skin conspired to wreck his concentration for the next millennium. He bent until his lips brushed her ear. The perfume of female fey filled him like an intoxicant. "Lark?"

Then she moaned slightly, flicking him away as she might a persistent fly. Jack sat back on his heels as she opened her eyes. Her unfocused look reminded him of the many times they'd awakened together. Memories of warmth and laughter—even a sense of peace—flickered like an antique film, out of place and unreal in the smoke-filled darkness.

"Ow!" Lark explored the cut on her head and winced. Her voice was hoarse with pain.

"What happened?" He caught her hand and held it. The way she was poking at her wound was making him twitch. His free hand found her cheek, cupping it gently to hold her still.

Lark cursed softly in her own tongue as she struggled to sit up. Jack helped her, sliding an arm around her shoulders.

Her heat mesmerized him, giving rise to an overwhelming urge to carry her away to safety and soft pillows. However, sitting up was as far as Lark could go right then. She leaned against him, blinking to clear her head. One more time, the scent of her blood nearly pulled him under.

"Never mind me. What's happening now?" Lark asked.

"The fire is still burning. Most of the onlookers have cleared out. I'm sure the palace is already spinning a cover story. The more important question is how to stop the fire."

"She said the fire will go out on its own. This is for show." Lark was struggling to stand. Jack supported her, taking most of her weight until she regained her balance. Lark winced and cursed again.

"Who said that?" Jack asked.

"I shot her but it didn't even slow her down. She must have walked away." Lark rubbed her cheek, leaving a smear of dirt. "After that tree blew up, no one would even notice one more injured person leaving this scene."

Jack wondered about the tree. He wondered about the whole incident—but getting Lark to safety was his first priority.

"Who were you chasing?" Jack asked, doing his best to be patient.

Lark hesitated, as if reluctant to say the name. "Drusella Blackthorn."

Jack sucked in his breath. Originally, there were five Dark Fey nobles who'd escaped the confinement spell a thousand years ago. Two still survived: Drusella and Egon Blackthorn, cousins to the Dark Queen.

"According to reports, Drusella always works with her brother," Lark said. "No doubt it was Egon who hit me from behind."

The Blackthorns. They'd been involved in the attempt to steal the wedding ring, and now they were back. Jack was about to ask more, but Lark had pressed her palms against her eyes.

"How badly does your head hurt?" he asked, concern banishing everything but her.

"My pride hurts worse," she confessed. "I was jumped like a rookie."

"Egon's a Dark Fey sorcerer. Give yourself a break."

"This has not been a good night."

She was entirely right, yet in that moment Jack found a shred of pleasure in the fact Lark was in his arms again and for once they were in harmony. She sighed, dropping her fine, slender hands from her face. They appeared so delicate, although she could pack a fearsome wallop when her temper was up. Lark was like a pearl-handled pistol, no less lethal for all her prettiness. Jack had never expected less of her than the other Company agents, and she'd never disappointed.

If Lark had been ambushed, it was only because she'd been up against villains with a thousand years of magical expertise. The thought of her alone with the Blackthorns turned his cold, dead heart to ice.

"We'll get them," he said, his voice dark with menace. "But right now, let's get you inside and then figure out why the Dark Fey set the arch on fire."

"Drusella said the fire will go out. It's not about destruction—this is just a sideshow. The real question is what the main event is going to be."

Despite her matter-of-fact tone, his chest tightened as she turned to him, her eyes dark and huge in her pale face. She was in pain, and every piece of him demanded she be safe and sheltered in his care. *No one else touches you but me.*

Chapter 10

Without warning, Jack slid his arms beneath Lark and lifted her. Sure, he was a vampire, but his casual strength still startled her. She might as well have been a kitten, for all the effort it took to pick her off the ground.

The sudden motion as he straightened made her pounding head reel. She curled into him, her cheek cradled against the soft leather of his jacket. Beneath the garment, the solid muscles of his chest moved like living iron. Iron had always been a fey's weak spot, and she wasn't in a mood to resist.

He carried her through a garden entrance and up a set of stairs. Once on the second floor, Jack turned down a side hallway that appeared to be used mostly by servants. A few passed by, but there were too many injured limping here and there in the chaos for Lark and Jack to stand out. Finally, they reached the end of a dim corridor and he moved to set her down. She twisted in his arms, sliding down his body until her feet touched the floor. She indulged in another few seconds of contact before unwinding her arms from his neck.

"Can you stand on your own?" he asked, holding her elbow until he was sure.

"I think so," she said, though she braced one hand against the wall. "Where are we?"

"Someplace safe." He unlocked a narrow door that might have led to a broom closet. Once inside, he locked the door behind them. When he turned on the light, she expected mops and buckets. Instead, the overhead glow revealed a small sitting room with simple but tasteful furniture. Through interior doorways, she could see a bedroom and bathroom. There were no windows, but that was a plus for the undead.

"Whose rooms are these?" she asked. "Yours?"

Jack shrugged. "The king keeps this apartment for Company use. So did his father and grandfather. The place isn't exactly a home away from home, but even spies and dead men need a place to sleep and take a shower."

Though an agent, Lark had never been assigned to the palace, so she'd never known the rooms existed. Still, she was slightly annoyed that she hadn't sniffed out all of Jack's lairs. The man had more bolt-holes than a fox.

She tried to frame an answer, but the afterglow of being carried in his arms scrambled her thoughts. She caught the faint scent of him, an exotic aroma as if he'd walked through a spice merchant's stall in some desert market. It wasn't a cologne or soap—it was just one more enigmatic quality that made up Jack Anderson.

Be careful, she told herself. *He's slipping more and more toward his demon side, and that means he's unpredictable.* All the same, his attraction held a dark edge that made her mouth water and her brain turn to mush. Yes, this was Jack—but he had her alone, in a hidden apartment with only one exit and no windows, and he had a demon on board. There was good reason to be wary, even if he was all solicitude.

His hooded eyes, with their long lashes, held her pinned where she stood. The room was too small, as if the walls were sucked inward by the tension between them. She raised her hands, palms out, in a gesture of self-defense. They almost prickled from the force of Jack's presence.

"I'm covered in blood. I need to wash it off," she said. "It must be driving you crazy."

The corner of his mouth quirked, and he gestured toward the bathroom door. "Please."

Lark took a first step, every instinct telling her not to turn her back. His mouth might be smiling, but she could see the tips of his fangs. Once a vampire's hunger was roused, it didn't fade until he was fed. Surrender to a vampire's bite brought ecstasy, but it also made one utterly vulnerable to their every whim.

Good sense told Lark to lock herself in the bathroom ASAP. Still, there were things she had to know immediately. The answer would decide what she did next. "Are you locking me up here?"

"I'm going to let you recover here."

That wasn't quite an answer. "I'll help you if you stop trying to put me in chains. You saw what's out there. We need to work together."

He gave a slow, reluctant nod. "For now. Until you give me a reason not to."

It wasn't much, but she'd take that crumb of trust—and push for one more. "You still have my guns, plus the one I borrowed from Princess Amelie's guard."

With a rustle of leather, Jack produced the weapons one by one and set them on the tiny hall table, and then set her clips next to the small arsenal. "Go wash up. I'm going to check in with the guards. Maybe they've uncovered something of interest."

There was nothing more to say. Lark forced herself to pretend she didn't notice the drowning black of his pupils as they dilated to take in prey. Fear tickled the back of her neck like a feather of ice, and once she reached the bathroom, she locked the door. That wouldn't necessarily keep him out, but it made her feel much better. Sort of. Desire and fear spiraled together like crazy DNA.

Pulling herself together, Lark looked around. The room was basic and stark white, but it was spotless. She stood in front of the sink and confronted the mirror. She was filthy, her hair matted and her coat stained where she'd lain on the grass. Blood had dripped down her collar and sleeve and smeared her forehead and cheek. With a mental apology to whoever cleaned the floor, she shed her garments one by one and let them fall, planning to deal with them when she wasn't covered with blood and dirt.

When she finally stood naked, she considered her reflection. She looked as she always had, pale skin over muscles toned with training. That was, and was not, the truth. Fey healed quickly and well, but without magical intervention it would have been a very long time, if ever, before the scars from the fire in New York had faded away.

She'd been told to simply use a glamour to cover the ruined mass of skin and muscle that stretched from her collarbone to her knees. The Light Fey were too weak to waste power, even on the only Company-trained agent the Light Court had. The warrior in her had understood and even prized the scars, but the woman in her had mourned her beauty. And appearance aside, what no glamour could cover was the pain. She was healed enough to power through the excruciating injuries, but anything that didn't hurt was numb and clumsy from the damage.

The Light had wanted her back in the field, and Lark wasn't one to shirk duty, even through acute discomfort— and a haze of painkillers. But on her way out of the Light Fey territories, Lark stopped at the library of her old school. There, half remembered from her studies, she had found the Dark Fey spell that would heal her.

Such magic was forbidden to the Light, so she'd traveled well away from her home before she'd used it. It had taken a sacrifice of her blood—something a convalescent couldn't spare—but it had worked. Overnight, she had become whole again, as sleek and healthy and pain-free as before. Of course the Light Court would find out eventually, but under the circumstances, Lark was prepared to sin first and beg forgiveness later. She'd always been the odd one out in the family—the orphan, the one who tried a little too hard, the one left uninvited if there was a more interesting guest. Lark had learned early to provide for herself.

But Drusella Blackthorn's words returned to her. *For those first few days after you arrived, your flirtation with the Dark made you incredibly easy to follow.* The spell that had ended her pain had also left a residue that made it possible for the Dark Fey to track her.

Lark's body tightened with frustrated anger. She leaned on the sink, hanging her head. *I should have known better. Dark Fey magic always comes with a price.* She should have realized Dark Fey could follow the stink of their spells long after they faded for everyone else. The fact that she had been full of pain, drugs and remorse for what she had done to Jack didn't make it any less stupid.

She tried to remember everywhere she'd been since she'd arrived, but her thoughts scattered like startled birds. Should she tell Jack? But how could she explain what she'd done and why, when he was so much a part of her reasons? He'd just take this as one more sign not to trust her.

She shivered, her exhausted emotions at their limits. Jack was on the other side of the flimsy door. If she lingered in here for too long, he'd know something was amiss. Lark stepped into the shower. Her head ached and stung as she washed the blood from her hair, but getting clean made her feel better. She washed quickly, gathering her wits so she could decide her next move.

Lark turned off the water and reached for a towel. As she stepped out of the tub, she froze, one foot a few inches from the thick white mat. Her clothes were gone from the floor. On the back of the door, a thick white robe hung on the hook. Jack had been in there while she showered. It was so like him to assume control of her personal space without asking.

She thought of the drowning darkness in Jack's eyes as his hunger rose, and her pulse galloped. She pulled on the terry-cloth robe and was glad to see it covered her from neck to ankles. Some men should only be confronted when both parties were fully dressed. Lark cinched the waist of the robe and went to retrieve her clothes.

Jack was sitting in the tiny kitchen nook, hunched over the counter. The posture showed the width of his shoulders and the clean lines of his profile. His cheeks looked slightly pink, as if he'd fed. Lark felt a pang of jealousy completely out of sync with the rest of her mood.

He was scrolling through the messages on his phone. "I still can't get a signal."

"For how long?"

"Since I lost it while driving to Company HQ." He tossed the device to the countertop in disgust. "I was talking to Kenyon."

Lark froze. She knew the names of all the Horsemen, though she'd only ever met Mark Winspear, who was a friend as well as fellow agent. "Where was Kenyon?"

"At a restaurant, I think. He said Ralston and Winspear are out of town." Jack rubbed his face, his voice constricted. "Odds are the Horsemen escaped the blast. That's the only thing keeping me sane right now. But I can't get anyone. I don't know who else made it."

Lark bit her lip. Faces flashed through her mind— friends, teachers, even the cooks who fed the few non-vampires in the tiny cafeteria. One more second and she would go to pieces—and that wasn't going to do a thing to stop the next attack. She forced herself onward. "It's all the magic pinging around. That's how I popped that electronic lock. Spells wreak havoc with the tech."

Jack dropped his hands from his face. He looked weary. "Yeah, I figured as much."

"Where are my clothes?"

His eyes swept over her, taking in the huge robe wrapped around her slender frame. The corner of his mouth twitched, almost a smile. "I got rid of them. The palace staff are bringing something in your size."

"Aren't we supposed to be saving the world right now? I could wait for fresh socks."

"Your clothes smelled like your blood. I couldn't afford the distraction."

Her breath caught, remembering the tension just before she'd gone to shower. "Ah."

The lines around his mouth tightened. "Yeah."

"Did you talk to the guards?"

"Not yet. There's no landline in this suite and the cell phones are down. I only left you here long enough to find a staff member."

"Why wait here? You could have left a note."

A possessive look flashed through his gaze. "I had to make sure you didn't pass out in the shower. You have a head injury. You need to rest."

Lark grimaced. "I don't need to rest. I need to kill Drusella Blackthorn."

"All in good time. Now sit down and let me look at your wound."

Grumpy now, Lark obeyed and pulled herself up onto the high stool at the counter. It wasn't an easy move in the robe.

Even at that height, Jack stood tall enough to check her scalp. "You've got a nice bump, but the cut's not deep. I could stitch it, but it's not really necessary."

"Good. Don't bother. We've got better things to do. If the fire was a distraction, it was obviously meant to spread the remaining security thin. With the Company disabled and the human guards running like headless chickens, what's been left unprotected?"

"Don't forget the police and fire were called in, too. The target—if there was one—might have been in the city. With the wedding so close, there are all kinds of dignitaries in town. Also banks. Casinos. Museums."

Jack was behind her, hands resting on her shoulders, when he paused. For a long moment he remained as still as only a vampire could be, and then one finger traced her neck, following the line until it disappeared into the collar of the voluminous robe. It tickled and, reflexively, she pulled the thick terry cloth tighter. Then she realized the collar had gapped when she'd climbed the stool, and he could see her shoulder. She suddenly felt far more exposed than she actually was.

"You said you were burned," Jack said softly, a faint note of distrust edging the words. "You look fine."

"Healing magic," Lark replied, her voice cool. She didn't need to say what kind. "I've only been back on my feet the past few months."

He touched her neck again, his fingers lingering at the side of her throat. Then he bent and kissed the spot, his lips soft and cool. "I've always admired your ability to survive. I saw what was left of the building."

"Came to dance on my grave?"

She heard the hitch of his breath and cursed herself.

"What happened that night?" he asked.

Lark slid off the stool, needing to move. She couldn't stand still while thinking about the fire, as if her fight-or-flight response confused memory with the here and now.

Jack wasn't asking about the moment she'd stabbed him, but her mind went there first. The dagger had been spelled to steal Jack's secrets. She'd expected to learn of an amulet or a charm that gave him his extraordinary strength. She'd been utterly unprepared for what had happened next.

Jack's eyes had transformed first, somehow growing dark and bright at once until they were as piercing as a sun and as cold as a star. Lark had frozen, not understanding what was going on. But then Jack had howled with pain, and the blue zigzags of power had burst from his skin, blazing so bright the afterimages had rendered her blind. The energy had come at her in hot waves, lifting her hair as if the winds of hell had risen. And all of it had been focused on her and the crime of her betrayal.

She'd discovered a demon.

Instantly, he'd slid a hand around her throat. His power had beat through her, crushing her pounding heart like a fist. Somehow she'd known that, with a thought, he could have squeezed it to pulp.

"Why did you do that?" The voice had not been Jack's, but an utterance of the abyss.

After that, her memory of the night shredded to nothing, as if the sheer voltage of his power had blown away her synapses. She'd come to her senses hours later, stretched out on her office couch, an afghan drawn over her like a blanket. Jack was gone. The wedding dress was gone—just like always, he had kept his word.

The detail of the afghan had haunted her ever since. She'd never been able to make up her mind if his gesture had been made with affection or irony.

She turned to him now, uncertain. "After you left, it was quiet. When I came to and finally opened my office door, everyone had gone. I was…I wasn't myself, as if parts of me were still unconscious. I was having a hard time stringing thoughts together. I started to walk around the place, not sure what to do next—and they jumped me. They were only human and I gave as good as I got, but there were too many."

Jack's face was hard to read. "I'm sorry."

His attack had made her vulnerable, but she had provoked it. "Don't be."

"Did you identify them?"

Lark shook her head. "They were Knights of Vidon—a handful of the crazy ones who want to keep the war with Marcari going—but it didn't take long to figure out from their conversation that they had some connection to the Dark Fey. I'd given my assistant, Bree, the case notes

I wanted to protect and you had the dress, so they didn't find what they were after."

"But they tried to make you give it up anyway," Jack said, making it a statement more than a question.

"Yes," she said. "They left me for dead, set the fire and left. No doubt they intended to hide any evidence of a murder."

Jack's eyes narrowed, his jaw flexing as if he clenched his teeth.

Lark forced herself to finish. "I tried to crawl out, but the ceiling collapsed before I reached the stairs. The Light Fey carry a contact amulet, a kind of in-case-of-emergency spell. The local fey were able to get me out before the humans found me. You know the rest."

He turned his face away, making a noise of regret and anger deep in his chest. "That night should never have happened. Any of it."

She folded her arms across her chest, hugging herself. "I'm sorry, Jack. I'm sorry about so much."

Unexpectedly, he smiled, giving her a sidelong look. "You know you turned Mark Winspear's life upside down when you gave that notebook to Bree. They had quite the adventure over it."

The change of subject felt like a white flag of truce, and she seized it. "I heard that story. I'm really glad they found each other. I'm fond of them both, and Bree's boy. He was nearly born on the floor of my atelier."

"I remember." Lightly, he put a hand to her cheek. "Keep the good memories of the atelier. It was a happy place."

Lark hauled in a breath. Remembering the good times— and everything she'd lost—was too bittersweet to bear. She'd thrown it all away and had still not helped her people. All those hopes were pinned on Amelie's wedding now.

She put her hand over Jack's where he touched her face. "Do you think you and I can work together now? Can you forgive me enough for that?"

He withdrew his hand, his expression growing hard. "I'll say this once. You could have asked me for what you needed back then. You chose betrayal instead. That's harder to forgive than any wound."

"That's true," she said. "But I can't take it back. I wish I could."

His nostrils flared, a mix of emotions passing over his face more quickly than Lark could read them. The skin of her arms prickled with the brush of his demon power. "Jack?" she asked softly.

"The devil of it is, I still want you. I can control so much of myself, but never that." He tilted her chin up with his finger. Their noses bumped slightly, and then his mouth was on hers. The faint tingle of power became a rush of sensation that engulfed her whole body. His hands rose to cup her cheeks, holding her as gently as a flower, but that delicacy concealed fearsome might.

It wasn't just supernatural power, but brute strength from his human side, too. The Crusaders of old had been hard men forged in the crucible of war, prepared to ride across a continent to take what they wanted at the point of a sword. That, too, was part of Jack's basic nature.

His tongue parted her lips, demanding more. The taste of him stirred an ache of rising need. Then she felt the smooth, hard slide of his fangs against her lip, a suggestion of the exquisite pleasure their bite could give. She stroked her tongue against them, shivering with the knowledge of the pleasure they could bring. That was vampires—dark and terrible as a jungle cat, and just as beautiful.

Lark pulled at his lip with her own teeth, teasing and pulling at him until he plundered her with his tongue. When she returned the gesture, meeting his invasion with one of her own, his fangs drew a drop of blood. Jack shuddered, the foreplay cycling to a new intensity as his hunter's instincts were aroused. The danger and darkness in him only whetted her curiosity, wondering how far he would go. Lark felt the shift like a crackle of static where their bodies met, her fey magic rising to meet his.

He refreshed the kiss, the pressure of his mouth drawing a different kind of fire through her flesh. Suddenly the robe felt too warm, her body pulsing with needs she hadn't felt since they'd parted. Her breasts ached, nipples too sensitive to bear the rough fabric rubbing against them. Lark made a needy sound deep in her throat, begging for more.

This might not be forgiveness, but it felt good.

Or perhaps not. Gently, he stilled her hands. "We shouldn't be doing this," he said, his fingers still trailing down her arm. There was a note of regret in his voice, but it was firm.

He didn't need to fill in the blanks. Whatever heat might be between them, it wasn't going anywhere. Now that the crisis was over, he was returning them to their previous footing.

"Who says you can't control yourself?" Lark fought a sting of aggrieved frustration. His diamond-hard principles were one of the things she loved about him, but she wasn't a fan right now.

"What I want and what's wise aren't always the same thing."

Ouch. Lark gathered her dignity. "Yes, well, maybe it's the bump on the head, but I think we should get down to business and figure out what the Blackthorns are up to," she said, pushing back her wet hair and wincing as her fingers found the place where Egon's blow had struck. "The burning arch isn't half of it. As she was ranting, Drusella claimed the Dark Fey are responsible for destroying the Company compound. Nothing we hadn't guessed, but it's confirmation."

Jack took a step back, inhaling a breath he didn't need. "They will regret that."

Menace thrummed through the simple words. Just like that, the lover disappeared and the agent snapped firmly into place.

"What next?" Lark asked.

"With the phones down, we'll have to go old-school."

"What does that mean?"

A muscle in his jaw jumped, a sure sign of tension. "Up till now, I've followed the chain of command, done everything step by step, but as you say, we're spread far too thin and the attacks aren't over."

"What are you going to do?"

"I'll ring the tower bell to summon the Company. It's the fastest way to find out who is still here to answer the call."

He didn't take the thought to its logical conclusion, but Lark said it in her mind. *We need to know if any of our friends are left alive.*

Chapter 11

Jack's chest tightened at the tolling of the bells.

Since the time of the Company's founding, the supernatural warriors knew the signal required them to muster at the deepest heart of the old palace. The high bell tower had been part of the royal residence since the middle ages, and vampire ears could hear the ancient bronze bells for miles beyond the city's borders. If any agents were nearby, they would heed the call.

But despite all the people hurrying through the halls—those not called outside by the fire—there was no flood of racing warriors. It wasn't a good sign.

Uneasiness roiled through his gut as he strode through the palace corridors. He wished Lark was beside him, but he'd left her waiting for her clothes. She needed the rest, but he knew she wouldn't take it. Stillness wasn't in her nature—especially not at a time like this.

If only he knew what was behind her presence here. He believed what she'd said about Therrien Haven, but there was more to her story than that. The Light Fey didn't need someone of Lark's caliber to track a missing person. Her specialty was surveillance and slipping into places she didn't belong—which raised more questions than Jack had time to ponder. Better to have her at his side, where at least he knew what she was doing.

Jack finally reached his destination. The old banquet hall—part of the original castle—still endured at the building's core. Jack had been there when the stones had been dragged from the mountains to raise the first keep.

Jack heaved open the iron-strapped doors to the windowless, cavernous space. The smell of cold stone wafted on the movement of air. He entered, his glance taking in the enormous fireplace and the bare rafters above. Nothing had changed. Every inch of the walls was covered with battle shields, the heraldic designs faded by centuries, but Jack found his at once—the black hawk of Marcari on a field of gold. It was the same shield that he had carried home from the Holy Land. He'd been a youngest son, battle weary and angry with the world, carrying a fortune in his pack and a curse on his head. That journey had been nine hundred years ago, but the memory still turned him cold.

The tapestry at the front of the room only made things worse. The colors were still brilliant—bright yellow stars shooting across an indigo sky. At the bottom was the fiery pit with tentacled monsters reaching up to snatch the souls of the damned. But most striking were the falling angels and what they had become—demons as vile as any creature of hell. They had walked the mortal world only a handful of times, and the swath of blood and destruction they had cut beggared description.

Jack turned away from the tapestry. He carried one of the Fallen inside him. Only his mortal will and the discipline of the Company kept him from toppling into the abyss and taking everything he loved along with him.

He waited near the huge rough-hewn table in the center of the room, hoping for some sign of the Company warriors running to answer his summons. The tolling ceased, the echoes seeming to cling to the high ceiling, reminding him he was utterly alone. Even with the conflagration outside, the bells could be easily heard for miles.

Jack looked around, apprehension making his mouth run dry. Was it possible that every last member of the Company in Marcari had been caught by the infernal blast?

The enemy had taken out Marcari's greatest protection with one masterful strike. Then they had created the distraction of the burning arch to occupy any remaining opposition. Whatever was happening was big, and it had been carefully planned.

Jack couldn't wait any longer. He surged toward the door, ready to search the palace himself. But no sooner had he moved than a figure appeared in the doorway.

"Kenyon!"

Faran Kenyon, the Horseman called Famine, stood taller than Jack. He was strongly built and had a werewolf's fluid grace, managing to look dangerous despite his fine clothes and the stylish cut of his fair hair. Obviously, he'd been out someplace nice—no doubt the restaurant Jack had heard in the background during their earlier phone call.

"You're all right?" Jack asked.

Kenyon stared at Jack a long moment, his blue eyes guarded and looking very much like the stubborn street kid he'd once been. "Yeah. Why wouldn't I be?"

Jack took two strides forward, grasping him in a hard embrace. Kenyon was like a son to him. Logic might have said he was safe from the blast, but Jack's heart had needed to see him in the flesh.

After a moment, he felt the rib-cracking pressure of the young werewolf's embrace and, for an instant, the world was good. The young man snorted. "Good to see you, too. Fuzzy balls, Jack, what's going on? Why the bells?"

"Where are Ralston and Winspear? You said they were away."

"Yeah, so tell me what's happening," Kenyon demanded.

Jack took a shaking breath. "You first. I need to know where my team is at."

The werewolf bowed his head, submitting to his leader—though he was a little grudging about it. "Winspear has taken the girls to Paris for some emergency wedding shopping."

"Winspear?" Jack asked, relieved Plague was fine but having trouble envisioning the ex-assassin anywhere near a shoe store. "Which girls?"

"Chloe, Lexie and Bree. And don't picture him carrying around a bunch of pink-wrapped parcels. He's just driving. He's got some medical thing at the university he refused to miss. They should be back sometime Tuesday."

Mark is safe. The women are safe. "What about Ralston?"

Kenyon pulled a phone from his pocket and dialed. He listened for a long moment and then put away his phone. "Still no signal. I haven't been able to reach him, but he's out leading thirty new agents on a training exercise."

"You're sure?"

"Yeah, why wouldn't I be?"

Jack fell back against the table with a sigh of relief. He could finally admit to himself he'd dreaded this moment, in case it had gone a different way. But it hadn't. All his Horsemen—and their women—were all right. He sent up a silent prayer of thanks.

Kenyon caught Jack's expression. "Now you tell me what the bloody hell is going on. Why are you so worried about everyone? What's happened since we talked?"

It had only been a few hours, but it felt as though a month's worth of events had been crammed into that single night. It was past midnight now, Jack's vampire senses telling him they had reached the deepest part of the darkness.

Jack swallowed and ripped off the metaphoric bandage. "There's no easy way to say this. Company HQ is gone. It's been destroyed, almost certainly by Dark Fey magic. There's nothing left but a hole in the ground. I saw no sign of survivors."

There was a heartbeat of utter silence as the blood drained from Kenyon's face. He backed to the wall and leaned against it, his movements deceptively casual. It was a long time before the werewolf spoke again. "Start talking."

Jack described what he'd seen. As he spoke, Kenyon's

expression closed off, assuming the blank mask of a man used to hiding his thoughts. "Is that why an email went out calling an ad hoc meeting of all Company staff?"

"I find it hard to believe it was anything but a lure to get as many Company members as possible into the building. Can you think of anyone who didn't go?"

Kenyon shook his head. "I skipped out and went into town for dinner. I came back when I heard about the palace fire on the radio. I just arrived, but so far I haven't seen anyone else from HQ."

Fresh grief slammed Jack like a fist to the gut. *So many must have died.* He turned away, fighting for calm. "That leaves thirty trainees and the Horsemen to guard a palace and a royal wedding with all the dignitaries and celebrities involved. King Renault put out the call for agents stationed in other countries, but it will take time to get reinforcements here."

"This is the Blackthorns at work, isn't it?" Kenyon asked.

"Yes. And they're responsible for the fire outside."

Swearing softly, the werewolf rubbed his forehead, as if a headache was starting. "Last time they cooked up a blood ritual in the palace maze. I can't wait to see this week's surprise."

"I can," said Jack drily. "After a thousand years, anything that still surprises me can't be good."

"I'd forgotten you were such a ray of sunshine."

"I'm more of a thunderbolt kind of guy."

That got a rueful laugh, but it died quickly. "You've been expecting something like this, haven't you?"

"I never expected a direct attack on Headquarters."

Kenyon flushed, looking suddenly very young. "There was one other person who wasn't at HQ. Winston Rathbone. I had dinner with him tonight."

"Rathbone?" Jack said curiously. He handled the finances of the individual agents. Rathbone had a supernatural nose when it came to return on investment, but he was hardly Kenyon's typical choice for dinner companion. It did, however, explain the werewolf's dress suit.

"I wanted to make sure everything was all right with me on the money side. I'm marrying Lexie," Kenyon said quietly. "In case you didn't already know."

"You've mentioned that a few hundred times." Jack swallowed around the sudden ache in his throat. *Married! Yesterday, he was just a mouthy kid with a talent for second-story work.* There was still mercy in the universe if Kenyon had picked tonight of all nights to check his portfolio. "She's getting one helluva guy. I'm proud of you."

"I hope you can squeeze our wedding into your calendar, now that you're on the Jack Anderson superhero comeback tour," Kenyon said. "Sounds like we're going to be busy playing Dark Fey Whac-A-Mole."

Jack felt a sudden, grim pleasure at that image. It was good to have at least one of the Horsemen back. "I will dance at your wedding. You can count on that."

Jack just hoped the Dark Fey wouldn't be dancing on their graves first.

Chapter 12

A knock came at the door to the banquet hall and Jack looked up as Kenyon answered it. Lark pushed past the werewolf, her gaze sweeping the room until she found him. She was dressed now, looking neat and pressed, but her eyes were wild. "Jack!"

His brain stalled a moment, still seeing the white terry robe—and the silky skin beneath it—in his mind's eye. Then he saw her looking at Kenyon, and he remembered his manners. "Jessica Lark, this is Faran Kenyon."

The werewolf's eyes widened. "Pleased to meet you, ma'am."

She leaned forward, planting her hands on the table as if she needed the support. She was trembling, light shivers moving up and down her frame, but her voice was controlled. "Forgive me for being rude, but we don't have time for pleasantries. I'd barely set foot in the hallways again before Captain Valois found me."

Valois was the head of the local police and a good cop. "With the arch on fire, I'm not surprised that he's here," Jack said.

Lark shook her head. "Valois is here for another reason. He got a ransom note and came to the palace to verify it. It was demanding the rubies of Vidon for the safe return of Princess Amelie."

"The princess?" Kenyon asked sharply. "What are they talking about?"

"A ransom?" Jack demanded.

"No way," Kenyon added. "That's not even logical. Amelie always has that ring on a chain around her neck. You couldn't kidnap her without kidnapping it at the same time."

A bad feeling was pooling at the base of Jack's spine. "Who sent the note? What were the details?"

Lark met Jack's eyes. "It was vague, saying there would be instructions to follow—but there's no question it's real. Valois says Amelie's gone. I came straight here to tell you."

Lark had barely finished speaking when Jack bolted from the room, Kenyon on his heels. Lark outpaced them—fey were faster than any other creature, even vampires. Her feet barely touched the marble floors as she darted through the palace. Blood pounded in her aching head, but she desperately tried to think.

Drusella had said Lark had been easy to follow—and what had she been doing but visiting Amelie time and again, telling the princess all about her fey heritage? Despite Lark's precautions, had they been overheard? *Was Amelie kidnapped because I used Dark magic to heal myself?* Shame wrenched her as she sped through the twists and turns of the corridors.

They were almost back to Amelie's rooms when she skidded to a stop, her shoes sliding on the hard floor. The passageway outside the royal apartments was crammed shoulder to shoulder with people, most of them in uniform. Without a doubt, something had happened.

Lark suddenly felt hollow, as if every scrap of blood and bone had vanished from inside her. She leaned against the wall, bracing herself before she sank to the floor. *I was supposed to protect Amelie and instead I brought danger to her door.*

Lark had barely finished the thought when she felt Jack's hands on her shoulders, holding her back when she moved to join the crowd. The deliberately gentled strength in his hands brought back intimate memories, and her breath hissed in as her flesh reacted to his presence.

"Stay here," Jack said softly. "Wait and think."

"Wait for what?"

"This had to be the Blackthorns," Jack said. "Magic is the only way someone could get to the princess so easily."

With a cold chill, Lark thought of the tricks she'd used to get into the princess's rooms. "I agree. And now we know why the arch was on fire. This is why they'd needed a distraction."

"The blaze drew the crowds away," Jack agreed. "It certainly worked on us."

"I left Amelie under guard just a few hours ago. I told her she would be safe." Lark pulled away and turned to face Jack. Her panic over the kidnapping was reflected in Jack's eyes, but they both had their professional masks on. Emotions weren't helpful now. "I need to start questioning witnesses."

"Let Kenyon pave the way with the police captain. You and I are dead, remember? Ghosts don't have much authority when it comes to official crime scenes. Ghosts are better at the sneaking and spying part."

"Speak for yourself, dead man."

"Ouch. That's a grave accusation." Their banter, half-hearted bravado to cover their fears, faded to silence. Then Jack spoke again. "Where would they take the princess?"

"To their turf. Somewhere they have control."

"Outside the capital, then."

Lark bit her lip. She had sources of information the Company didn't know about. There were rules against sharing, but she mentally kicked them aside. This wasn't the time to hold back. "The Light Fey have intelligence that servants of the Dark are setting up shop near the gates to the Dark Fey realm. I'd say that's where we need to look first."

"In the mountains?" asked Jack, his voice surprised.

"Yes."

"That's a long way. Why go there when the wedding they're trying to stop is here?"

"I think it says something about their confidence. They don't care so much about the wedding itself anymore." Lark was already exhausted, her head pounding from Egon's blow. "They think they can free the Dark Queen before the wedding takes place."

Jack swore. Lark agreed. So much depended on the wedding and the coronation that would follow, and so much on Amelie keeping her fey blood a secret.

After a few minutes, Kenyon's request to Valois bore fruit. Everyone but a handful of Captain Valois's best detectives was cleared from the hallways outside the royal apartments. Immediately, Jack entered Amelie's rooms to search for clues.

Lark hunted for the invisible traces only a fey could hope to find. Ambulance attendants were bent over the guards who were slumped outside the princess's door. One of the unconscious guards was in his middle years, but she recognized the younger one as the guard who'd loaned her his backup weapon. She put a hand to the young man's throat, feeling for a pulse. It was there, but it was faint and slow.

But that wasn't all she felt. There was an oily film of Dark Fey magic clinging to his skin. "He's still alive, but you should get him to a hospital right away."

"What's wrong?" Jack asked, emerging from Amelie's rooms.

"We call it a Sleeping Beauty spell. It should wear off, but it's hard to say whether it will be a matter of days or weeks." In the old days, victims usually died of dehydration before the magic dissipated. At least now they could put the victim on an intravenous drip. She moved to check the other guard and found the same result.

"Isn't there any way to remove it?"

"Not my kind of magic," Lark replied. "And the thing

about a kiss breaking the spell—it only works about half the time, even with royal blood involved."

"You can count Kyle out as a volunteer," Kenyon announced, emerging from the direction of the prince's rooms. "He's gone, too. The place is trashed. There was definitely a struggle."

Lark rose to her feet. At her signal, the ambulance attendants brought stretchers for the fallen guards. "Why take Kyle?"

"To ensure Amelie's cooperation?" Kenyon suggested.

"I'm not sure. She might have been drugged. I found this in the trash," Jack said, holding up the empty bottle that had held the potion meant to disguise Amelie's fey blood. He held it toward the light in his gloved hands, studying the dregs. "I can't figure out what was in it. It doesn't smell like alcohol."

Lark's heart quailed, imagining the princess drinking the potion in an effort to protect herself. How frightened she must have been! And how smart. Light Fey blood doubled her value as a hostage, since the Light Court would be just as frantic as King Renault for her return. That made Amelie almost too valuable a prisoner to give up, no matter the amount of ransom.

The potion would only last a few days, but that was a few days the Dark Fey couldn't confirm the princess's bloodline. Regardless of whether or not Drusella had seen Lark visit Amelie, that would create doubt until the potion wore off. Delay meant an opportunity for rescue—or so Lark hoped.

"Smells herbal," said Kenyon, sniffing the bottle. "Not cooking herbs, either. I don't recognize these."

Lark took the bottle in her ungloved hands, all too aware she'd handled it before.

"Fingerprints!" Jack took it back with a dark look for her amateur mistake. "Do you know what it is?"

Lark just shook her head and Jack dropped the bottle

into an evidence bag. "I need to keep looking," he said as he disappeared back into Amelie's quarters.

Lark followed Kenyon to the prince's apartment, where Kyle was staying until the wedding. It was a mess. Even the heavy drapes were torn from their moorings.

"I don't get it," said the werewolf. "Something like this should have caused a racket. How come no one noticed?"

"A cloaking spell," Lark replied. "The place stinks of it. They must have taken both the prince and princess at the same time and covered their tracks with a glamour that made everything look and sound normal. I've used that kind of spell myself."

"Huh." Kenyon kicked a velvet throw cushion out of his path. "Something doesn't sit right. I'm still not sure why they'd take the prince."

"I have one theory," Lark said. "The rubies hold the spell to open the gates, like a container. The Haven family of the Light Court wove the magic, which is why their blood is used in the rituals. But to activate the spell, you need a token or representative from each of the major races. That way no one race can decide the fate of the Dark Fey. They all have to agree."

"Which means what?"

"To open the gates, the Blackthorns will need a vampire, a werewolf, a Light Fey of the Haven line and a mortal prince. Not a princess—the spell was written with the original kings of Marcari and Vidon in mind. So I think they need Kyle for the spell."

"That makes sense," Kenyon agreed in gloomy tones. "They had Kyle's brother the last time they tried the gates. Too bad they didn't keep him. The guy is a goof."

Lark bent and picked up a framed photograph that had smashed on the floor. It was a picture of the princess leaning against a bright red Porsche, a wide smile on her face as she preened for the camera. That look was meant for Kyle, not a casual observer. An inexpressible sadness lodged in

Lark's chest. She set the photo facedown on the end table, careful of the shattered glass.

Jack appeared in the doorway. "Look at this." He had a bundle of white fluff in his arms. "I found this little guy in the back of the princess's shoe cupboard."

"That's Lancelot," Lark said. "Amelie's dog."

"Lancelot?" Kenyon said in mortification. "I bet he gets teased at doggy day care."

The poor thing was shivering in fright, giving it the look of a hysterical bedroom slipper. "Check out his collar," said Jack.

"Hey, little brother. Everything's going to be okay." Kenyon drew near, rubbing the dog's ears until the creature stopped shaking. Then he unbuckled the thin strip of jewel-studded leather and held it up. "The princess knew Lance here would be smart enough to run and hide."

Lark's jaw dropped. The ruby wedding ring was hooked around the collar. It was a stroke of brilliance, and it changed the game entirely. "She's left us a bargaining chip."

But their momentary elation didn't last long. "This means the kidnappers wrote the note to Valois after they took the princess. The captain just told me that he got the note two hours ago. That means they have at least that much of a head start."

"They'll get to their stronghold before making any more demands," Lark said. "We need to intercept them before they get there."

"We're only assuming they're heading toward the hidden gates," Jack said. "I'd like more proof, but if we wait any longer, we'll lose the chance to catch them on the road."

"Which road, exactly?" Kenyon asked. "Does anyone know how to get to the Dark Fey kingdom?"

"The entrance is in a lake at the heart of the Derrondine Pass," said Jack. "I was there when the original spell was cast to lock the Dark Fey inside."

Kenyon gave a low whistle. "That's deep in the mountains and as remote as it gets."

"Which is why we have to catch them. No doubt the Dark Fey are counting on that isolation to work the ritual in secret." Jack's eyes seemed to burn, for once his anger barely banked. "We may be all that's left of the Company in Marcari, but guarding the princess remains our duty. We leave at once."

Chapter 13

Jack commandeered an armored Land Rover Defender from the palace garage and Captain Valois offered enough supplies and weapons to equip an invasion—which wasn't far from their goal. Jack had done battle with Selena, Queen of the Dark Fey, back in the day. Sometimes more was better.

"I should be going with you," said the police captain. He was somewhere in his forties, with nondescript brown hair and worry lines that matched the creases in his uniform.

"You're understaffed and under attack." Jack might have added that the police were out of their depth, but he could tell Valois already knew it. "Keep the palace and its guests safe. We'll get the bride and groom back here in time for the wedding."

Valois gave him a shrewd look. "You are very confident, vampire."

"You've seen us in action," Jack said, gesturing to where Kenyon was loading supplies into the vehicle. "The Horsemen always come through."

Valois nodded. "True. Kenyon was hellish messy and kept turning up naked on the palace lawn—but he got results."

Nevertheless, the police captain produced a piece of paper from his jacket pocket and handed it to Jack. "Here's what we know so far. There was a late-model black Chevrolet Suburban seen leaving the west palace entrance at exactly the time our kidnappers would have left. What caught the interest of our patrol was that the drivers of the vehicle appeared to be loading large bags of laundry. Not the usual laundry company. The patrol wrote down the plate number and went to confront them."

"What happened?" asked Jack.

"He just remembered the incident five minutes ago. Can't remember actually speaking to anyone or what they looked like."

"Fey mind tricks." Jack took the paper with the plate number from Valois. "Leave pursuit to the Company. This type of situation is what we're good at."

"Ah, but the enemy got to your headquarters first, didn't they? It seems not even the vampires are invulnerable this time."

Jack had no reply to that.

Valois folded his arms. "There is one thing I don't understand. Why would Dark Fey need a regular vehicle? Isn't there a spell they could use to travel faster?"

"That seldom works with human passengers," Jack replied. "The risk would be too great."

"Good to know they have limits. Is there anything else you need?"

Jack needed the drones and choppers and everything else that had been destroyed at HQ, but there was no point in saying so—the locals didn't have anything close to that level of tech because the Company had always provided that. Valois was doing what he could. His most trusted team had already taken on the forensic work involved in processing the HQ crime scene.

"Keep this mission under wraps," Jack said. "If no one knows we were here, and if no one knows the prince and princess are missing, we have a far better chance of success. The last thing we need to deal with is news hounds and public panic."

"Understood." Valois frowned. "I know the Night World

likes its secrecy, but I have to say that burning arch was hardly discreet."

"If this group wins, the whole world will know about the Dark Queen. I don't think they care."

The police captain grew pale. "Good luck, Jack. Do what you do best."

Jack flashed him a feral smile. "The Company gets justice. It's what we've always done."

Lark bolted upright from a light doze, her head pounding from the merciless bouncing of the vehicle. The Land Rover was climbing a steep road toward the foothills of the mountains. Jack had driven for the rest of the night, trading off with Kenyon hours ago. Rough terrain made the ETA at the Derrondine Pass hard to guess, and they had no sense of how likely they were to overtake the kidnappers. Kenyon was barreling along right at the edge of safety…and a bit beyond.

Lark straightened up, fumbling with the seat belt that was threatening to strangle her. She was in the back of the Land Rover, chilled by air-conditioning and sheltered by the murky glow of tinted windows. The tinted glass privacy panel behind the driver's seat was shut. Faintly, she could hear music pounding through the sound system with Kenyon accompanying in a surprisingly good singing voice.

She'd been dreaming about the time she'd gone riding with her uncle Soran's sons. Her cousins were everything fey warriors were supposed to be—strong, fleet and fearless. She'd tried to keep up with them, fallen off her horse and broken her arm. Lark wondered why she'd had that dream now. Maybe the out-of-control situation had reminded her of that wild ride. Or maybe it was the fear she would fail.

Jack was next to her, slumped against the door and inscrutable behind his sunglasses. She studied his face, admiring the clean lines of his features. She was tempted to trace them with a fingertip except he looked so grim, the set of his mouth an unhappy slash. His restless twitching suggested he was having bad dreams, too.

"Jack!" she said.

One hand went to his eyes, knocking his sunglasses askew. He sat up with a grunt.

"Jack, wake up."

"I'm awake," he snapped, then pulled off the glasses and rubbed his eyes. "Or now I am."

Lark watched him, wondering if he remembered fey could sometimes read a sleeper's dreams. She'd never penetrated his, but she could sense them like a distant storm. She gripped the seat as the Land Rover hit a bump. "Nightmare?" she asked.

He closed his eyes, his expression resigned. "Is there any other option, given the mission?"

"Impossible odds don't keep you up. You're cool as a perfectly chilled chardonnay."

A crease formed between his brows. "How long have you been waiting to use that line?"

"Don't deflect. What's up?"

He grunted. "Some questions are on my mind."

"Like what?" Lark asked.

He shot her a grumpy look. "For an isolated people determined never to get involved, the Light Fey know a lot—like the fact the Blackthorns are setting up shop near the gates. Just how deep in this situation are your people?"

So they were back to playing spy on spy. "With the Dark Fey rising, we need to be vigilant. Our forces are ready for battle at the first sign of attack."

His expression softened slightly. "Good to know. You used to be the best fighters of anyone, but what numbers can you put in the field today if things go wrong?"

"The council hasn't shared that information with me." Lark pushed her hair back, suddenly weary. "You know they'd never let me tell an outsider anyway. The Light Court is pathologically secretive." Even a hint of their vulnerability would give someone like Drusella ideas.

A lift of his eyebrows said he noticed her unusual bluntness. "Rumor has it your numbers are declining."

"We did ourselves a disservice by remaining isolated. That much is plain."

Few understood how that mattered—or how Amelie's kidnapping was a disaster deeper than anyone but the Light Fey could know. The wedding and coronation had to happen, or they were in trouble beyond anything the Dark Fey could devise.

Jack noticed her mood. "What's wrong?"

"I'm afraid," she said truthfully. "I'm afraid of the Dark Queen. I'm afraid of my own mistakes. I'm afraid the good guys can't pull together in time to save each other." *I wish I could tell you everything, but Amelie's secrets aren't mine to tell.* And the slightest hint about the princess's bloodline would put Amelie and all her future children at risk. Lark wasn't ready to do that, not even with Jack.

He bowed his head. Even in the gloom of the car, it was easy to see his hair would have been streaked with gold if the sun ever shone on it. But too many years had passed in darkness, and now it was the brown of winter loam. Transfixed by the memory of its feel, Lark couldn't help herself—she pushed aside the strands that fell across his forehead. His head jerked up, his expression wary.

"The Light Fey are vulnerable," she said, risking as much frankness as she dared. "You're right, we're deeply worried about the Dark Queen returning. The council has suspected this might be coming for a long time. And that's exactly why they sent me to you."

"Did you join the Company just to get close to me?" he asked. Despite his light tone, she could hear the bitterness beneath.

"Yes. I didn't care why they sent me at first. I was beside myself with joy at getting picked for such an important mission." Moral qualms about her role had struck her much later, when she'd finally met the fearsome leader of the Horsemen. "I broke every rule and wanted you for myself. Whatever happened in the past, or happens now, you have to believe that much."

Lark took a deep breath, waiting for his reaction, even if it was anger. She was glad to give him what truth she could. She owed him.

He studied her from behind his dark glasses, his mouth turned down. "And now that you've had a glimpse of what I am?"

"It was a shock," she said bluntly. "But I don't give myself lightly, Jack, and I won't sever that bond until you show me I chose the wrong man. Whatever you are, you've never done that." Even after she'd stabbed him, he'd covered her with a blanket.

His mouth dropped open slightly, an expression of profound surprise. She felt a twinge of satisfaction. Jack wasn't easy to catch off guard.

"You can't say that, Jessica. It's not that simple." His voice was hard, drawing a line he forbid her to cross.

Then the vehicle swayed and he caught her, his hands finding her waist. His touch had nothing in common with his tone. For once, their contact felt utterly natural, without hidden meanings. She melted into his embrace, softly closing the space between them. He let her nestle there, adjusting his position so she would fit all the better.

"Don't tell me what I feel," she replied softly. "My private feelings are the one true thing I have in this world of spies."

He took a shaking breath—a sure sign of emotion in a vampire. Slowly, his fingers began to trace a pattern up and down her back in a slow, gentle caress. Lark didn't speak. For once, she'd said the right thing at the right time and she wasn't going to ruin it.

She tipped her chin to look at his face. His expression—or what she could see of it—was thoughtful. The shades had to go. Sliding upward, she pulled off his sunglasses and kissed him.

The effect was instant. His fingers tangled in her hair, drawing her close. Lark's pulse began to pound, a giddy pleasure tingling through her body. The warm electricity coursing in her veins found a home low in her belly at the same time his fingers slid beneath her shirt, seeking out the lacy edges of her bra. Her fingers curled in the soft cotton of his shirt, gathering bunches of the fabric as she leaned in, savoring his flavor.

"Can we ever stop being agents?" he asked suddenly. "Truly?"

She froze, her lips millimeters from his. "Why not?"

"I never know what's real with you."

"Does it feel as if I'm seducing you for nefarious reasons?"

"You've done it before." The lines beside his mouth were unbending. "Are you here to get something else from me?"

The words burned her worse than any fire. "No."

He kissed her brow, lips soft against her skin, but the gesture was faintly mocking. "Are you sure?"

He was silent as she eased back to her side of the car. Once she was settled, he slid the sunglasses back on, disappearing behind the mirrored plastic. Regret pooled like something toxic in her gut. "I care about you."

"We've already proved how well that works out between us."

She stifled a sigh. "I think one day you're going to have to forgive me, Jack. For your own sake."

He didn't speak. With those sunglasses on, she couldn't even tell if he was looking her way.

She leaned back in her own corner of the car, folding her arms across her stomach. "My head hurts. I'm going to get some sleep."

* * *

As Lark closed her eyes, Jack stretched out his legs as best he could and leaned back against the door. The vibrations were like a massage to his shoulders, and he should have relaxed, but that wasn't in the cards. Not after that conversation.

He'd not been kind and he knew it—but sometimes questions had to be asked. And—it had to be said—he was used to the idea that Lark was in the wrong. He'd grieved for her, but she had done the unthinkable. Being the wounded party had given him power over the pain she'd dealt him.

And yet…here she was. The Lark who had come back to him was different. She seemed subdued, even restrained, like someone who'd been through a lot. That made sense—but perhaps recovering from the atelier fire wasn't the only reason for the change. Might his memory of her be flawed? Anger and distrust had a way of distorting the past. He might be remembering a wily seductress who'd never actually existed.

Or am I willing to overlook the truth because I want to make love to her? Because he did—her presence, just an arm's length away, burned like heat thrown from a flame. The softness in her glance said his touch would be welcome. His reluctance alone kept them apart. And yet… she had seen what was inside him. Logic said she should run away.

So why was she still here? He didn't know. With most women, a knife to the gut meant goodbye.

Closing his eyes felt good. Vampires weren't meant to be awake during the day. Daylight acted on him like a monstrous hangover and made it hard to think clearly. Direct sunlight wasn't fatal, but it could deliver a nasty burn.

The bump and lurch of the heavy tires was oddly soothing, like a rocking cradle. Or maybe it felt like home. Although he'd been born in what was now Marcari, Jack had been a traveler almost as soon as he could sit a horse.

Exhaustion and regret swamped him like the stuffy air inside the Land Rover. His last fading wish was for a dreamless sleep. He didn't get one.

Jack stood on the battlefield somewhere in the Holy Land, the sun beating down on carnage straight from hell. His mare was dead, flies already buzzing though her foam-flecked sides had barely stilled. More horses—big destriers as well as light-boned Arabs—were crumpled in the dust like broken toys, with arrows in their flanks. The stink was like a wall of corruption.

And for every horse there were three men: peasants, priests and mercenaries all there for their own reasons. Some came for faith. Most were there for money. Jack had been sent because he was one son too many and had to make his own way in the world.

The dead were everywhere he looked. Jack fell to his knees, his legs suddenly unstrung. He wasn't sure how he'd made it through the battle, but sun and thirst were going to kill him. The thought was distant, edged with a remote panic that couldn't claw its way in through the fatigue.

His helmet was baking hot, the narrow eye slit no relief. He raised his hands to remove it, but his arms were trembling with exhaustion. When he finally fumbled the thing off, he sucked in a rasping breath of air that tasted of sand and death.

And that was when he saw the man standing a few yards away, his eyes blazing like twin stars. The stranger was dressed in the light robes the Saracens wore, the breeze plucking at the thin fabric. Folds of cloth covered his face, shielding it from the sun and sand and leaving only a slit for those unearthly eyes. He held out a leather-covered bottle. "Drink."

At that, fear kicked in, full colors flying. Jack staggered to his feet, his survival instinct dredging up fresh strength. "No! I know who you are."

"So?" the man asked.

"I know what you are," he whispered. "Demon."

The man put a hand to his chest, mockery in his star-bright eyes. "You wound me."

Jack took a staggering step back, putting distance between himself and the water skin that held cool, refreshing, damning relief. "Wound you? I wish I knew how to kill you."

The man laughed, but the sound held an edge of impatience. Suddenly the figure looking back at Jack wore his own visage, dressed in modern jeans and T-shirt. "Liar. You look in the mirror every day and see my eyes looking back at you. You and I have become one."

Terror speared Jack worse than any battlefield wound. He flinched back another step. "That's never going to happen."

"It happened."

"I've kept you bound, Asteriel."

"Don't be an imbecile. You don't even exist anymore. All you are is a handful of memories and a good jawline, human. The rest of you is me."

"I'm not one of the Fallen. You are."

"You keep saying that like it's going to change something. You're me. We're one." Jack's twin swept a hand around the ancient scene. "You're nine centuries too late to go home."

"Are you sure about that?" Jack drew his sword.

His demon self rolled his eyes. "We have a bargain. One you're going to need very soon."

"Why?"

"Haven't you figured it out, Jack? There are two things we have in common besides your physical body. One is that we both think your fairy is hotter than a dragon barbecue. Stop vacillating like a nervous schoolboy."

"About what?"

The demon's teeth—Jack's teeth—flashed white and

sharp. "You ache to throw her onto your bed and possess her, body and blood."

Jack felt the burn of shame rising to his face. "She betrayed me."

The demon snorted. "Don't judge a soul by one mistake. You of all people should know better than that."

Jack ground his teeth. "I don't take relationship advice from demons."

Said demon folded his arms. "Judgment has a curious way of slicing the hand that wields it."

Jack bowed his head. Anything that came out of the demon's mouth was suspect, but there was the ring of truth in those last words.

He ground his palms against his eyes, blinded by the sun and rippling heat that sucked every scrap of moisture from the air. All he wanted was escape from the dream, but experience said it wouldn't end until the vile creature had finished talking. And the conversation, as far as he could tell, had gone seriously off track.

"And what else do you and I have in common?" Jack asked.

"You know me. Think about it."

His jaw was beginning to ache from clenching his teeth. "I don't like guessing games."

"You saw that hole in the ground where your headquarters used to be."

"That was Dark Fey magic."

The demon waved his hand in dismissal. "Around the edges. Do you really think the Blackthorns have that much power?"

Jack didn't reply for a long moment. They were finally getting to some sort of point, but he couldn't figure out what it was. "I don't know their limits."

The demon gave a derisive chuckle. "You're going to

need me before this is over. Prepare to embrace your dark side, my knightly friend."

"Explain yourself!" Jack demanded.

"Nighty-night, knight." And the dream was over.

Chapter 14

"Phones are back up," Faran Kenyon said, arching his back until it cracked. "Either we're far enough away from the magical interference or it's died down."

Lark was rummaging in a plastic storage box full of snacks. Whoever had stashed it in the Land Rover really liked granola bars but not chocolate, which seemed utterly perverse. Jack was still asleep in the back.

"Good," she said. "I need you to phone your girlfriend."

"Why?" Kenyon asked uneasily.

Lark turned to look out over the foothills. It was midafternoon and they had stopped at a lookout to change drivers. There was a reason this spot was marked on all the tourist maps. With the tall peaks looming ahead and the silver ribbon of the river below, it looked like the cover of a fantasy novel. All it needed was a flock of dragons. "I've been searching for Therrien Haven, but he's gone missing, and we need blood from one of the Haven clan to work the spell."

"I thought we wanted to keep the gates shut," Kenyon said uneasily.

"We may need to open or close the gates, depending on how this mission unfolds. Lexie's blood won't be as potent as her father's because she's half human, but it will probably work."

A stubborn look came over the werewolf's face. "I'm not asking Lexie to come here."

"No, I think she should stay as far away as possible, but she's with Mark Winspear. He's a doctor. He could draw a vial of her blood and bring it when he comes."

Their plan was to rendezvous with the other two Horsemen ahead. There was one crossroad where the winding mountain highway—using the term loosely—connected with a road going east toward Italy. The Company members out on training still had choppers. Most would go back to help Valois guard the palace, but Sam Ralston was an experienced pilot who could navigate the mountain peaks. It was their best chance of getting ahead of the Blackthorns. Of course, their plans depended on getting a cell signal through the mountains. It was a good thing the Company carried the best possible equipment.

Kenyon was already dialing, taking advantage of the reception before they headed deeper into the range. It took him another ten minutes to reach both the other Horsemen and explain what they wanted. It said something about the team that they asked few questions despite the werewolf's catastrophic tale. Meanwhile, Lark got behind the wheel and began adjusting the seat and mirrors. It was her turn to drive.

Finally, Kenyon put his head in the window. "If everything lines up, we'll meet the others in a few hours. The pass is due north. Just follow the road. I'm catching some sleep."

Lark nodded. There was no telling when the next opportunity for shut-eye was going to come around. No sooner had Kenyon retreated to the back than Jack slid into the passenger seat beside her. It was daylight, but the tinted windshield would keep the sun from doing him any real harm.

"Drive," Jack said, folding his arms across his chest, his mood no better than before. "I've slept long enough." He was clenching and unclenching his fingers.

She pulled out of the lookout area and turned onto the

highway. "Really? I seem to recall times when it was hard to get you out of bed."

The sunglasses hid his eyes, but one corner of his mouth quirked up in a self-mocking smile. "You know how to keep a good man down."

"At regular intervals, as I recall." Lark smiled to herself, taking the curve in the road just a little too fast. The roar of the powerful motor suited her mood. "Do you recall that place in Connecticut?"

It had been a historical manor redone as a hotel fit for royalty. Jack, of course, had booked the best suite. She had a mental image of him stretched out on the dark blue sheets of the canopied bed, pale skin like sculptured marble.

"That place was supposed to have quite the rose garden," he mused.

"I don't remember that."

"We never got around to looking at it." The quirk of his lips almost made it to a smile. "That didn't bother me at the time."

"It would have been nice to go back." But that would never happen now. She didn't even know why she'd brought it up.

Unexpectedly, he put a hand on her knee. "I would have liked that, too."

"Really?"

He didn't answer. Lark cursed the need to keep her eyes and mind on the road. She could only take a glance at his face, but it gave away nothing. And yet, unless she was very mistaken, it was almost as if he'd made an overture of peace between them. The knot of tension inside her eased a degree.

The conversation paused as she shifted down to navigate the steeper grade of the road that skirted the base of the first real mountain. The melting snows revealed its flanks of piercing green foliage, but scraps of white still clung to the top half of its slopes. Lark turned off the air-conditioning, suddenly chilled.

The river valley was far behind them now, the view ahead a sunlit meadow to the left and a wall of mountains to the right. There was little traffic, which made the surreal beauty of the scene all the more intense. Beautiful, except for one of the tallest peaks to their right. It was bare and black as pitch.

"What's with that mountain?" she asked.

"They call it Dragon's Tooth," Jack said in a flat voice. "It was a battle site of the old wars. A demon destroyed the dwarves that lived beneath it because they would not surrender their gold. Nothing has lived there since. Not even a scrap of moss."

"And the dwarves?" Lark asked, not sure if she should.

Jack paused a moment before speaking again. "They're extinct. That's what demons do. They destroy things utterly."

The road snaked back and forth along the contours of the rock formations, and both of them were silent for the next hour. The strained atmosphere was finally broken when Jack pointed forward, all his focus on a black speck miles ahead. "Look there."

"Is that the Suburban?" she asked.

Dusk was just starting to gather, lending a purplish hue to the light. Vampires could see well, but this was a stretch even for the undead. Jack pulled a set of field glasses from the pocket of the car door, slipping off his sunglasses long enough to peer through them. "Yes!" he said triumphantly. "I can't see the whole license plate. The angle's wrong, but the first part matches what Valois gave me."

Lark urged the Land Rover to go faster, pushing it until she felt the vehicle lurch on the corners. The motion must have woken Kenyon, because he pounded on the privacy panel. Jack slid it open.

Kenyon's face appeared in the opening. "What's going on and do I need a crash helmet?"

"We've got eyes on the vehicle," Jack replied. "It won't be easy to catch them, but it's a start."

He was right. It wasn't going to be easy because the winding road—while wonderfully scenic—multiplied the distance between the two vehicles. Frustration hunched Lark's shoulders.

"Sit down and buckle up," she ordered, slowing the vehicle. "This isn't a Land Rover for nothing."

"What are you doing?" Jack asked uneasily.

She waited until the Suburban went around the edge of the next curve and disappeared from sight. That meant, by extension, the Suburban couldn't see the Rover. If she was going to make a sneaky move without blowing their cover, now was the time.

"There's some land—I'm roving on it."

And with that, she bumped off the edge of the road and began cutting across the open meadow, lopping off a meandering section of road that was nothing but a waste of precious time. Fighting the wheel, she gritted her teeth and hoped the vehicle was as good as its reputation. The ruts bounced her into the air a few times, but she gamely pushed the Rover forward, her eyes locked on her destination. Dead ahead, the landscape changed again where the road threaded a narrow gap between two mountains.

"You'll be hearing from my chiropractor," Kenyon complained after a few minutes of relentless bouncing.

Lark flashed him a grin in the rearview mirror. "Where's your sense of adventure, Horseman?"

They were almost across the strip of meadow, the shadowy passage between the mountains dead ahead. The land had dipped, but now it was rising again. Lark stepped on the gas to make it up to the crest. The tires chewed the earth, fumbling for traction, but when she changed the angle of the wheel they finally grabbed. The Rover raced up the hill, gathering speed—and then the land dropped away over a narrow but very deep fissure in the earth. Lark gasped but gunned the motor, launching the vehicle into the air. Her stomach plummeted to the soles of her feet.

Jack cursed, knuckles white on the door handle.

The Rover landed with an unholy thump and bounce that was sure to leave seat belt bruises. The motor made a bizarre cough, almost as though it was clearing dust out of its throat, and then the tires caught and they shot forward again.

Reflex alone kept Lark steering. "Didn't see that one coming."

Jack made an inarticulate noise of disgust. "It's just as well I don't have blood pressure." But his expression was fierce, his eyes dark with the joy of the chase.

They had made up time, and on cue the Suburban looped back into view—its back end a tempting target directly in front of them. If the drivers ahead wondered where the Rover had come from, they gave no sign.

"How do you want to play this?" Lark asked.

"Carefully." Jack's Walther was in his hand. "If the prince and princess are in the vehicle, we have to stop it, not crash it into the mountainside."

A sharp corner loomed, and Lark had to slow to take it cleanly. The loss of speed chafed, and she muttered under her breath. They needed to make up only a few minutes and they'd be on the Suburban's bumper. The vehicle had tinted windows, but she could almost make out figures in the back.

"Chopper!" Kenyon stuck his head out the side window for a better look, twisting to see upward past the walls of rock hemming them in. "It's ours. Sam made good time."

The sudden breeze from the open window whipped Lark's hair, tickling the back of her neck. She risked a quick glance up and to her left. Sure enough, one of the Company's black helicopters was pacing them above. They were supposed to have met at the rendezvous point in another fifteen minutes, but Sam Ralston must have spotted them on the road and moved in as air support. That hadn't been part of Jack's plan for a stealthy ambush. She had a sudden flash of worry for the hostages. "What do we do, Jack?"

"Slow down," he said urgently. "Bad timing. The Suburban will have spotted the chopper, and they'll react if they feel trapped."

She didn't like taking her foot off the gas, but she obeyed. She felt distance opening between them like a tearing wound, but it turned out to be the best thing. The Suburban suddenly put on the brakes. Lark reacted instantly, tires protesting, but she couldn't brake fully before the doors of the vehicle ahead flew open and two men leaped out, assault rifles blazing.

Kenyon pulled an automatic rifle from the storage compartment behind him and slammed a magazine into place. "I'd say our cover's blown."

Chapter 15

Jack and Kenyon opened the Land Rover's doors. The racket of the gunfire roared in at a painful level. The men started shooting back, using the doors as shields. Thankfully, the Rover's armor plating held up.

A bullet struck the windshield, making Lark jump and leaving a spiderweb of cracks. Lark drew her Smith & Wesson and pushed the button that would slide open the sunroof. She needed to stay close to the wheel in case they needed a sudden retreat, but she wasn't about to miss all the action.

Meanwhile, the chopper drew closer, dropping altitude to hover directly above. There was no room to set it down, but the pilot was blocking any chance of escape. The sound of the rotors finished off what was left of Lark's hearing. Waves of dust and leaves kicked up, swirling through the firefight.

Then one of the shooters suddenly dropped, felled by a bullet angling from the sky. Distance, wind and motion had done nothing to spoil the shooter's aim. Lark thumped the steering wheel in triumph. Such impossible marksmanship was the Horsemen's trademark. A surge of hope made her eyes sting. They might pull off this rescue yet.

But then someone rolled out of the Suburban, keeping low to the ground. Jack shot at the figure, but the bullet seemed to veer off, ricocheting wildly against the rock wall. The dark-clad woman found her feet and rose from her crouch. *Drusella!* Lark clutched her weapon, surging up through the sunroof to take aim.

Lark fired, but it was too late. Drusella launched a ball of blue flame at the chopper's tail. The missile pulsed, coruscating with veins of orange and white as it spun. Lark summoned her power and threw a bolt after it, but it was like a spitball chasing a nuclear warhead. Her stomach rolled, an agony of helpless fury eating its way through her. Both spheres of power seemed to travel with agonizing slowness, but maybe that was because Lark guessed what was coming next.

So did the others. Jack and Kenyon leaped back into the Rover. "Back up!" Jack roared. "Get out of the way!"

She hesitated a split second, cursing her weakness—but weapons magic simply wasn't her strength. Bitterly she dropped back to her seat and slammed the Rover into Reverse, tears blurring her vision. With a roar, the vehicle sped out of the path of disaster.

And just in time. Lark's ball of energy sailed uselessly onward while Drusella's blew the back rotor to smithereens. Lark flinched at the smoking debris that dropped just feet from the front bumper. Bits of rock and metal pinged against the hood and skidded off even as Lark gunned the Rover backward and out of harm's way.

But the show had just begun. Like a dragonfly executing a solemn ballet, the chopper began to wheel in the air, spinning in erratic circles and nearly scraping the mountainside. Lark was aware of Drusella running for the Suburban, which was already in motion. The two gunmen lay dead and abandoned on the ground, the second one felled by Jack.

The chopper's drunken trajectory brought it closer and closer to the rock face. The air inside the Rover thickened with wordless horror.

Almost as if it tripped in midair, the helicopter tilted nose down. It was the worst possible move. Within seconds, the main rotor hit the mountain. Lark's face went numb with shock as the blades sheered off, shooting into the air like giant matchsticks. The effect was instant. The chopper dropped like a wingless insect, crashing nose first before rolling onto its side. Her breath stopped utterly, certain this nightmare couldn't get any worse.

But no. There was a moment of silence, as if the universe held its breath—and then in a gout of roiling black smoke, the chopper burst into flame.

Jack jumped out of the Land Rover and sped toward the wreckage. A glance told him the Dark Fey's Suburban was disappearing in a trail of dust, but there was no chance of getting the Rover past the burning chopper. In any event, he wasn't about to leave friends trapped inside a flaming wreck. Jack had come too close to that fate himself in the car crash that had nearly ended his existence.

He leaped over chunks of smoking debris, making for the main body of the craft. The door had blown off, leaving a hole in the side of the cockpit. Jack pulled his leather coat up over his head, tucked his hands in his sleeves and pushed through the wall of flame.

There was only one figure slumped inside the wreck. The inside of the cabin was searing hot, every surface a brand waiting for vulnerable flesh. Jack refused to let himself think or feel. He simply grabbed the body of the pilot and tried to haul him free. He was conscious that something had caught fast on the man's clothes. Using his sleeve like a oven mitt, Jack grabbed and yanked, using his supernatural strength. Whatever it was came free with a grind of metal and they were good to go. Another burst of strength and speed, and they were out of the wreck and safely clear of the flames.

Only when the pilot was on the ground beside the Land Rover did Jack allow himself to look at the man's face. It was Sam Ralston, the Horseman named War, and one of his closest friends. He was also the vampire Jack's niece, Chloe, had come to love.

Ralston's flight jacket was still smoldering, the sheepskin collar reduced to crisps of ash. It was a mercy he was unconscious. Jack shrugged off his own coat and used it to smother the embers, the action forcing him to take stock of his friend's condition. Part of the helicopter—perhaps a piece of the shattered door frame—was sticking out of Ralston's chest. That was what Jack had torn out of the cockpit. Cold dismay seized him. Vampires could survive a lot, but this was pushing the limit.

Lark was suddenly there, her hand firm on Jack's shoulder. "How bad is it?"

She sounded worried, but steady. He looked up to see her dark eyes filled with concern. All at once, he was grateful for her presence. She could pull her weight in a crisis, and he was going to need help to get Sam through this.

"He needs medical help fast," he said. "Where's Mark Winspear? He should have been on board."

"Kenyon saw Winspear jump. He's gone to search up that slope." She pointed.

"Okay." Jack cleared his throat, words all but deserting him. He'd thought Ralston and Winspear were safe because they'd been out of town—but once again, he'd been hideously wrong. It had just taken longer for Fate to find them.

The fear and pain rising with volcanic force inside him threatened to open the gate for the demon. A fierce prickling under his skin escalated to a harsh burn. The first spark of blue fire flickered across his skin. He sucked in breath, mentally willing his emotions down.

Lark squeezed Jack's shoulder. "I'll get some water from the Rover," she said, and moved away with her usual silent tread.

The brisk, practical words steadied him. His skin cooled, almost as if her touch carried the spirit of the promised water. He glanced at her retreating figure, moved by the beauty of her slim form.

Under control again, he pulled out his knife and began slicing Ralston's clothes away from his wound. He'd barely got Ralston's jacket off when he heard a shout from the rocks above. He looked up to see Dr. Mark Winspear, also known as Plague, being helped down the slope by Kenyon. The doctor was tall and dark haired, a vampire who was equal parts assassin and healer and, though limping and dirty, he was mostly unhurt. The two of them slipped and slithered the last dozen yards down the mountainside, kicking up a wash of dust and pebbles. When they got to the bottom, the doctor hesitated before putting weight on his left foot, as if marshaling his defenses against the pain.

Kenyon offered his shoulder to Winspear as a support. "Next time try a parachute, genius."

Lark was on her way back with several bottles of water balanced on the first-aid kit. She set down her burden and shaded her eyes. "Were you trying to fly?" she called to the doctor.

"Vampires can float," Winspear replied. Even from a distance, Jack could see his face was pale, even for the undead.

"You were floating straight down pretty fast," Kenyon said drily. "For a moment there, I thought we were finally rid of you."

"Your concern touches me to the quick." Winspear's gaze found Jack. "Death," he called, using Jack's code name. "How good to see you. You might have mentioned you'd survived a flaming car wreck."

"I would have expected a little more enthusiasm over my miraculous resurrection."

"We're named after the riders of the apocalypse. There's nothing about the two of us that says muffins and bluebirds."

Winspear had never been exactly cuddly, but Jack could

hear the anger beneath the ice of his words. Just as Kenyon had said, the other Horsemen didn't appreciate being left out of the loop. "I apologize for disappearing the way I did."

Winspear, still limping over the stony ground, gave a curt nod. "What's an extra funeral when you live forever?"

Jack rose to meet him. "How is your surgical mojo?" He gestured to Ralston.

Winspear froze, his expression going blank. At once, he was at Ralston's side, examining the metal shard piercing his chest. "Damn it all, this is too close to his heart. If I pull it out without proper medical equipment, he'll bleed out."

Kenyon turned and walked away, running his hands through his short, fair hair as if he meant to tear it out.

Lark made a helpless gesture. "What if he fed?"

Jack flinched. "You're the only one here he could feed on." He sounded abrupt, but the image he had in his mind's eye, of Ralston's fangs in her flesh, put a spear of rage through his brain. It wasn't logical—she was being generous—but the urge to fight Ralston for her rose like a fever. She'd been his lover, and no vampire surrendered his claim so easily.

"I know," she replied, her tone calm and firm. "It might save his life."

"It's a good theory," Winspear replied. "Fey blood is potent, but unfortunately he'd have to take too much. You're just one donor. I need to get him back to the city…and quickly. His best chance of recovery is in an operating room."

Jack knew he was right. There weren't many ways to kill vampires, but extreme damage to the head or heart would do it. Delay could be just as dangerous as it would be to a human. "We've only got one working vehicle."

The doctor glanced up from examining his patient, his expression all business. "And?"

"You should take it. It's far more useful as an ambulance than as a means to chase the Blackthorns."

"Not that I object," Winspear replied, "but explain your reasoning."

"It's going to take forever to clear the road and get past what's left of the chopper," Jack said. "You'll have to handle getting Ralston back to base on your own. The rest of us will keep going on foot. We'll be relying on you to send help as soon as possible."

"On foot?" Kenyon asked, and then shrugged. "Whatever you say."

Jack studied the land around them, now fading to blues and purples as the sun dipped behind the peaks. "They've seen us, so they may go off script—or off the highway. We can track them better this way."

The werewolf gave a slight smile. "Tracking is my specialty."

The doctor finished stabilizing Ralston's wound and rose, favoring his sore leg. "Then, let's get my patient to the car."

Jack turned to Lark and Kenyon. "Grab what supplies you can carry. We need to get moving."

It only took a matter of minutes. Backpacks were stocked, a space cleared and a makeshift bed made for the patient. Then Ralston was lifted inside and made as comfortable as possible. In the end, Winspear did draw a few vials of Lark's blood, but just enough to keep Ralston going until he was back in the city. As the procedure was underway, Jack forced himself to examine the glowing remains of the chopper in search of anything worthy of salvage— but all that was left was as charred and gutted as his mood.

As they prepared to part, the doctor clasped Lark's hands. "I am delighted to see you are alive, old friend. Bree will be thrilled to see you, as well."

Lark hugged Winspear. "We'll catch up later," she said. "I promise. I have so much to say to you both."

"So do we," said Winspear, kissing her on the cheek. "Until later."

Then Winspear turned to Jack and Kenyon and removed a hard case from inside his jacket. "It was just good fortune that I got your call when I did. We were driving back at the right time for Sam to intercept our journey and pick me up to meet you here. But before the ladies took the car back to the city, I was able to fulfill your request."

He opened the case. A stoppered vial sat nestled in the contoured case. "It's Lexie's blood."

Winspear snapped the case shut and handed it to Jack, who slid it into a zippered pocket inside his own coat.

"I hope you know what you're doing," the doctor said. "I remember the Dark Fey. There were a few left roaming the world when I was still human. In terms of unpleasantness, they made the Black Death look like a sniffle. Not a situation I care to see again."

Jack nodded. "I will slam the door on them."

"I wish I was at your side," Winspear said. And then he clasped Jack in a rough hug. "It's good to see you, old friend."

Jack closed his eyes, knowing what a gift such open affection was, coming from the taciturn Winspear. "Good to see you, too. Take care of Ralston."

With that, the Rover drove away, leaving the rest of them standing next to the smoking ruins of the chopper. The doctor would call for help and hopefully get Ralston into a medical chopper, but communications were notoriously sketchy in these mountains. His biggest advantage was that the Blackthorns wouldn't be interested in two injured vampires alone on the road.

Jack cast a glance through the gathering night at the road where the Suburban had gone. The Dark Fey had long disappeared from sight.

The good guys had a lot of catching up to do.

Chapter 16

It was a mystery to Lark how a werewolf could separate the scent of one motor from every other motor on the road, but Kenyon claimed he could smell which way the Suburban had gone. It probably helped that traffic was limited to a car or two every hour, and less now that it was approaching midnight. Lark was footsore and cold, but at least they knew they were going in the right direction on this gray ribbon of road lit by a waxing moon.

They were walking in a line, Kenyon in the lead and Jack guarding the rear. Kenyon stopped, putting his hands on his hips and waiting as the others caught up.

"Something change?" Jack asked.

"Yeah." Kenyon shuffled uneasily. "They stopped here. The vehicle drove off but I'd say some of the passengers got out."

"Why?" Lark wondered. "There's nothing here but trees."

Kenyon shrugged. "I'll need to check around to see if their scent leads away. There's nothing to say they didn't get out just to stretch their legs for a minute."

"Check it out," Jack said.

With a nod, Kenyon left his backpack and set off, tensed in a way that said every nerve was trained to the task at hand. Lark dropped her pack and sat on a boulder beside the road. Though the doctor hadn't taken much of her blood, she could feel the added edge to her fatigue. Being in nature healed any fey, and the clear air and starlit sky was like a tonic to Lark, but she had barely left her sickbed. She could have done with a little less nature and a little more couch in front of the television.

As she caught her breath, Lark mulled over something that had passed between her and Winspear before he'd left them there on the road. She and the doctor were old friends—not romantic ones, but comrades from her early days with the Company. As such, she knew how to read his expressions.

She'd seen the label on the vial of Lexie's blood. She'd shot him a look, and he'd raised an eyebrow, confirming her guess. Then he'd put a finger to his lips, signaling silence. It was then she'd known the blood draw hadn't been done after Kenyon phoned him. Winspear already had the samples with him, and the label belonged to a private clinic that specialized in mixed-species pregnancies. There was only one conclusion Lark could come to: Faran and Lexie were expecting, and the mother-to-be wanted to be the one to deliver the news. That should have made her happy, but instead it made her want to swathe Kenyon in bubble wrap and send him home to his wife-to-be.

Jack sat beside her, jolting her out of her thoughts. There wasn't a lot of room on the boulder, and Jack's legs pressed against hers. "It's a nice night for a walk," he said.

Lark huffed. "If you don't mind the homicidal fairies and crashing helicopters."

Jack squeezed her hand. "Don't worry. We're quick on our feet. Always have been."

"I'm admiring the Dark Fey's handiwork. You have to appreciate the planning."

"Queen Selena's got nothing else to do. Plotting really good revenge tends to be a time suck."

Lark studied his profile, wishing they were alone somewhere safe. She ached to touch him—it was an ache that ran deeper than any physical hunger. "Is the Dark Queen communicating with her people outside the gates? Is that even possible?"

"Given what we've seen, I believe the Dark Fey have wedged the gates open a crack. The seal on the gates, though incredibly strong, was never completely impervious. We didn't have the power." He seemed to be looking far away, gazing into that distant past. Sometimes it was hard to remember how very long he'd been walking the earth. "We concentrated our energies on making absolutely sure Selena herself couldn't leave."

"Was it hard to get all the races to agree to the banishment?"

"No. It sounds almost cartoonish to say, but Selena really was after world domination. She enjoys fear, both for its own sake and as a means of self-protection. If she gets out, we're going to need all the help we can get to stop her, including the Light."

"The Light doesn't have a lot to work with right now."

Jack gave her a curious look that said she'd let too much slip. Lark cleared her throat. "What I mean is, if I could have stopped Drusella Blackthorn, if I was better..."

"Do the Blackthorns know what you can do?"

"Not really," said Lark. "I'm not the same kind of magician. Ask me to cast a glamour and I'm top of the charts, but taking down a helicopter isn't my best game. You saw that."

"Let them underestimate you, and then play to your strengths. That's when you'll get them."

"I hope so."

"For fear of sounding as ancient as I am, I knew your grandfather," Jack said. He brushed his knuckles along the back of her arm. "His power was more like yours, more about illusion than strength, and yet he won the battle of the Star Tower."

The story was famous—one her uncles held up as the example of all a fey should be. Her grandfather had stood at the gates of the Star Tower, raised his sword and lit it like a torch with his magic. Then he'd held the entrance for three days and three nights, spending his life energy until he burned away to nothing. Light Fey were light made manifest and breathing, and he had ignited himself to save seven hundred innocents from Selena's army—for the Dark could not abide the touch of his brilliant spirit.

"I'm no hero of legend," Lark said.

Jack shook his head. "Your grandfather had courage, but he couldn't throw a fireball to save his life. That didn't mean he wasn't as stubborn as they come. Sometimes refusing to give the Dark what it wants is all that counts."

The moment stalled. Lark sat very still. Jack's hand lingered on her arm; their sides touched. She wanted to lean into him but feared disturbing the truce they'd found. The slightest push might remind Jack how little he trusted her.

Before she could decide whether to risk more contact, Kenyon returned. "There's a path a little ways up the road. It heads straight into the trees and then turns directly up the mountain. I smell fey, but I also smell humans. I think they're taking the prince and princess overland."

"So the kidnappers leave the Suburban and the driver carries on thinking we'll follow the vehicle," Lark said. "Meanwhile, the kidnappers march the prisoners through the mountains?"

Jack turned to look where Kenyon was pointing. "That's the back door to the Derrondine Pass. The kidnappers might have found another route through the mountains, because I can't see them doing that climb with prisoners. It's straight up the rock face."

"We won't know until we find them." Lark rose stiffly, slinging her knapsack over her shoulder. "It's into the woods we go."

Kenyon made a face. "I think there are a lot of stories where that ends in tears."

"Yeah," said Jack drily, "and I think most of those involve the big bad wolf."

* * *

The path wasn't a trail made by axes or even by the steady traffic of wildlife—it was made by fey. Someone had commanded that nothing grow there, and by the shiver up Lark's spine when she set foot on the bare dirt, the earth heartily resented the intrusion. *Dark magic, then.*

Even with the clear path, the route was a long, hard slog that meandered through the trees, angling ever upward along the toes of the mountain. Hours later, Lark's feet were sore after a night of walking, and now the rising ground demanded she use saplings and tufts of grass to help her climb. Jack walked behind her, guarding the rear. Her pack grew steadily heavier.

Just as the sky was turning a pearly gray, the path ended. It wasn't as if it had arrived at a destination; it just stopped where the trees thinned, a patch of trampled weeds showing where a group of people had stood.

"Security," said Jack. "No point drawing a straight line to their door, but this gets them through the worst of the undergrowth. Wherever they went from here was easier to find."

"Not by scent," said Kenyon. "Bears live around here. I can't smell a thing past that stink."

"Then, shift and put your wolf nose into it," said Jack. "We'll rest."

Rest? Lark didn't need to be asked twice. She shrugged off her pack and sat on the grass, trying to summon the energy to reach for her water bottle. Kenyon headed off into the trees to get furry.

Jack paced restlessly, his iron vampire strength barely tapped by a dusk-to-dawn hike up a mountainside. "If they were on foot, they can't be all that far ahead of us," he mused. "And they had prisoners. That must have slowed them down."

Lark tilted her head up to watch him patrol the tiny

clearing. Within seconds, he had made her dizzy. "If you sit down and relax, I'll see if I can sense them," she offered.

"Can you do that without being noticed?"

"I'm a spy," she said a trifle impatiently. "It's my job to be sneaky."

Jack gave her a look. "All right." He didn't sit, but he stopped and leaned against a tree. At least he was still, and that would have to do.

Lark closed her eyes and extended her perception. She was aware of the mountain, the birds, trees and insects, the animals and the nameless energies that dwelled as part of the earth and yet separate from it. The Dark Feys' path slashed like a scar over the earth's surface, throbbing with a painful spell. Lark silently promised to break it once her mission was done. It had ever been thus, the Dark taking while the Light healed.

Lark felt a gentle tug, pulling her attention north. At first she wasn't sure why, but then she sensed Kenyon running in wolf form, a sleek gray bullet scrambling up a rise so that his eyes could confirm what his nose was telling him. An image flashed, the wolf paused, its elegant beauty outlined against the dawn sky—and then the visual faded as quickly as it had come.

Lightly, she explored beyond that point, letting her consciousness dip and float seemingly at random. Even a sentinel on the lookout for magical interference would have a hard time sensing her as she drifted past the wolf, past the scrub and toward the point where the forest met the steep wall of the mountainside. Indeed, there were caves, and surely that was where the Blackthorns and their prisoners had gone.

And yet something was wrong. Lark reeled her consciousness back slowly, trying to detect what was bothering her. She moved with extreme caution, fearful of a trap that would catch her there, vulnerable without the protection of a physical form. She had a sudden sense that her adversaries were not where she expected them to be. In fact, they'd reversed their course. A prickling chill ran through her and she risked a faster retreat, a mounting panic telling her she might need to move fast.

Kenyon howled, a deep-throated, mournful cry that resonated through the jagged mountains. The sudden sound snapped Lark back to herself. She was on her feet before she was fully oriented, and grabbed Jack's arm for support.

"What is it?" he demanded.

"They've doubled back on their trail."

The werewolf howled again, this time with an edge of rage. With unspoken consent, they raced toward the sound. Lark surged ahead of Jack, following a trajectory through the trees until they reached the base of the rise where she'd seen Kenyon in her vision.

"This way!" she pointed, but they didn't get much farther. Egon Blackthorn stood at the top of the rise, a silver chain in his hands. On the other end of the chain was Kenyon in wolf form, snarling, ears back and with long ivory fangs bared. He was lunging against the chain, smoke rising from where a silver collar touched his ruff. The sound he made was terrible—a long, outraged growl broken by bewildered whimpering. His claws scrabbled at the ground as if digging for escape. Teeth snapped at Blackthorn, toward Jack, at the grass. The beast was obviously maddened with pain.

Egon looked utterly in command. He was a tall, bald mountain of a man with black eyes as cold and impassive as flint. "In time, he will obey me just to make the agony stop." His voice was just as hard as his expression. "Go home before you end the same way."

Jack's gun whipped up, an iron bullet leaving the chamber before Lark could even form a thought—but it didn't matter. A wisp of smoke was all that remained where Blackthorn and Kenyon had been.

Jack roared, scrambling up the rise to where the fey had stood, but it was pointless. Kenyon was gone, another prisoner.

Jack and Lark were the only ones left to fight.

Chapter 17

Disbelief jolted Lark, leaving her frozen where she stood. She lifted a hand to sketch the air where the wolf had been, unable to find words. The helpless gesture was as far as her strength would go, and all she managed was a soft, outraged cry.

Exhaustion welled up in a sudden black wave and Lark's legs buckled. Jack reached for her, but she hit the ground anyway, knees thumping to the soft earth. She curled forward, putting her head in her hands. It would have felt good to weep, but grief and panic blocked even that slight relief.

"They've got us all," she said, barely giving the words voice.

"Not all of us," said Jack. "We're still in play."

"I'm not sure that matters." Lark could usually find some scrap of hope. Not this time. Jack was a great agent, and she was very, very good—but the Dark Fey had so far been unstoppable—and they had Amelie, where all her people's hope rested.

She heard Jack's clothes rustle as he crouched beside her. When he slipped his arm around her, she forced herself to look up and meet his eyes. In the pale dawn, she could see the strain in his face.

"What now?" she asked, barely able to rise to her knees so that they faced one another. Jack took her arms, his strength alone holding her up. Lark bowed her head. "Are we running straight into a trap?"

He swallowed. "We go forward or we go back to the city. There aren't a lot of choices."

The idea of turning around and heading back to safety was as pointless as it was tempting. If the Dark Queen won, none of them would be safe. Not the prince and princess, not Kenyon, not any of them. In very little time, the whole world would be at the mercy of the Dark.

She closed her eyes, her strength failing her. "I don't know."

"Listen," said Jack, shaking her a little. "It's up to you and me."

You and me. She'd wanted to hear those words on Jack's lips. She'd longed to be his partner again, working with instead of against him. She'd yearned to be in his arms. But this mission seemed insurmountable.

And yet, if she had to put her faith in anyone to see her through this test, it was Jack. Besides, the Light Fey were counting on her. She was the only trained agent they had. "I promised Amelie I'd keep her safe."

"And?"

Lark dug deep and crawled to her feet. "I vote we make Egon and Drusella eat their trap."

Jack grinned. It was a quick flash, bright and sharp as light glancing from a blade. Lark's stomach leaped at the sight.

"Onward, then," he said with deceptive softness. His fingers touched her cheek, leaving an electric tingle in their wake.

They retrieved their packs and trudged down into a broad shallow of land that lay between them and the vertical face of the mountain. They swished through long grass dotted with pale flowers that seemed to glow in the false dawn. Jack pushed hard, but the meadow was wider than it seemed. The grass spread to a rippling sea that felt endless until they found the fey path again—which seemed to start as abruptly as it had ended in the woods.

The trail steered them to the base of the cliff, where a thin strip of trees clung like a foot rug to the mountain. Even though the route was direct, it took them the better part of an hour. By then the sun was rising, and Lark was buckling under her fatigue. They'd been hiking almost around the clock.

The moment she saw a large rock, she sat. "Just give me one minute."

"We need rest," Jack said, sounding as tired as she felt. Dawn hit vampires like a brick wall.

Lark shook her head. "I already feel guilty for sitting here."

The corners of his mouth quirked down. "In another half hour, we'll be hunting for a path through the mountain. Once we find it, we'll be crawling in dark places and meeting up with who knows what."

Lark surrendered. Jack was old and strong enough to power through the daylight fatigue, but it would drain him of strength he'd need later. "Then, let's get off this track," she agreed.

Jack held out his hand. Wearily, she took it and let herself be hauled upright. Her hand felt good in his, as if his touch loaned her a bit of his resilience.

After another ten minutes, they found a cluster of trees that offered shade and concealment. Lark sank gratefully to the thick bed of ash leaves. "I'll set a perimeter spell," she said. "I don't think either of us is up to keeping watch."

Jack started to protest, but then nodded agreement. "I'll keep watch, but a backup is a good idea."

He sat, his back against the trunk of a tree. The shadows were thick there, making him almost invisible against the roots and bark. After wearily setting a few trigger charms, Lark scooted back against a boulder, then tried to use her backpack as a cushion.

He held out an arm. "I'm softer than a rock."

A smart remark hovered on her lips, but she was just too tired. Instead, she curled against his shoulder, finding he was just as good a cushion as she remembered. "This break is only for a few minutes."

"Right," he said. "Because we have supernatural stamina."

They were both asleep in under a minute.

Lark drifted into Jack's dreams. She'd never done so before, but they were touching and too exhausted to keep barriers in place between them. She found herself wandering through an ancient market, the sun so hot and bright it felt like a weight against her skin.

Lark spun around in an effort to take in the scene all at once. Delight bubbled through her. She'd caught glimpses of other people's dreams before, but nothing this detailed or vivid, and never Jack's.

There were a few low buildings framing the square, but mostly she saw endless tents of colorful silk. Between and in front of those, brilliant carpets were spread on the dirt with wares arranged for sale—metalwork and pottery, spices and strange musical instruments that Lark could not name. The square was crowded with all manner of people, from nimble dark-skinned children to huge men with forked yellow beards. And the hot air reeked of animals, every one of which was cackling or bleating or grunting. Someone had brought camels.

Judging by the robes and armor, they were in the far distant past. She took a second look around, examining faces more carefully this time. Sure enough, there was Jack, looking haggard and dirty and...human. Lark's breath caught. Nothing about him was ever ordinary—that was just impossible—but as a mortal he looked oddly vulnerable. All of Jack's features were the same, but the dark, fierce spark of his vampire side was missing. And yet...so was the steel wall he kept between himself and the world. This was his basic, unguarded self.

His eyes met hers, the pale blue bright in his deeply tanned face. Alarm crossed his features—almost panic—and he immediately came toward her. He wore a long tunic of chain mail that jingled as he moved, and over that a surcoat embroidered with a black hawk on a field of gold. He was clearly dressed for battle.

"You shouldn't be here," he said, his voice sharp.

"I'm so sorry," Lark said at once. "I don't mean to invade, but we were both so exhausted. There's not much I can do about it until one of us wakes up."

He looked around the crowd, on the alert for—what?

"Jack, this is a dream. Nothing can happen." Lark turned her attention back to the scenery. "You were really here, weren't you?"

He took her elbow and began steering her though the crowd. "I was a third son. It was this or the monastery."

That was a detail Lark had never known. Vampires tended to keep quiet about their human lives. "What did your older brothers do?"

"Squabbled over land. I got the fun-filled vacation with complimentary siege warfare."

She moved her arm so that it was wound through his, turning his grip into something more companionable. "I never dreamed of actually meeting a knight in shining armor."

That seemed to amuse him. "Well, I'd definitely avoid the ones covered in rust."

Then he froze, staring at a figure who was idly fingering the wares of a knife maker at one of the colorful stalls. It was Jack again, but this version of him was pale as ivory and dressed in richly embroidered robes. Slowly, he turned to face them, a blade still in his hand. His graceful manner made Lark think of the black-feathered hawk sewn on Jack's surcoat—beautiful and predatory.

"Ah. I see you've brought a friend," this figure said to the knight. His bright, piercing eyes shone as if they were lit from within.

"Leave her out of this," Jack said, stepping in front of Lark.

Lark, of course, immediately shifted so she could see what was going on. She had a sudden feeling she wasn't the only intruder in Jack's dreams. Whoever this doppelgänger was, she could feel power pouring off him in pulsing waves. Not human, then, but something else. Something very dangerous.

He held up the knife, the sun blazing along the blade. "A pretty thing, this. Most useful."

"What do you want, Asteriel?" Jack snarled.

"I approve of your fey. Very lovely."

Jack tensed. Suddenly his arm was rock hard, his muscles poised to fight.

The richly dressed double laughed, his smile as sharp as the weapon he held. "Does she know about my gift to you? Most important, do you remember what I said the last time we spoke?"

Lark felt Jack's thunderclap of alarm. It threw her out of the dream and she sat bolt upright, fully awake with her skin prickling in fright. The position of the sun said they'd been asleep for a long time—far longer than the dream itself. The shadows said it was late afternoon. With a sense of profound disorientation, she pushed her fingers through her hair.

Jack was sitting up, too, his look one of utter horror. Slowly, his gaze focused on her face. "Are you all right?"

She gazed at him curiously, still trying to figure out what had just happened. "What was that?"

"A dream."

A dream where nothing much had actually occurred. Still, the feeling of menace had sunk deep into her bones. "Who was your twin? Was that supposed to be someone real?"

Jack sank back to the ground. He pulled off his sunglasses and bent an arm across his face. "Yes. He just wears my face in my dreams."

The words—and the way Jack said them—sent another chill over her skin. "What did he give you?"

Jack moved his arm but didn't replace the glasses, simply shutting his eyes instead. The sweep of his dark eyelashes brought back memories of other times, and other beds. Lark's throat ached with the memories.

"Treasure," he said without expression. "Spoils of war. He made my fortune."

Lark felt the balance of push and pull between them, of trust and secrecy. She'd seen something she shouldn't have. The question was whether Jack would pull away or let her in. Lark could barely breathe, wanting to comfort but unsure whether her touch would be welcome after such an invasion.

She swallowed. "For someone who made your fortune, you don't sound happy about seeing him."

Jack's face grew tight. When he spoke, it sounded strangled. "No."

Taking a gamble, Lark leaned against Jack again. To her relief, he wrapped an arm around her waist. "The odd thing was that he wanted to make amends. He thought I could do good with all that wealth. He asked me to take it and relieve all the suffering I could."

"But?"

"It didn't work." There was finality in his tone that closed the conversation, but she couldn't resist pushing it one step more.

"Why did he pick you?"

Jack was silent for a long moment. "I'd seen too much death. I must have looked like a man who needed a respite from war."

"But?"

"It turns out I'd only seen the tip of Death's tail." Jack

opened his eyes, which held echoes of the stranger's brilliant, unearthly gaze. "He showed me the rest."

The sight of those eyes chilled Lark's blood and she understood. "He's your demon!"

And the figure in the dream had been holding the knife she'd used to betray Jack's secret. Was that a message meant for her?

Chapter 18

Asteriel hadn't lied when he'd said he and Jack were one. Their two souls had worn away over the centuries until they fit seamlessly together. It was hard now to tell whose memory was whose, or even if they could be pried apart. And yet, once in a while, Jack's subconscious set the demon free of his mortal half's relentless will—at least in dreams. That was when the nightmares came to remind Jack what was at stake.

Theirs had been an unusual bargain: gold for willpower. Jack got a fortune on the condition he used it for good works. In return, Asteriel got a chance at redemption—the real, get-to-Heaven deal earned with repentance and good deeds. The deal had appeared perfect. The fallen angel thirsted to see justice done in the world, and so did Jack.

And the chance to help an angel find peace? After seeing so much death and war, Jack couldn't refuse that kind of wonder. All Jack had to do was take the creature with him when he left the desert for home—as a passenger inside his body. Good deeds had to be done personally to count toward redemption. Uniting with Jack—and Jack's natural self-discipline—ensured the Fallen wouldn't be tripped up by his cursed nature. After all, he'd tried to be good before, but something had always gone wrong.

True to form, the Fallen had failed to mention the consequences if Jack died. They had been murdered not long after reaching Jack's home.

"What are you thinking about?" Lark asked, interrupting his reverie.

She was lean but soft, the curve of her fitting exactly against his chest. He knew her smell—so much like the woods themselves on a May evening, clean and sweet and beckoning to pleasure. The protective ache rising in his still heart was as pure as springtime. It was fey magic, or maybe it was just female. He held her like a talisman against his thoughts.

"The past," he said. *The first time I woke up to that rattling, horrified gasp of air into my dead lungs. To that moment I realized I was fused into one being who was half human and half demon and thirsting for blood.* Mortality had been the only thing keeping their two souls apart. In that moment of waking, Jack had understood that the Fallen were truly demons, and now he was a creature of foul hungers wearing a man's face. Ordinary vampires had a touch of the demon inside, but he was more, made not from a bite but from something far more infernal. He was a vessel for one of the Fallen.

"Our past?" Lark asked. "Or a long-ago past?"

He allowed himself a half smile. "Memory is a strange thing when you get as old as me."

Lark raised a brow. "You make yourself sound senile. Do you remember my name?"

"I can just about bring you to mind."

He shifted his hands against her slender waist, the curve of her back inviting him to draw her closer. The shadowed light of the grove turned her dark brown eyes to near black. He knew there were a thousand reasons to walk away, to keep a brutal grip on his self-control, but holding her was too sweet. All caution slipped away in a receding tide. "Jessica," he said softly, letting a sliver of his longing betray him.

One corner of her mouth curled up. "I almost don't mind that name when you say it."

"It's beautiful."

"It's not mine. Fey only ever take a first name to live among humans—or, rather, human computers. They go crazy without something to fill that data field."

"Lark, then," he said. "Though I think you're too fierce to be a songbird."

"We always sing at daybreak," she said with a sly wink. "Vampires should find us frightening."

She smiled, and it was like dawn—bright and fresh and untouched. Jack's chest tightened. Seeing her face light up like that was like feeling an unspeakable burden lift from his shoulders.

"We find you terrifying," he said. He couldn't help himself—he kissed her soundly, rolling them both so that he was on top, the soft leaves and grass cushioning her from the ground.

"Jack, what are you doing?" she asked, her fingers feathering through his hair.

"Defending myself." Neither her voice nor those teasing fingers indicated she wanted him to stop, so he kept going. That was one good thing about being dead—he didn't need to come up for air.

Eventually, though, she broke the kiss. "Jack?"

"Shh." He was exploring her skin ever so slowly, kissing his way along the clean angle of her jaw. All women had their beauties, but this was one of Lark's. The soft skin of her throat met the delicate architecture of her ear just *there*, and the fine skin of her temple *there*, and the flare of her cheekbone *there*. The fey had skin that was almost translucent, and the fine blue tracery of veins was visible and tantalizing. In an instant, Jack was swamped by the tangled needs for flesh and food and affection. Hunger rose, as all consuming as a three-alarm blaze.

And then her lips caught his, and the pressure of them made him focus again, even as the taste of her destroyed any hopes of sanity. She was cinnamon and heat, and Jack began to feel his own flesh warming as her fingers dug into the muscles of his back and shoulders. As her teeth caught his lower lip and bit down, he felt his fangs begin to descend. It had been a long time since he'd tasted fey blood, and his control began to unravel.

"Be careful," he murmured.

"Always," she said, but that was pure fiction. The fey could not be Turned, and Lark had never denied him. Perhaps she had no idea of the damage a lust-crazed vampire could do—or didn't care. The fey were wild creatures and regarded a slippery slope as a fun ride.

Vampires should find us frightening. Yes, absolutely. Everything that kept Jack himself depended on his control, and Lark could make him let go of those boundaries like nothing else. Mortal men could be driven to sweet despair by a fey lover, and Jack knew well that she could unmake him with a kiss.

Already he could feel the madness of her passion rising. It was ephemeral, like pheromones or electricity, but it acted on him like a drug. How much was magic or biology or just Lark herself was impossible to know, and it didn't matter. And it didn't matter what else was going on in the world right then. He had to possess her.

He began with his hands, stroking her hip and feeling the flare and dip of her curves. The fey were willowy, but Lark had an athlete's muscles. Jack had always liked the contrast of strength and fullness in her body, and moved upward with lingering touches to explore the arch of her ribs and the soft riches of her breasts.

Lark found the juncture of his T-shirt and belt and worked her hands beneath the cloth. Her hands were cold against even his flesh, and he flinched. She laughed, the sound becoming a buzz where their lips met, and then he was lost to the feel of her fingers against his back, urging him closer. A deep burn of need pooled in his belly. Even at his angriest, his body had missed Lark. Having her here now, alive and wanting him, was a dizzying relief.

His mouth slid to the collar of Lark's shirt, tasting the salt of her skin and the musk of female beneath. She'd changed into practical clothes for the journey and was wearing a soft cotton work shirt over a tank top and jeans. He could still smell traces of soap in the folds, and that only added to a sense of comfort and rightness. She was everything he had to have. His hands found the shirt buttons and began working with determined speed.

The rise and fall of her breath pressed her body into his with every gasp. The dark pools of her eyes were wide, her lips swollen and parted and begging to be kissed again—but there was something he'd never seen in her before. She had always been proud, wild and fierce, and all of that was still there. Yet there was also uncertainty. They had been apart, and the road back had not been a smooth one.

He wanted to say something but faltered. Jack ran a finger down Lark's cheek, tracing its smooth curve. He licked his lips, experiencing an uncharacteristic twinge of nervousness. Lark was strong, but he'd never seen her eyes so vulnerable before now. It changed every dynamic between them, even if just by a hair.

"I want you." It wasn't poetic, but it was one of the few things he was certain of.

Doubt flickered behind her eyes, as if she didn't trust his welcome.

"I mean it."

She put her hands on his face, tilting his head to look straight into his eyes. "Stop talking, Jack, and prove it."

That would be a pleasure. Jack opened her shirt and sat back as she pulled off her tank top, unveiling a confection of pale green silk beneath. The notion of such daintiness hiding beneath plain cotton only made him hotter. He moved in, taking her in his arms once more. He had to taste the heat beneath that silk.

Still, as his fangs scraped against the lace, he made no move to tear it away. With an iron hand, he held his need to a slow burn, spooling out the experience a bit at a time, forcing himself to give as well as take.

He licked and teased, tasting her through the whisper of cloth. Her nipples pressed against the silk, roused and ready even as a sheen of perspiration began to slick her skin. She stirred beneath him, writhing and bucking as he reacquainted himself with all the moves she liked—and there were many. The scent of her desire filled him, extinguishing every thought save his need for her. Her fingers worked at his zipper, and the sudden freedom brought a moan of relief from his throat.

But there was something he needed first, an impulse so basic not even his will of iron could deny it. Inexorably, her pulse drew him to a vein. It slipped under her translucent skin, a running river of life. He needed it, wanted it, desired it as intimately as he craved every other part of Lark. His fangs—sharp, long and lethal as only the eldest vampires possessed—slid neatly through her skin. Lark murmured and arched against him, giving him better access to the fresh flow of her warm life. A vampire's bite gave erotic pleasure few could resist.

Jack's brain all but exploded at the sensation of her warmth inside him. The taste was sweet and velvety, but fey blood was as potent as strong liquor to his kind. He took no more than a sip, letting it slide down his throat. He didn't need more, and she had already given blood to heal Ralston.

That was the wrong thought to have. A fierce pang of jealousy tore at him, causing him to take a second swallow. She was his, *his*, and the heat of her life inside him proved it. She shuddered beneath him, responding to his claim with a cry of completion. A dark fierceness deep in his belly filled with satisfaction as he held her, rejoicing in what he could do with just a tiny bite. There was so much more in his repertoire.

But one thing at a time. He pressed his mouth around the wound, licking it closed. Lark moved, blinking at him with pleasure-drugged eyes. She didn't speak. There was no need. He was as hard as a spear now, and she was all but melting as he slid inside her. It had been too long since he'd felt such a powerful need, and he needed all his concentration as he pushed home, taking her all over again. He had drawn her essence into him, and it was time to complete the circle by leaving his with her.

The sun was failing, leaving him stronger. His senses were sharpening as the shadows lengthened, and he was growing aware of the rustling leaves and shushing wind. Tension hung in the air, but he was with his woman. He was a hunter fixated on his prey. The world might have been ending, but he had a mission to complete.

Somehow they'd shed half their clothes, and he felt the heat of Lark's thighs against his waist as he moved. There was warmth and wetness and pressure building inside him. Jack changed his angle, and as he withdrew to stroke again, he caught the glisten of her fluids clinging to his skin. By all the evidence, her pleasure was at the triple-A rating.

Jack growled his pleasure and went for the gold star. She cried out, spasming around him, taking him greedily as deep as he could go. And Jack came. He roared, fangs bared, the leash of his control finally loosed as he claimed her again.

For a wild, reeling second, his heart pounded, kicked by blood and passion back to a semblance of life. The giddy sensation forced Jack to gulp in air, and he reeled like a drunkard, balanced on the knife's edge of pain and pleasure. Lark was sprawled beneath him in a loose-limbed daze of satisfaction, her hair tumbling like waves over her breasts.

Taking her hand, he kissed it gently and pressed her palm to his chest, where the beat of his pulse was already slowing back to nothing. He cleared his throat, the speech center of his brain balking like an ancient computer. "Never doubt that I want you. You're life itself."

Chapter 19

Lark listened with wonder to the last beats of Jack's heart as it returned to its silent resting state. "I've never felt that before. Why—"

He cut her off, putting one finger to her lips. "It is a peculiarity of what I am."

In other words, something about the demon made him more alive than a vampire should be. Passion had let its power slip free.

"Why haven't I felt that before?" she asked again.

His mouth curved in a look of pure male possession. "Maybe I wanted you more than ever."

Or maybe it was one more sign that he was losing control of the demon. Yet what had passed between them was as exquisitely blended as fine liquor, everything in balance. She was beginning to understand the complex creature Jack was, with his human reason navigating impulses no mortal could understand. Small wonder he was stubborn. He needed that strength of will.

Lark swallowed back a lump of complicated emotions, caught unawares by the sudden insight. It seemed to demand words, something profound, but nothing she could find measured up. Helplessly, she ran her hands down Jack's chest, letting her fingers trace the swell and dip of his muscles.

"I missed you," she said, devastated by her lack of eloquence.

"Hey," he said, brushing at her cheek with his thumb.

Lark touched her face and realized she was crying, all her pent-up emotion finally finding release. "I'm sorry," she said, embarrassed by the tears.

"Hush." Jack kissed her, his lips lingering on the tracks of her tears and teasing her mouth until she returned his smile. If he meant to banish her sadness with affection, it was working. Despite the dangers that lurked ahead, she felt a flicker of hope.

When he finally let her go, she could feel his mood changing, his gentleness turning to hard purpose. "It's dusk," he said. "We should get moving."

By the time she dressed and picked up her pack, the light had faded to a purplish hue, washing the reds and yellows of the landscape to gray. The first stars pricked the sky between the branches overhead. Jack pulled her into the circle of his arms, kissing her forehead. It was a fond gesture, but his body was strung tight as a bow, ready for battle. Even so, he took her hand as they set out.

With little conversation, they found the path and pushed through the forest toward the mountain. It was a hard slog on rising ground, and Lark's muscles protested. Now that they were closer to their destination, a pall of gloom seemed to hang in the air. Beneath that, energy buzzed in a soft, sinister murmur.

Jack stopped, the cliff face only a dozen yards ahead. They studied the rock face in the growing darkness. "See any secret tunnels?"

"Where should I be looking?"

Jack pointed northwest. "The Derrondine Pass is on the other side of this mountain. The gates to the Dark Fey kingdom are in the lake. That puts the Blackthorns' hangout dead ahead."

Lark bit her thumbnail. "Give me a minute. I'm sensing something nearby, but I'm having trouble getting a fix on it."

"Go for it."

Lark cast her senses outward, trying to get some sense of where the buzzing was coming from. The pull of the magic was definitely to the north. "That way," she said, pointing.

Jack put a hand on her arm, stopping her before she could move. "Should we be trying to avoid the source of this magic? What's your read on it?"

Lark shook her head. "Recon only, but if that's where the party is, we need to know who's dancing. I don't think it's just Dark Fey. There's a taste of other energies, too."

Faster than her eye could follow, Jack dropped his hand and drew his weapon. "Other energies?"

"Shifter, maybe sorcery. It's…unusual."

They moved silently through the woods side by side, and kept the mountain to their left. Lark saw the light first. It seeped through an inch-wide crack that outlined a rounded doorway at least twenty feet high. In daylight, they would have missed it. The door itself was made of the same material as the face of the rock and there was no handle or knob.

She stopped, crouching in the shadows next to the rock. Jack took a position next to her, his shoulder brushing hers. "Speak friend and enter?" he suggested.

"You do know the fey regard Tolkien the way vampires do Stoker, right?"

Jack shrugged. "I don't suppose they'd open the door if we knocked politely?"

Lark was silent, thinking hard. Her brain almost clicked as a plan suddenly presented itself. It was a horrible, awful, dangerous and idiotic plan, but those very qualities meant it might just work. She turned to Jack. "Did you bring any explosives?"

Despite being a vampire, Jack paled.

"The more suicidal a plan is, the better you like it," Jack grumbled half an hour later, dusting dirt from his fingers. He'd spent half his time looking for surveillance systems and hidden cameras. The man didn't trust even the toadstools.

"You're the one who won't leave the house without a brick of plastic explosives somewhere on your person," Lark retorted.

"And aren't you glad I have interesting hobbies?" Jack pushed a button on his remote detonator and a large patch of brush, rocks and dirt flew into the air with a hearty rumble.

Lark loved working with Jack. He knew how to do everything.

Exactly fifteen seconds later, the sliver of light around the door grew as the heavy rock slid forward with a loud scraping sound. It didn't open all the way—just enough to let someone pass through. But that was okay. Lark hadn't expected anything more.

A half dozen figures in dark clothing crept out, automatic weapons at the ready. They advanced with an efficiency and coordination that spoke of military training. Muzzles swept the trees and shadows, searching for the source of the noise.

"Night World mercenaries," Jack murmured. "Shifter or fey?"

Lark studied their faces, picking out what details she could in the darkness. There were plenty of lone wolves, half fey and other unaligned creatures willing to sell their services to the highest bidder. The Company butted heads with them on a regular basis.

"A mix," she returned, taking a firm grip on his forearm. "Come on."

With that, she cast a glamour on them both, rendering them invisible just like she had at the palace. Two mountainous guards still stood by the door, weapons at the ready, but there was enough room to creep behind them. Lark waited until a gust of wind stirred the leaves, and then she and Jack slid through the door, the dry rustling hiding the noise of their passage.

Once inside, they found no one. Rather than the network of caves they'd expected, the smooth shaft ran through the rock. Electric lights hung along the walls, providing the illumination she'd seen from the outside. Lark and Jack hurried forward, holding hands and moving as quietly as they could. The place echoed like an empty auditorium.

Lark struggled not to think of the mass of rock over-head. Fey were woodland creatures, not fond of enclosed spaces, and being underground was already working on her nerves. Her only comforts were Jack's hand around hers and the knowledge that they were cutting miles off their journey with every step.

"Do you think this was built with magic?" Jack asked quietly, a disembodied voice beside her. "No troll or goblin made this. It's too perfectly done."

"Magic made parts of it anyway," she replied. "Though, I'm not sure who has that kind of power. A sorcerer?"

"Hard to say," Jack replied. "Most of them are crazies sitting around in pajamas and a pointy hat talking to toads all day. I'm thinking bigger."

His words seemed prophetic when the long tunnel abruptly ended and the passage through the mountain widened into a cavernous room. This looked more like a huge cave, but one that had been outfitted with doors, lockers and—Lark blinked when she saw it—a coffee nook complete with microwave. By the number of doors, corridors and signage in several languages, they were seeing just a tiny sliver of an enormous complex. Soldiers and laboratory workers hurried down the corridors and across gangways like determined ants.

Jack was looking around curiously. "This reminds me of something from one of my dreams."

"You dreamed of this place?" Lark asked.

"No. It was something Asteriel said… *Do you really think the Blackthorns have that much power?* Someone helped them blow Company HQ as completely and quietly as they did, and someone built this. It's not the Dark Queen, because she's still locked up. They're working with another ally."

They pulled aside as a group of black-clad soldiers marched past, wheeling a two-tiered trolley piled with equipment. Lark felt the pressure of Jack's fingers, and heard his grim whisper in her ear. "This place looks as if it's ramping up for action. They have a window of opportunity before the Company's other locations can send reinforcements to Marcari."

He was right. If the Dark Queen was smart, she'd make her move immediately. They didn't have much time.

She felt the quick pressure of his fingers again. "Look to your left," he said.

There was a sign pointing down a long hallway. The legend—in French, English and two dialects of Fey—read Custodial Cells. The prison. Lark's heart jolted with wild hope and horror in the same beat. If Kenyon, Amelie and Kyle were in this place, that was where they would be held.

"Shall we?" murmured Jack.

Chapter 20

Something felt wrong.

It didn't feel wrong all at once, or Lark would have protested the detour. She and Jack had turned left, leaving the main path through the mountain and entering a bare, tiled hallway that looked like something out of a second-rate hospital.

As soon as they did, though, her nerves began to hum. There was foul—or, more accurately, fouler—energy here in this part of the complex. The corridors were set around a circular bank of desks and monitors, radiating out like the spokes of a wheel. Lark guessed it was a command center of some kind. Black-clad soldiers crowded the area, marching in groups or hurrying by with computer tablets or armfuls of supplies.

Jack and Lark followed another sign pointing toward the cells, and her misgivings went from caution to high alert. The path grew darker and full of twists and turns. Doors lined either side of the hallway, spaced a dozen steps apart. They were heavy gray steel and had narrow, high windows and keypad locks crackling with spells. Jack swore softly and pulled her aside as two mercenaries wearing heavy weapons belts—shape-shifters, from their massive size—swaggered toward them. Their wide shoulders filled the passageway from edge to edge in a wall of scowling black.

Lark's heart squeezed with alarm. Her glamour made them invisible and masked their scent, but it wouldn't survive direct contact. Jack pressed himself into the slight depression made by one of the steel doors, sucking in his breath as the pair drew close. Lark slid off her backpack and held it in one hand as she plastered herself against the tile wall. Clutching Jack with her other hand, she stilled her breathing despite a pounding pulse. If only the guards would hurry up and pass by—but they were deep in conversation.

"He's in the medical unit, boy. He won't be going anywhere," said one guard to the other, gesturing toward the doorway where Jack was standing.

The pair stopped. "Should we check on him?" the second guard asked.

She felt Jack tense, his fingers twitching. She guessed the problem—the guards were too close for him to move away if they went for the door. A bead of sweat trickled down the small of her back as the larger of the two shifted his weight and the baton in his belt brushed her arm. An inch more and he'd realize someone was standing behind him. She barely dared to inhale.

"No point," the first guard grunted. "The medics have been in and out. Prisoner or not, he's past needing a guard."

"Then, why bother coming down here at all? Cells are empty except for the one."

Jack's hand tightened around hers, lending her strength. She squeezed back.

The first guard coughed and sniffled, wiping his nose on his sleeve. "Listen, boy, a mindless wander around these parts is better'n some tasks. Get on the wrong side o' some folks and, well, who's going to argue for the likes of us, eh?"

"Get on the wrong side of who?" The second guard shifted nervously, nearly stepping on Lark's foot.

Lark shrank into herself, desperate not to make a sound. The baton tickled her elbow, teasing her like a prodding finger. She was exquisitely aware of Jack's tension as he readied to spring to her defense.

The first guard made a rude sound. "Stop asking questions, boy. Asking just gets you more work."

"That would be a tragedy."

"Spoken like the green soldier you are. Just wait a few years and you'll realize that high ground you're on is a pile of—"

"Yeah, yeah, and you walked miles to school through a troll-infested swamp."

"Smart-ass. You're buying the first round tonight."

The guards moved away, and Lark all but gasped with relief. Cloth rustled, and Jack pulled her into his arms, holding her hard. It was odd, embracing without being able to see him, but she closed her eyes and let her sense of touch fill in the detail. Her fingers explored the leather of his jacket, the soft cotton shirt that fit tight over the swell of his chest. His hair brushed her cheek as she leaned into his arms, her body suddenly alive with the memory of their lovemaking.

The need to touch Jack burned through her with the force of panic. It was an animal demand born of fright, but at least some of it was a rebellion against the wrongness of the place. Her soul needed something sane and right, because this nest of threat beneath the mountain surely wasn't. Her hand stroked his cheek, finding the nape of his neck where his hair curled as soft as a child's and pulled him down to her.

Jack's lips brushed her brow, then worked their way down her face in tiny light kisses. She tilted her face up as she would to a warm spring rain, letting him find her mouth. Perhaps they didn't have time for this—they were in enemy territory—but the stolen moment seemed all the sweeter, bolstering her courage. She allowed herself a tiny moan of gratitude.

And nearly jumped out of her skin when the lock behind

Jack gave a sepulchral clank. They darted aside, fingers still wound together, as the door swung open with a slight whoosh that said the room beyond it was airtight. Lark caught the scent of antiseptic and blood as well as the unmistakable tingle of magic. This had to be the medical unit the guard had mentioned, but it wasn't ordinary medicine going on in there.

They watched as a tall, thin figure in a gray uniform and white lab coat emerged. He looked like a half fey, with elegant features and long, supple hands. Instead of a computer tablet, he had a slim binder with papers clipped to the front. He frowned and flipped through the pages as he walked away. Lost in thought, he didn't seem to notice Jack catch the door before it clicked entirely closed.

According to the guard, this was where at least one prisoner was being held. They slipped inside without a sound. The room beyond was dim except for a curious piece of medical apparatus in the center. A visual sweep confirmed they were alone.

"Cameras?" Lark asked softly.

Jack took his time looking. "No. There's probably too much ambient magic for that kind of tech."

With a sigh of relief, Lark released Jack's hand, letting the glamour fade. She needed the rest—all at once, her head was pounding again.

Silently they approached the huge machine that rose at least ten feet from the cold tile floor. Lark circled to her left, trying to make sense of it. There was a large white control unit attached to a tilted platform. Blinking lights and dials were everywhere, but much of the detail was lost in a tangle of wires and tubes. But Lark quickly forgot all that, for she saw a figure strapped to the platform, arms and legs outstretched and strapped with thick leather and iron buckles.

Iron robbed fey of their powers. With a sudden rush of dread, Lark darted forward to get a better look at the prisoner. He was male, wearing only a scrap of towel despite the chill of the room.

It was Therrien Haven. Lark's heart all but stopped. "By Oberon!"

Instantly she was at his side, feeling for a pulse despite the banks of monitors all around him. She wanted the evidence of her own senses that he was still alive.

Therrien Haven looked about thirty, though he was centuries old. He was one of the red fey, with pale skin, green eyes and hair the fiery color of the sunset. Like all the Light Court, he was handsome. Or had been. Captivity had wasted his flesh and dulled the flame of his brilliant coloring. But as Lark touched him, his eyes flicked open, his expression wary despite whatever drugs he'd been given.

"Fair greetings, Haven," she said in their own tongue.

Jack quickly moved to the other side of the platform. "Did you say Haven?"

Lark nodded. "We've found Therrien Haven."

Haven gave a slight cough and replied in English. "I probably don't look much like my driver's license at the moment."

"We'll get you out of here," Lark said, pulling her gloves from her pockets so that she could handle the iron restraints.

"Wait," Haven said. "If you release me, every soldier in this mountain will descend on you."

"But your blood will open the gates," Lark said. "We can't let the Dark Queen have you."

To her horror, he laughed—a dry sound that scraped over her nerves. "Look around you. The Dark Queen has me in every way possible. My essence is what's fuelling this whole place."

Lark's gaze slid over the tubes hooked into ports in Haven's veins. Clear saline was going in, as one would see in any hospital. But the tube coming out held tiny, individual globes of light suspended in a clear liquid. For a crazy moment, Lark thought of tiny Christmas lights—until she realized what she was looking at. Her grandfather had blazed his light all at once, burning in one mighty effort until it killed him, but Haven's essence was flowing from his arm to machines ranged at the head of the platform, one tiny drop at a time. The fey's natural strength would keep him healing faster than a mortal—for a while. But no one could survive being drained forever.

"They're draining his life," Lark said, despair creeping into her voice, "The same fey energy that went into keeping the Dark Fey contained is being reversed here, used to help free them."

Haven nodded, his gaze darting feverishly from Lark to Jack. "They don't have the gems used in the ritual, so they can't blast the gates open, but through me they can crack them a little at a time."

"Are the Blackthorns in communication with Selena?" Jack asked.

"Yes," said Haven. "I've heard them talk. They behave as if I'm not here."

Because Haven was as good as dead. They wouldn't let him live an hour beyond his usefulness.

"We won't leave you behind," Lark said firmly.

"Lexie?" the fey asked, his voice faint.

"She's safe," said Jack. "She's going to be married."

Married. Lark's mind filled with the image of Kenyon captive. There was a child on the way, too. A sick feeling rolled through her, but she kept her emotions off her face.

Haven squeezed his eyes shut. "I knew they were after her. The only way I could protect her was to put myself in their path."

"And she is fine," said Jack in a gentle tone. "Your efforts worked."

It was exactly the right thing to say, but she could tell Haven was weak and tired. Tears slid from under his eyelids, and she leaned forward to brush them away. His skin felt like paper.

"I can't come with you," said Haven. "I couldn't walk, much less run. I am not worth the rescue."

"Our mission begins with saving you," said Jack. "But it will end when we stop the Dark Queen."

"Then, leave me where I am." His voice regained a tiny bit of strength as he said it. "If you succeed in destroying her, I'll count the price a bargain."

He was right, but Lark didn't like the fact one bit. The idea of leaving Haven behind made her chest ache.

"There is a door to the outside near here," he murmured. "I've smelled the green of the forest in the air now and again."

"Good," said Jack, encouragement warming his voice. "That's good information."

Haven looked feverish, as if giving up the chance of res-cue was one blow too many. "There are other prisoners, but the Dark Queen is holding them close to her until she can escape. They've taken them through the gates."

Lark felt suddenly dizzy. "They're in the Dark Fey realm?"

Haven grew agitated. "The portal is open wide enough to get in, but not out again. Don't think about securing your passage back with my blood. If you take as much as a drop, they'll know. The equipment is protected with spells."

Lark swallowed. They had Lexie's blood, and they had the ring. "We'll manage."

Haven turned his face away. "I wish I could help more."

"Your job is staying alive." Lark wasn't sure how she'd gotten the words out. Her throat was clogged with grief, and leaving him strapped to this infernal machine was going to break her heart.

"We'll do what we must," said Jack firmly, "and we'll come back for you."

"One promise. Please." Haven closed his eyes. His voice was fading.

"What?" Jack asked.

"Hurry. The Dark Queen is only the beginning of the danger."

"What do you mean?" Lark asked, bending close to catch his words—but Haven lost consciousness before he could say more.

Chapter 21

When Lark summoned her magic to put the glamour back on herself and Jack, it felt as if something inside her was tearing apart. After using her ability for so long a stretch, she needed real rest, and that wasn't going to happen. At least Haven's information about a nearby exit was correct. The steel double door, complete with panic bars, looked like a delivery entrance from the inside.

"No guards," Jack said. "I don't see any cameras."

Lark gratefully released the glamour again. She put a hand to her aching head. White lights were dancing through her vision, the first sour hints of nausea creeping up the back of her throat. "What about alarms?"

Jack was carefully examining the door frame. "Just a sturdy lock." He bent to work on it. There wasn't much he couldn't pick.

The sound of footsteps penetrated her thoughts. "I think the guards were making their rounds again. They're a way off, but they're coming in this direction." She took a breath, pushing panic to the side as best she could.

"How's your head?" Jack asked, still poking at the lock.

"Not great." She kept her voice steady, though her stomach lurched on a queasy bubble.

At that moment the lock clicked. Jack straightened. "Piece of cake."

And it should have been their first clue that something was wrong.

The door opened to a lot of night sky, the stars a dizzying blanket so close they seemed touchable. There was an immediate drop to a rushing river so far below that the trees on its banks looked like a lumpy dark carpet.

"It's their waste-disposal system," Jack said without emotion.

Lark shifted her backpack uneasily. She could hear the footsteps clearly now—at least two guards, maybe more. She couldn't see them yet, but they'd be there any second. "Now what?"

He smiled, but he wasn't happy. "Don't scream."

Alarm numbed her for a split second. "What?"

Jack grabbed her tight, wrapping his strong arms around her waist and pulling her so tight that he nearly choked the breath from her lungs. And then he hurled them both through the door and into a sickening, horrible plunge.

Terror was a poor word for the frozen blank of Lark's mind. All she could see was the sky wheeling overhead, the thick carpet of stars swirling as they fell. Icy mountain air rushed past, deafening her and clawing at the skin of her face. Blood pounded in her like a clock ticking down her seconds left to live, but with each beat came another sensation. Something dark, powerful and *other* surged from Jack like a crackling mist. Magic, certainly, but nothing she'd encountered before. Despite hurtling to a certain death below, every nerve in her body sang in response to him.

A split second later, their fall became a tumble and they were spinning and rolling, end over end. Jack was still grasping her close, his hard grip painful as they were flung through space. Lark squeezed her eyes shut, feeling as if her insides were shaking loose when they thumped into something solid. Jack took the brunt of the shock, but then they were rolling, one over the other, at least a dozen times until the rising ground slowed them to a stop.

Jack still held her, his thickly muscled arms pressing her to his chest. She was lying on the ground, her left hip digging into the ground. Logic said it wasn't moving, but her head still spun.

Lark cracked open her eyes and rolled to her back. The stars shone above, interrupted by a few tree branches. *Wow.* There wasn't much else to think.

Slowly, she sat up, letting her stomach settle and taking stock of their position. She could see the mountain where they'd been, but it was at least a mile away. Lark looked around in confusion. There had been a broad, fast-flowing river below the door when they'd jumped. They were on the other side of it now. They hadn't just fallen, but traveled across the water. They'd *flown.*

Suddenly Jack moved, the action as quick as a pouncing lion. Lark turned to see him, doubled over as if his stomach ached. Alarmed, she crawled over to where he was kneeling. His head was bowed, giving no indication he was aware of her approach.

"Jack?" She reached out to touch his arm. "Are you hurt?"

He flinched as if stung. And then he looked up, and Lark's entire body turned to ice.

His eyes looked as if they'd trapped the stars. They shone with a cold, remote light, piercing and inhuman. It was as if a different presence had suddenly taken Jack's place and was looking at her now with an intelligence far older than even the fey, and far more powerful.

She'd seen those eyes before, most recently in his dream. Her scalp crawled with fear, and she snatched her hand back. "Asteriel?"

"At your service." The voice was Jack's, but the way he spoke was subtly different. More precise, as if he didn't get much practice speaking. Then the brilliance of his eyes softened as if a filter had been slid in front of so much light.

Shock throbbed through Lark and she sagged back onto her heels, battered by the power that rolled off Jack like a surf. This was the creature she'd seen in New York the night she'd stabbed him. It wasn't threatening her now, but she still felt the skin along her arms prickle with fear. But not just fear—there was a darkly magnetic pull to him, as if he tugged on a string that went right to her core. Demon Jack was undeniably sexual.

His gaze was amused. "You always wanted to know what made Jack so strong a vampire. Here I am. Your lover was never bitten, but blended from pure essence of demon."

"Give him back." Even his scent was rich with desire. This close to him, she felt as if she were still hurtling through the air, the ground nowhere to be found.

Jack's smile flashed in the dark. "You make it sound like this is some bargain-basement possession. It's nothing of the kind. We have a gentlemen's agreement."

"And deals with demons always end so well." Lark swallowed, not sure what to do. Memories of his hand around her throat crawled through her mind. "Why did you save me just now?"

"That shining knight is still part of me."

"Where is he right now?"

The demon wearing Jack's face reached out, brushing the hair from her eyes. It was a gesture she knew well and, more than any other evidence, made it clear just how much the Fallen was part of the man she knew. "He will be back as soon as I am done. Since you know our secret, you and I must have words."

Her flesh chilled. "About what?"

His eyebrows gave a playful lift, but his tone was serious. "First, you must understand that it is my choice to give him control in return for sharing his life. Life is important to me because it is my only chance for change, but the stakes are real and they are high. If Jack is destroyed, then so am I. If I fail to redeem myself, I am damned forever. This partnership is my only chance to change my fate."

Lark caught her breath. His star-bright gaze bored into

her, searching every feature. "Do you understand?" he asked.

"I'm not sure."

"You changed the game when you stabbed us."

Alarm froze her. Lark remembered him holding the knife in Jack's dream. "How?"

He answered so softly, it sounded apologetic. "You opened the way for me to take control. The truth spell on the blade means he cannot hide me anymore. Not if I give in to temptation."

Lark's mouth went dry. "Is that why his control is slipping?"

"Yes."

A wave of sick realization made Lark reel. She buried her face in her hands. "No wonder he doesn't want to forgive me."

"No man wishes to show the woman he loves that he is truly a monster. At the same time, a man needs a little monster when it comes to a fight."

"And there will be a fight."

"Yes, and then the temptation to be what I am, terrible and ripe with power, may destroy all that we have achieved after so many years together."

And it was so much. As a star agent of the Company, Jack had saved more lives and righted more wrongs than anyone Lark could name. He could be inflexible, maddening and difficult, but he was unquestionably good.

And possibly she had undone the salvation of his darker half. Lark had no idea how to answer, but hid her face with her hands, wishing the earth would swallow her. Was there no end to the evil she had wrought that night in New York?

Never mind Jack forgiving her. Would she ever forgive herself?

A long time passed before Lark felt gentle fingers pull her hands away from her face.

"Are you all right? Were you hurt when we fell?" he asked. And this was the Jack she knew. Asteriel was gone.

"I'm fine." Lark felt tears on her face, their heat almost burning against the chill air. "I'm not fine. I've caused you so much pain."

He was silent, a shadow against the backdrop of stars. His eyes had faded back to their normal hue, but now they held profound confusion. "Tell me what happened."

"You saved us. You flew, not floating like Mark Winspear. You *flew* us across the river."

He let go of her hands, rising to lean against a tree. He looked exhausted. "I remember that part. It was the conversation afterward that's fuzzy."

She got to her feet, forcing herself not to weave. She could still feel the motion of their dizzying flight like a fading afterimage. The urge to beg forgiveness welled inside, but so did a sudden fear she didn't deserve it. She ducked her head, grabbing instead for a simple question. "Does Asteriel always appear to you wearing your face?"

"Demons and angels can appear in any form they please." He made an abrupt, impatient gesture. "Our backpacks are gone. The straps broke in the force of the fall."

She didn't care about the packs, but understood the conversation was done. "We'll manage. I don't think we have much time to worry about supplies anyway."

Jack went still. She could feel the energy between them shift subtly. Instinctively, she knew he was lowering his guard a degree. "I'm sorry."

Lark frowned. "For what?"

"I'm not what you thought." His voice was tight.

"You're exactly who you've always been to me." She drew closer, wanting to see his expression. His features were washed in starlight, the clean lines stern and beautiful. Maybe that was one reason why he'd been chosen by the Fallen—he looked the part. "I've known who you are for years. You're the one who saw what I could be when I walked through the doors of the Company. You made me think better of myself."

Lark didn't give Jack a chance to argue. She leaned in and kissed him gently on the cheek, a featherlight touch of breath and skin. "Tonight you saved my life. There is no need for apologies or explanations."

Jack's reaction was instant. Suddenly it was her leaning against the tree, his arms trapping her on either side. All at once, his demon didn't seem so very far below the surface. He leaned in, his forehead touching hers. "Remember, there is a part of me that is a shark biding its time in an all-too-flimsy net."

"Remember, I like sushi."

"Hmm." He kissed her eyelids, then her lips, and she felt the walls between them melt away. His mouth was soft and needy on hers, drawing her in with the slow, sweet magic of a man who was entirely in the moment.

He stepped into the embrace, no longer leaning but letting his hands slide up her sides, careful and possessive. She could see his eyes now, the sweep of lashes where they touched his cheek. She knew the architecture of his face well enough, but now he seemed different, as if every feature had undergone a subtle shift.

"Jack?" she murmured.

"What?"

"Don't you think there will be guards from the mountain looking for us? We left the door open when we fell."

His eyes flashed, echoes of Asteriel. "Why should they assume it was intruders? They'll put it down to someone's carelessness. Even if they do suspect something, how many people do you think survive a fall from that doorway? They won't waste the manpower looking for trespassers who should have tumbled to their death."

"That sounds overconfident."

"They couldn't spot us inside their own facility. What makes you think they'll find us in the wilderness?"

She heard the defiance in his voice, a predator's taunt against the hunters who dared to try to cage him. The demon wasn't far beneath the surface, and it wanted to flex its muscles—mission and danger be damned.

"We barely escaped with our lives," she pointed out.

"Then, celebrate." He nipped her ear, his body warm with sexual heat. "Let me show you how."

"Jack, shouldn't we be moving ..."

"How come you can still talk?" His mouth moved to the angle of her jaw.

Lark held her breath, fascinated and wary. Jack's control was shredding before her eyes, the demon pushing to the surface to claim its due. She could run or she could surrender, and both seemed perilous choices.

Jack's fingers trailed over the arch of her collarbone, tracing it as if he was committing it to memory. His movements were unhurried, almost mesmerized. He brushed her breasts lightly, as if marking his territory for later. His touch did something to her insides, sweeping every other thought away. All at once time and urgency meant nothing. She was his task of the moment, and he wouldn't be rushed. She didn't want to try.

And yet, some small voice of reason refused to be silent. "This isn't why we're here."

She hoped the words would call to Jack, help him back into control, but he laughed instead. It was a soft, wicked sound that stroked things low in her body. "Since when do the fey avoid temptation?"

"Temptation is dangerous," she countered. "You told me that yourself."

His eyes flashed again. "Am I dangerous?"

The question made her catch her breath. Lark leaned her head back, pressing it into the bark of the tree so she could tilt her chin up and meet his brilliant eyes. He was so close, their noses touched. Speaking nearly brought them into another kiss. "I think I like your demon, Jack."

His fingers fastened on the lapels of her coat. In a moment, he'd pushed it off her shoulders, letting it fall to the grass below. Her shirt followed, leaving only her tank top. Lark shivered when Jack's mouth found her bare shoulder. His hips rolled against her, the hard bulge in his jeans proving just how much his demon liked her back.

Jack pulled Lark tight to him, and she reached up to wind her arms around his neck. His hands cupped her cheeks, running his thumbs along the fine ridge of her jaw. She could feel the pulse in her neck flutter against the pressure of his fingers, as if alerted to his predator's touch.

The immense power lurking just beneath Jack's skin was oceanic in its depth and mystery. Lark was all but immortal, but she was still young even by human years. Jack had been a vampire for centuries, and the demon within him was more ancient still. All that time had honed his power, distilling it to frightening purity. She could sense the demon's presence as she never had before, a swirl of power that could engulf her with the slightest effort of will. The vibration of it was erotic all on its own, but it was also terrifying.

His mouth found her neck, leaving nips as he tasted her flesh. "I want you."

The words shuddered through her with tectonic force. There was so much need in his voice, so much loneliness. Lark was glad of the tree at her back holding her up. It was the voice of an angel condemned to darkness, wanting to be loved for his own sake.

The tension between Jack and his demon, of dark and light, sparked in the air around them. Asteriel had gained the upper hand tonight, and Lark knew with the thin shred of logic left to her that her next move could change everything.

"Trust me," he whispered, his voice a rasp of need.

She was overwhelmed, terrified, but she understood this dark side was part of Jack. After all, she had exposed it with her blade. Now, when the demon was near the surface, she had a chance to heal that wound. She could beg for forgiveness, but that was for herself. With sudden clarity, Lark knew that her energy was much better spent showing compassion.

She ran her hands under his shirt, feeling the smooth skin pulled taut over furrows of abdominal muscle. Those muscles flexed as he pulled off his shirt and jacket, the gesture showing the flare of his shoulders as he lifted his arms. He grabbed her by the waist, lifting her feet from the ground as if she weighed no more than a leaf. Lark wrapped her legs around his middle and found his lips again, drinking in the shattering presence of him.

His hands roamed up her ribs, skimming off her tank top so he could claim every inch. Eventually, he found the silk of her bra and pulled down the gossamer fabric, exposing her breasts. His mouth closed over her nipple, wet and greedy, the pull of it shooting sensation deep into her core. She rocked against him, mindless with exquisite, pleasurable distress. Her hands raked through his hair, then fell to his shoulders, then slowly ran down his arms, caressing him until she cupped his hands where they held her waist.

He released her nipple, leaving it peaked and wet in the cold air. Demon brightness lurked in his eyes. "What do you want?"

The question was gentle, though filled with darkest heat. It went straight to the molten lust in her belly. She could only manage one word. "More."

Though they had made love before, all of Jack—even the part he hid—was present now. The moment felt new and forbidden as he lowered his barriers a little further than he ever had before.

He unhooked the front catch of the bra, letting her breasts fall free. The garment fluttered to the ground as he palmed her flesh, kneading and sucking until she was blinded by tears of pure need. "More," she whispered.

"Like what?" he replied, the rumble of his words more felt than heard.

Releasing her grip on his waist, she braced herself on his shoulders and slithered down his front until her feet touched the ground. Then she found the front of his jeans and began working on the fastenings. Jack inhaled sharply as he sprang free into her hand. She drew her palm slowly up his length, making him growl low in his chest. The sound alone nearly broke her.

Lark released him and stepped away, undoing her own jeans and shimmying them over her hips. She stepped out of them, toeing off her boots. It wasn't the best striptease ever, but the time for coyness was long past.

In a quick, sinuous movement, he pulled her down to the grass. Jack knelt, one hand on either side of her head, and straddled her legs, blocking out the stars overhead. Raw desire set Lark's pulse pounding. The scent of the night, of Jack's skin and the wild mountains filled her like an intoxicating drug. Wherever their skin brushed, she could feel the prickle of his power, bringing every hair on her body to attention. So much magic—dangerous magic—sent her senses reeling. A rush of heat crept over her, making her slick and ready.

"Is this what you want?" he murmured, tasting the soft skin at the hollow of her collarbone with tongue and lips.

He raised himself, looked down at her. His face was lost in shadow but for the brightness of his eyes. She reached up, tracing by touch the lines of old scars that crisscrossed his chest. Souvenirs from his mortal days, no doubt. Her light touch made him shiver, hardening his nipples into peaks. Then she let her hand drift until she found his velvety hardness. "This is what I want. Now."

"Good." He pushed her knees apart, urgency making him rough.

She guided him as he pushed inside, growling herself as his size filled her. Her nails dug into his shoulders, the instinct to brace herself warring with the desire to pull him closer. Her grip only made him move harder, his first thrust a lesson in how much his control had slipped. Alarm surged, but only for an instant. Her fey wildness responded eagerly, welcoming this new roughness. Her muscles clenched around him, the delicious agony in every nerve turning her vision to starbursts.

The ragged thrusts settled into a rhythm, each hard and greedy, as if he was devouring her very essence through the act of desire. She cried out exclamations of surprise and need, but she had gone far beyond proper words. A storm gathered within her, one of wetness and heat and pulsing flesh. Spasms quickened deep inside her as his rhythm broke and he began to pound relentlessly. Hard. Fast. Harder. Faster. The raw frenzy savaged her will and remade the remnants into helpless, mindless need.

Lark surrendered, tears streaming as release hit without mercy, blanking every nerve in exquisite torment. It was perfect.

Chapter 22

Hours later, Jack led them away from the river and down a steep path through the trees. They were obviously heading into a valley, though she couldn't tell yet how deep it was. "Are we anywhere near the Derrondine Pass?" Lark asked. After crossing the mountain and the river, she had all but lost her bearings.

"We're in the pass right now. The site where we did the ritual to close the gates to the Dark Fey kingdom is straight ahead." Jack pointed to a line of tall pines about twenty yards away.

Lark barely noticed the massive trunks, and Jack was the reason why. Every man had his demons when it came to relationships, but Jack's was literal—and yet his dark side had proved it could give pleasure with an artful and generous tenderness. Trying to think after that was like trying to see after staring into the sun.

The demon was hidden now, nothing of those star-bright eyes remaining in Jack's gaze. Still, memories clouded Lark's perceptions. Jack had been dark and dangerous before, but now every thought of him scorched her.

She took a deep breath, calming her racing thoughts. "If we're so close to the ritual site, why can't I feel it? It should reek of magic."

"The craftsmanship of the spell was careful, so that no energy was wasted. We wanted the spell to last." He took her hand and guided her down the path, holding branches out of her way. "There are no leaks to betray its presence."

They'd made it to the edge of the trees, and the view opened up before Lark. The scene was beautiful, but not what she'd expected. The trees sheltered an alpine valley filled by a lake, the water a mirror image of the starry sky. It was still—only the slightest ripple revealing the presence of a breeze. She could smell the snows that fed it and shivered. "Where are the gates?"

Jack pointed at the lake. "They're not literal gates made of metal or stone. We pass through the water to the other side. It looks still, but the undercurrent is wicked."

"The passage will be difficult," she said, speaking her fears aloud. "Fey portals try to separate and confuse intruders. It's part of their defense system."

Jack slid something from a pocket inside his jacket and held up the handcuffs. "If we use these to lock our wrists together, it can't separate us."

Lark narrowed her eyes. "You just like cuffing me, don't you?"

"I can't risk losing you."

The seriousness—and heat—in his tone made Lark's breath hitch. "Really?"

He responded with a teasing curve of his lips, the look adding a sensual layer behind his practical reply. "We'll be on your turf once we're there, and I'll need your guidance. I'm not fey."

"I'm not Dark Fey," she pointed out, but he was right. She understood the complicated and often deadly rules of the fey courts. Without that knowledge, few survived long.

He lowered the handcuffs. "Your call. Last chance to back out."

Lark swallowed. Entering the Dark Queen's realm was a mad errand with little chance of success or return. But far more important to Lark was the fact that Jack trusted her.

And she trusted him. All of him. His demon had cradled her in his arms.

Lark held out her left wrist. "We're in this together."

The dive was long and freezing cold. Jack remained awake through the deep dive, but then vampires didn't need to breathe. Lark lost consciousness just as the magic of the gates pulled them into the realm of the Dark Fey.

As Jack had predicted, the cuffs alone had kept her in his grasp through the crushing blackness. The portal spit them out eventually, dropping them to the dirt and leaves. They should have been dripping wet, but the magic of the gates had kept them dry.

Now Jack sat cross-legged on the forest floor, Lark's head in his lap. She lay in an exhausted sleep, her face turned up to his. Her mahogany hair fanned about her like a mermaid's tresses. He was lost in the contemplation of her cheekbone, of the curve of her ear. The fey were exquisitely beautiful, but one never truly noticed just how much until they were still—and with Lark that rarely happened. She was always in motion—laughing or fighting or rushing into the next adventure.

He'd taken the cuffs off. They'd left a welt on both their wrists, but his had already healed. Hers was still red and raw. Jack lifted her hand and kissed her wound, tasting the sweetness of her skin. They needed to move, but he hated to end the moment. He pressed his cheek to her hand, rubbing against her fingers. Everything in him screamed to get Lark far away from this realm and the insanity of what they meant to do, but she was every bit as much an agent as he was. If he admired her courage, he had to let her use it.

He left a kiss in her palm as he lowered her hand, reluctant to let her go. He brushed the hair from her forehead lightly with his fingertips.

"You are extraordinary," he said softly.

Her eyes flickered open, their dark, soft brown reminding him of darkest coffee. She focused on his face, at the sky above him. Then her expression grew wary as she sat up. "We made it?"

"We are in the kingdom of the Dark Fey," he replied.

She looked around. "How do you know? It looks just the same as where we were."

"Not quite." They got to their feet. It was warmer here, more like April than February. Flowers dotted the forest floor with stars of palest blue. "The nature of the Dark Queen's influence is subtle, but it is perverse. It's quite pleasant right here, but I'd stay away from the vegetation farther on. Some of it is mobile and not very friendly. Also, beware the rabbits. They looked hungry, and for once I don't mind being already dead."

She shot him a look of alarm as she straightened her clothes. "So what do we do first?"

"Explore?" Jack said. "Since we've lost our supplies, we need to find safe provisions."

Lark would need food and water, but nothing in a fey realm could be trusted, and poison was the least of it. Some foods were spelled to bind one to eternal servitude; others were laced with charms that could turn one to a moose or a mushroom according to the caster's whim.

"Right," she said, glancing around. "That looks like a path."

It was more of a deer track, but it would do. They set out with Lark leading the way. She would detect magical traps before he did.

They did not have to go far before the landscape changed. It was as if the ordinary world had spilled over near the gates and all traces of what was normal dwindled deeper into the Dark Queen's territory. Spotted toadstools sprouted thickly from the forest floor, some growing nearly as high as Jack's knee, and the air was heavy and oppressive, scented with a white trumpet vine that smelled like decay.

"There are spells here," Lark announced. "I've been

disabling them as we go, but if they had their way we'd be wandering in circles until we dropped from exhaustion."

Jack wasn't surprised. "Then, this road must be going somewhere, if they don't want us to reach the end."

"There." Lark pointed. "I can see the edge of the forest up ahead. And I think that's where we want to go."

Jack saw the castle at once. It was a pale blue shadow on the horizon, its outline like something from a picture book. There were turrets and towers, a drawbridge and moat. Jack, who had lived in his fair share of castles, studied the fortifications with a practiced eye. Whoever had built it knew their business.

A few minutes later, they stood with the last of the trees behind them, and a rolling meadow stretched between them and the castle gates. Jack glanced at the brooding purple sky, thick with clouds so low they brushed the castle's highest tower. It was either twilight or about to storm or neither. This wasn't true sunlight, because it had no effect on his vampire physiology.

"What do you think?" Jack asked, his gaze settling back to the castle. "If I were an evil overlord, I'd hold my prisoners there."

"Incoming!" Lark whipped around, her weapon out and ready. Jack instantly drew his, scanning the trees for movement. Every few feet the air shimmered, as if from waves of heat, and a handful of figures materialized. Jack recognized two of them at once: Egon and Drusella Blackthorn.

"Maybe we can help by extending an invitation." Drusella held a long spear with a leaf-shaped blade of bronze—a traditional fairy weapon, but it looked odd in her hands. An assault rifle was far more her style.

Jack snarled, fangs out and coiling to launch himself. All of the fey took heed and stepped back. All but the Blackthorns. Drusella thrust the spear forward to keep him at bay. Jack snatched at it, but succeeded only in knocking the weapon aside. Drusella was fast.

"Hold!" Egon commanded in a deep voice. "There is no need to fight. Her Majesty would be delighted to entertain you."

Jack and Drusella stepped apart, but not before Drusella got in one last jab. Egon awarded his sister a quelling look. "It's not every century we get visitors. When you emerged from the lake, the queen was impressed by your courage in coming here."

It wasn't a huge surprise that the portal was watched, so Jack got straight to the point. "You have hostages. We have come to get them back."

Egon raised his eyebrows. "That's a conversation best had with the queen."

"Maybe." Jack eyed the cluster of other warriors—a half dozen figures with bows and arrows. Primitive, but a good shot was every bit as deadly as a rifle. "She needs to work on her people skills."

Jack drew closer to Lark, careful not to foul her aim but ready to hurl himself in the path of any weapon that flew her way. Then he pulled his Walther.

Egon gave him a withering look and drew a heavy sword from a sheath slung across his back. "You can put those guns away. Firearms don't work here. Something to do with the amount of magic in the air."

Unease crawled through Jack as he aimed at the ground and pulled the trigger. It gave a click, but nothing more. He tried again with the same result. Disgusted, he thrust the gun back in its holster. "And here I left my crossbow on the nightstand."

With a derisive lift of his eyebrows, Egon turned and led the way to the castle. The others followed, herding Lark and Jack along at spear point.

To Lark, the Dark Fey kingdom felt out of tune, and the disharmony grew as they approached the castle. The Light Court was almost arcane in its love of ritual and protocol, but they embraced the forests and wilds. Here nature was twisted, from the bruised clouds to the meadow of dead grass.

Jack walked next to her, reining in his stride to match hers. She could feel the layers of his mask slipping as they walked toward the castle. There was intrinsic violence in his every move, his grace and strength poised to lash out and to protect. Even his hands were half curled at his sides, ready to grab and strike at the least sign of danger.

Once he had to catch her when she stumbled. The ground was rocky and treacherous, the path hidden by dust. The grass was dead and white as ash. It crunched like breakfast cereal and yet, when Lark glanced down, it seemed to reform the moment she passed, springing up again in sere, shriveled spears.

The drought extended to the castle walls. The moat was dry, the drawbridge flanked by guards in livery of black-and-white. Jack was looking around curiously. "This is all wrong."

"How?" she asked.

"It's too quiet. There should be people and livestock everywhere in a working castle."

He was right. As they passed beneath the great stone gate tower, she could see the yard was almost empty of life. The wind keening between chinks of stone drowned out any incidental noise. It sounded lonely, as if the castle itself was in mourning.

Egon led them through the huge doors and into the great hall. Here the silence abruptly ended, as if someone had flipped a switch. This room was crammed with guests in outlandish, colorful dress—and they were all talking, squealing or chittering with excitement. Many were from the lesser tribes of the fey, and so were all sizes and shapes, from the tiny winged fey that tended flowers to the grotesque lizards that haunted desert mountains. Wings, antennae, scales and tails were draped in glittering finery.

The Blackthorns marched Jack and Lark down the center aisle of the hall. The noise rose to an ear-splitting pitch as the crowd parted, drawing back to show an aisle paved with dark-veined marble. Lark felt the prod of Drusella's spear between her shoulders, and she quickened her steps. She tried not to look around, but it was impossible not to see the glittering eyes fixed on them, and the leers of anticipation. Everyone had known they were coming and expected a show.

Black-and-white banners hung from the rafters, unremarkable until Lark saw they were enormous bats with their wings outstretched. In the center of the aisle, about halfway along, was a marble fountain. Gold and silver goblets sat on its rim, as if inviting guests to drink. She felt Jack stiffen as they passed. The liquid in the fountain was warm, scarlet blood.

At the head of the aisle, on a dais made from a latticework of bone, sat a great golden chair. There, Queen Selena reclined, her slender body barely filling half the throne. She was exquisite, glittering with gems at her throat and wrists and in the mass of her shining golden hair. Her large eyes were gray, her fair skin flawless as mountain snow. She was dressed in silks of deep indigo with silver mesh stitched over her bodice and sleeves.

A savage poke to the back from Drusella's spear brought Lark to her knees. Jack knelt beside her, but it was a stiffly courteous gesture, holding little true respect. Lark looked up under her eyelashes as Drusella and Egon moved to flank the throne. The queen paid them no attention—her gaze was locked on Jack, a faint smile playing around her lips. Lark knew they had been foes during the bloody wars of olden times, but their hostility hadn't ended there. From behind her prison gates, Selena had sent tentacles into the Knights of Vidon, the Company and even the human police to achieve her ends. Now she had attacked *La Compagnie des Morts*, Jack's home for as long as it had graced the earth. To see Jack kneeling at her feet must have seemed a final triumph.

But there was more to come. Selena flicked the billows of her skirts aside to reveal one last cruelty. At her feet lay a wolf in a silver collar, shivers running through its body as if it was racked with agony. Its golden eyes were flat and dull, no fire left within them. Lark gave a strangled moan. They'd found Faran Kenyon.

Jack sprang to his feet, but the leaf blade of Drusella's spear was immediately at his chest, pressed directly above his heart. "Stay where you are, vampire."

Queen Selena stepped to the edge of the dais and looked down on them, eyes wide with amusement. "So," she said in a voice as pure and soft as bells, "after all these years, you have come to amuse me, Silverhand. How very kind you are to blunder into my waiting arms."

Chapter 23

"We're not kind, and this isn't a social call," Jack replied.

"I know that well enough," said the queen, her eyes turning cold with warning. "That is what I like the least about the men of the Company. It takes so much effort to put you in an agreeable mood. But then, I suppose there are fewer of you left to annoy me."

That did nothing to improve Jack's frame of mind. "Give me the wolf."

"No." She turned and waved away her courtiers. They cleared the hall, leaving only a handful of guards posted along the wall. Suddenly the place felt cold and echoing, the only sound the thick burble of the blood fountain. "No, I like my new pet. I think I shall keep him."

Rage stirred—the closest thing to a father's anger Jack knew—and he felt his fangs slip free. Faran had been a troublesome, stubborn, wonderful youth who had grown to manhood under Jack's watchful eye. Jack would rather be chained there himself. "I demand him."

"And again, no." The queen drew herself up. "He is a mortal who has eaten of the food of the fey. By the laws of our magic, he is mine to command. He will not even remember who you are unless I will it."

Horror crawled through Jack's bones. A low growl thrummed in his chest.

Queen Selena was not impressed. "Your situation is precarious. That is why courtesy was invented, vampire. It helps one navigate choppy waters."

The way she said *choppy* brought knives to mind. Jack flinched inside, but forced his face into a neutral mask. "Then perhaps we can move directly to business," he said, wiping all emotion from his voice. "I do not have time to waste."

"Time," said the fey queen. "Time is all I have had, and all I would have if the leaders of the mortal realm had their way. You have locked my people in here for a thousand years with no connection to the living world. All that is left to us is death and dissolution."

"This realm is as broad as you require, Your Majesty. Whatever you need—food, supplies, even treasure—is here. That was all part of the terms."

"We are forgotten and fading from existence. I refuse to suffer this indignity one moment more."

"I am sorry your banishment is so tedious," Jack said, though he frankly didn't care if Queen Selena shriveled and died. During the early wars between Vidon and Marcari, the Dark had torn entire villages to pieces, scattering bones and flesh over the countryside like a horrifying rain.

"How kind." She gave a bitter smile. "But I will not mistake polite words for leniency. Nor should you underestimate me. I will not rest until I am free."

"Your position does not come as a surprise."

What did surprise him was that she hadn't slain him where he stood. The queen had too many advantages—the prisoners, the army in the mountain, Haven and even a window of opportunity while the Company was in shambles. There was no reason to waste time talking to him and Lark. She wanted something they had—something she couldn't take by force. Jack's gaze shot to where Kenyon lay stiff and suffering at the foot of the throne. *Take the queen and tear out her throat. Now. Before it is too late.*

But she had the royal couple. If they struck before he

could protect them, the other fey would kill them all. Reluctantly, Jack decided to play her game to see where it would lead. "If you will not let me have my wolf, then will you return the prince and princess?"

Queen Selena looked amused. "No, because as long as I have them, I have your attention. It's hard to establish a bargaining position from exile beneath a lake."

"Bargaining position?" Jack asked.

Lark turned to Jack, her tone urgent. "No bargains. We'll never get what we want in the end. That's how it works. It's a point of honor with the Dark Fey never to strike a straight deal."

"Is my word as a fey and a queen not binding?" said the Dark Queen, giving Lark a poisonous look.

"Your word binds to the letter and only to the letter," Lark replied.

"Just so," Selena said, her words as silky as a mink stole. "Let us wager the least of our prizes so you can see me in action. I swear a solemn oath that any larger deals will be conducted in precisely the same way."

Lark stepped on Jack's foot to get his attention. Her face was white with dread. "Jack." The word was a desperate plea that he would decline.

The Dark Queen snapped her fingers. Kenyon's head rose at once, ears swiveling forward. "Come, wolf."

Stiffly, he rose, moving as if he was ancient instead of a creature in his prime. Jack guessed with a sickening lurch that contact with the silver chain was slowly poisoning the wolf's blood. The great beast hobbled down the steps, nails clicking on the marble, to sit at the queen's feet. It was so large, its head nearly reached her shoulder. The yellow eyes were blank, stripped of will. The queen patted his head. "A beautiful animal, don't you think? I've kept him in wolf form since he arrived."

If Jack was appalled before, this was doubly bad. His hands curled into claws, aching to shred and tear. "Werewolf physiology is delicate. They have to shift, at least for a few minutes a day."

He had a sudden vision of red-haired Lexie, Therrien Haven's daughter. She was already planning her wedding with Kenyon. Her love would give him a real home and family. That was everything Jack had ever wanted for his ward—everything the young man had wanted for himself—and the queen was about to make a mockery of those dreams.

"Or he will get stuck as a wolf, or stuck partway. Yes, I know. That gives me some assurance you won't dither. Make your bargain quickly or I build a kennel. Your choice."

Jack looked into the wolf's eyes, searching for some remnant of intelligence or personality. There was nothing there. Horror crawled along Jack's bones. Lark slipped her hand into his and he clasped it, grateful for the anchor.

"What is your price for his return?" Lark asked, quietly taking the lead. This was her area of expertise. "And by that I mean his return to our custody, whole and intact, with no enchantments upon him or ties to you or your realm, your court or magic—and no lasting effects for him or his descendants, relations, loved ones, friends or associates, property or business interests for all time."

The queen laughed. "He is lucky you are here, Lark of the Light Fey. You bargain with skill. The price is simple. I will throw a banquet tonight, and you and Jack will dine with us. There will be no enchantment on the food, no tricks. In fact, I swear that you can eat and drink in perfect safety while you are within my borders."

"Swear the same for Kenyon and the prince and princess," Jack demanded.

The queen looked annoyed but nodded. "If you dine with us."

Lark spoke next. "And how long in mortal hours will the banquet last?"

The queen sighed. "No more than three."

It was a good catch. It was possible to end up a permanent guest at a banquet without end. Jack and Lark exchanged a long, troubled look. The one thing that gave Jack comfort was that the queen wanted their trust. If this was a preliminary deal, a gesture designed to lure them in, there was a good chance she'd let them win.

"There will be a trick here somewhere," Lark said, obviously not sharing his opinion.

"I know." Jack stirred restlessly. He was better with a weapon in his hand. "But if we don't throw the dice, the game is over before we start."

Selena wound her fingers through the beast's collar of silver chain and twisted, pushing the silver links against its skin. The wolf whined, and Jack could see pink, raw flesh where the fur had already burned away. *I am going to kill her. That's a solemn vow.*

"We'll attend your dinner," he said in an even voice. "You can stop strangling my friend."

He saw the flash of dismay in Lark's eyes, but there was no other possible course of action. "I'm sorry. Something has to be done."

"It certainly does." The queen laughed softly, an amused sound that raised the hair along his skin more effectively than any evil cackle. "And this is just the first item on my list."

Jack couldn't wait until they got to the big-ticket items.

Scratch that. He dreaded the answer.

Chapter 24

"You don't understand," said Lark, waving her hands in exasperation. "You don't dine with fey. For some clans, dinner parties are considered dull unless somebody dies."

Jack looked up from where he reclined on a puffy piece of furniture somewhere between a couch and a bed. "Suddenly I'm not so anxious to join your family for Thanksgiving."

"We don't have Thanksgiving. We have the Feast of the Dead." Dispirited, she fell onto the cushions beside him.

"Was that before or after you poisoned your guests during the appetizer course?"

Lark clapped a hand over her eyes. "Don't joke about such things."

Jack grunted, letting it drop.

They'd been shown to this room to rest—and be good little prisoners—until the banquet. Instead, they were treating it as an opportunity to regroup and plan. Lark needed it. Whatever she'd expected, Selena's castle wasn't it.

If circumstances were different, their chambers might have been nice. The walls were draped with tapestries and the floor strewn with soft cushions. A sunken bathing pool of dark green marble steamed in one corner, separated by a curtain. Fey liked their luxury baths. It reminded Lark strongly of the bedchambers back home.

Home seemed like an impossible dream. She'd been on missions before, but none so far from any chance of rescue. She wondered if Sam and Mark had made it back to the capital and if reinforcements had arrived from the other Company sites. Had they identified the dead from the head-quarters' blast? Would she live to find out?

"What do you make of Selena?" Jack asked unexpectedly.

Lark blew out her breath. "I think she's everything I was warned about and more. She's lying about the kingdom being completely sealed. The Blackthorns are here. They'd never come through the gates if they thought they couldn't get out again."

"Therrien said the gates are cracking open. They're just farther along than he thought." Jack folded an arm behind his head, showing the thick muscles of his biceps. "Selena can't get out because the spell was focused on her, but her two strongest lieutenants can squeak through. It probably takes a hideous amount of power, which is why none of the other Dark Fey are escaping."

"That opening will only last as long as Therrien does," Lark said softly. Her heart wrenched at the thought of the trapped fey. "The queen has limited time to put her plans in motion before that crack in the gates falls shut again." When Therrien died.

"No wonder she's forcing our hand." Jack said, shifting closer so they touched. His solid presence comforted her, easing her sadness. "And yet there is a reckless element I don't understand. I remember the queen as a precision planner. Grabbing Amelie and Kyle was a huge risk."

Lark tensed. "It could be her people suffer beyond the intent of the banishment."

"How so?" he asked.

Lark shifted away, suddenly needing space. Jack frowned. "What is it?"

She hesitated, still caught in the habit of silence. And yet, at the heart of the Dark Queen's realm, the cost of saying nothing might be too high. "Without an anchor in the mortal world, the fey do not thrive."

"An anchor?"

"A complex subject. It is enough to say we need contact with the mortal realm to keep our strength."

Understanding flickered in his eyes. His words in the Land Rover came back to her. *Rumor has it your numbers are declining.* "As long as I've lived and dealt with the fey, I never understood how that worked."

"There's no reason you would. The point is that if Selena is any kind of queen to her people, she'll try to end the banishment for their sake as well as hers."

Jack's eyes went icy. "I've seen what the Dark Fey— what Selena will do. We cannot let her out."

A frisson passed down Lark's spine. He was absolutely right. The queen's first move would be revenge.

Lark shifted nervously. Between them, she and Jack had almost everything with them that it would take to open the gates. Selena hadn't searched them yet, but Lark was certain that would come before the day was over. It was time to take precautions.

She leaned across and kissed Jack's cheek, dropping her voice to a whisper. "I need to hide the ring. Just in case we're being watched, I need a moment of privacy."

Only the slightest nod showed that he'd heard her at all. She rose, enjoying Jack's attention as she stretched with catlike languor. "I need to wash up. It would be an insult to arrive smelling like I've been thrashing through the woods for days. Which is exactly what I've been doing."

"You're seriously going to wear the clothes they brought?" His eyes were bright with interest.

Jack's outfit wasn't too bad, though it looked like the height of fashion from the Dark Ages. Lark's appeared to belong to a *Sword and Sorcery* centerfold. "At least they're clean."

She slipped off her overshirt, letting it drop as she padded to the bath. Once in the room, she looked around for peepholes. She found none, but that was no guarantee there was no surveillance. After drawing the curtain around the bathing pool, she cast a spell on the water, raising a fog of steam to confound any watching eyes.

She waited until the fog had thickened, then stripped off the rest of her garb and emptied her pockets. There was little of value except for Amelie's ring, which she quickly cupped out of sight in her right hand. Motionless, she concentrated on the slender band, whispering a spell. The magic was Light Fey craft, quick and precise as a diamond cutter's blade. The burst of power would be gone before anyone detected its presence.

The ring turned, spiraling through the meat of her hand until it disappeared inside her flesh. Lark gagged at the pain, covering her mouth with her other hand to stifle any cries. Sweat chased gooseflesh across her skin as waves of agony surged through her. She sank to her knees, barely aware of the hard stone floor. By the time the spell ended, she was panting.

Lark remained where she was for a long moment while her head stopped spinning. Then she stepped into the pool, hoping it would wash away her discomfort. It didn't disappoint. The bath was deep enough to stand in, and the water buoyed her up, hot and comforting.

She flexed her fingers, relieved that they still moved, if painfully. A small white scar marked the spot where the ring had gone in, but that was hardly remarkable. The ring was effectively hidden.

She let herself sink beneath the water, rejoicing as the water sluiced the grime from her hair. She rose up, pushing her tangle of dark locks from her eyes just as the curtain drew aside.

Jack had shed his clothes, and she took a moment to appreciate the view. At this close distance, the steam rising from the water did nothing to obscure detail. The fact that they had made love hours before only gave fresh clarity to her imagination.

Jack climbed the steps down into the bath, displacing the water so that it lapped higher, reaching Lark's collarbone. She pushed herself backward, drifting until her back rested against the marble side of the pool. She caught the lip of it, steadying herself.

"Shouldn't you get a lady's permission before invading her bath?" she asked.

"Better to ask forgiveness after."

"That hardly seems the act of a gentleman."

"It seems to me a gentleman's task is to ensure satisfaction."

His hands circled her waist, lifting her from the water as if she was no more than a reed. His lips pressed to her belly, his tongue capturing the water that trickled from her skin.

"Put me down," she protested, but wasn't sure that was what she wanted. This was a dangerous place, filled with spies. They had plans to make. She'd only come here to hide the ring—but that was hard to remember with Jack touching her.

He let her slide gradually, an inch at a time, the muscles in his arms working with the effort to hold her in place. And the places he let her slide were designed for perfect friction. Lark flung her head back, her breath shuddering in as his mouth took its due along every step of the ride.

His lips found the notch at the base of her breastbone. Her muscles tightened, exquisitely alive to the hint of fang in the kiss. Her legs wrapped around his waist, asserting some control.

"I thought you wanted down," he murmured.

"I changed my mind."

He lifted his gaze, no doubt on the cusp of more sarcasm, but she bent and stopped his mouth with her own. His hands found her breasts, rolling her nipples with his thumbs. She shuddered, wanting him inside her again.

And then her back was braced against the marble, his mouth working down her body, this time with more teeth. A vampire's fangs emerged sometimes in hunger and sometimes in lust, and she suspected Jack was feeling both as he dipped beneath the water, the brush of his hair erotic as the water stirred it against her skin. No bubbles rose, as he didn't need air, but tiny blooms of blood rose through the steaming bath.

He knew how to use the prick of those needle-sharp points for pleasure. Tiny fires erupted along her hip, the crease of her thigh, her most private places, and finally at the vein of her thigh. There was a white-hot pinch, and she gasped, pleasure slaying her as she felt him drink. Ripple after ripple of pleasure took her as the water, the warmth and Jack's expert touch left her weak and wanting more.

Finally he emerged, streaming water, his mouth at once locking onto her breast, the sudden greedy suction drawing a cry from her lips. He released her only to push inside her sex, his shaft full and demanding, stretching her until she was sure she'd reached her limit, and then easing in another inch more. He had been urgent and demanding earlier, but now he seemed bent on extracting maximum pleasure from every move. Lark gasped as he grabbed her hip with one hand and the lip of the marble with the other and began working her, thrusting and withdrawing with a glacial slowness that hit every nerve inside her body with fireworks.

"By Oberon," she breathed.

"Shh," he said. "It's my name I want to hear."

She tried to reply, but her words trailed into a meaningless groan.

She arched into his rhythm, her body taking over as her brain dissolved to mist. Her hands were braced on his shoulders, her nails digging in. The feel of them seemed to spur him on, even as red stripes showed where her grasp had slipped. It was the same for her, the tiny fires where he'd bitten her swirling with the friction of their lovemaking.

And then a glow of light bloomed from his fingers, coruscating over her limbs with a thousand tiny pinpricks. This was not the harsh blue demonfire she'd seen before. The snaking coils of lightning were dark pink and bright yellow, snapping and exploding into more colors, diving through her flesh and Jack's. She sucked in her breath, alarmed for a moment until she felt the hum of his power rippling through her. It was like trails of molten desire winding along every nerve in her body. They clustered in her belly but didn't stop there. They spread to every corner of her—along her jaw, her wrists and the backs of her knees until every fiber of her was sensitive to the least contact. And then Jack touched her there, and there, and there. She shuddered with the enveloping pleasure of it, weakened until only he held her up.

Her surrender ripped a satisfied growl from deep inside him. His slow, patient strokes suddenly quickened, building into an act of possession so absolute Lark could only grab on for the ride. He took Lark with an appetite bordering on fury.

He made a wild, torn sound that might have been a laugh. The water around them steamed now from the heat of his power, as if the storm within him was manifesting in the world. Through the haze, Lark glimpsed the bright stars of Jack's eyes.

The net had slipped, and his demon had surfaced once more. It seemed that even without a magic blade, she had the power to strip Jack of his iron control.

She gave a single throaty cry, biting down to silence it as her body abandoned all reason.

Chapter 25

When they finally came to rest some time later, they were back on the couch, one of the tapestries tangled around them. The wall hangings had suffered during a subsequent bout of lovemaking, and the room looked as if a swarm of imps had been through.

Consciousness came back to Lark in degrees, her awareness first taking in Jack's embrace, then the room and then how they had gotten there. Finally came the hammer blow of what they had to do before they'd ever know true safety again. The yearning to bury her face in Jack's shoulder and dive back into oblivion nearly broke her will.

But instead, Lark gathered herself, withdrawing an arm, then a leg and finally easing away until she was on her feet. Jack slept on, quiet as an effigy. The stillness of a sleeping vampire was eerie until one got used to it. Lark stood for a time, studying his face. He was in a dreamless sleep, finally enjoying true rest. She would not wake him.

She pulled on the clothing the Dark Fey had left. The outfit was little more than a long gauzy skirt, slit to the hip, and a short tunic that fastened with a jeweled clip at one shoulder, leaving her other arm and a good deal of stomach bare. The fabric was an iridescent rainbow of color. She combed out her hair and slid her feet into the soft slippers her hosts had left for her.

She knelt beside Jack, letting her hand rest on his hair. Power still hummed along his skin, as if now that it was awakened, it would not be silent. She had felt a lick of that power as she'd lain in his arms, and she knew the full strength of it unleashed in rage would be unimaginable. Jack's will was all that kept the world safe from it.

Lark pressed her lips together. It was her betrayal that had first uncovered the demon, and every time she made love to Jack, the demon showed itself more. Was that what Asteriel had meant when he'd shown her the knife in Jack's dream? Was her yearning for Jack putting them in danger?

She didn't know, and there was no time to ponder. Lark glanced at the window high in the wall, and the sky appeared darker. The hours traveled oddly in fey lands, but she assumed it was nearing the start of the banquet. She had to hurry if she meant to do some reconnaissance. She found Jack's jeans and slid his lock picks from the pocket.

She hesitated a second time. She didn't want to leave Jack alone in the Dark Queen's castle, deeply asleep and vulnerable. They had been careless to risk sleeping at all, but passion had left them exhausted. However, the reality was that Selena wanted them at the banquet to get whatever concession she was after. It wasn't in her best interest to betray them yet. The time for that would come later.

Lark crept to the door and put a careful finger on the bronze handle. There was no enchantment. A quick shove opened it and she looked out. There were no guards in sight. Taking a deep breath, she cast a glamour of invisibility and pulled the door shut behind her.

Lark touched the painful spot where the ring had sunk into her hand. Gently, carefully, she cast a seeking spell. Amelie had worn the ring constantly, the chain holding it next to her heart. Now the magic in the ring pulled toward the princess, drawing a golden line in Lark's mind and showing her the way. She wasted no time, her soft slippers making barely a whisper against the stone floors.

Amelie's room was unguarded, but it was locked. Using Jack's lock picks, Lark was inside in a matter of moments.

Amelie gasped in shock when Lark appeared in front of her. The princess looked disheveled but uninjured. Lark saw at once there were chains around Amelie's wrists, shackling her to the wall.

"How did you get here?" Amelie exclaimed, but quietly. Despite the circumstances, the princess had kept her wits about her. "And what on earth are you wearing?"

Lark fell on her knees, cupping the young woman's face between her hands. The princess's violet eyes were haunted. "Are you hurt?" Lark asked.

"No, but I'm scared witless." The princess was drawn, as if she hadn't slept for days. "They're furious I don't have the ring."

"Lancelot brought it to us."

"What an excellent friend he is." Amelie closed her eyes, just managing a smile. "And so are you. You were right to bring me that potion. They keep taking my blood. They've heard rumors that my mother had fey ancestry and they think that makes me more valuable as a hostage."

Guilt stabbed through Lark, and she buried her face in her hands. She cursed herself again for using the healing spell. She'd caught the interest of the Blackthorns and led them straight to the princess. "Don't worry. The potion is strong."

As long as Selena couldn't confirm anything, the Dark Queen would make no decisions about the princess. That bought them time. Lark lowered her hands and put on a confident smile. "Besides, we're going to find a way to break you out of here."

"What about Kyle?" The princess closed her eyes, her chin trembling. "He disappeared when we came through the lake."

Lark winced, remembering Jack's handcuffs. "Portals tend to scatter people around. He probably woke up a mile or two away." Her insides twisted at the thought. A mortal lost in a fairy world would be in deep trouble.

"You have to find him," Amelie begged. "I can't leave until you do. I won't risk the gates closing with him on the other side. Promise me, Lark!"

"Jack and I will do everything we can."

"Jack's here?" Hope flashed in Amelie's violet eyes.

"Yes." Lark couldn't stifle a grin she was sure told more secrets than she'd like. "With bells on."

The door rattled. Lark spun around, reaching for her glamour, but it was too late. Drusella Blackthorn was in the doorway. The look on her face made Lark's stomach plunge.

"I heard that," Drusella said with deceptive softness. "I think we need to put a bell on you instead."

Jack awakened to find Selena lounging in a nest of cushions, watching him with hungry eyes. He sat bolt upright, grabbing the tapestry with one hand and groping for a weapon with the other.

She waved a dismissive hand. "Relax, vampire. I'm not after your life or your virtue. Not at the moment, anyhow."

Jack froze, foreboding pounding in his veins. His first, only and immediate thought was simple. "Where's Lark?"

"She decided to have a look around. My people will find her and bring her back in time for dinner."

"Unharmed," Jack growled, vowing to have words with Lark for creeping off alone.

"Don't snarl, Jack, surliness doesn't suit you. My orders are to leave her in one piece." Selena plumped a pillow that had slithered off the couch and added it to her pile.

Jack's growl deepened.

The queen waved an impatient hand. "I should point out you might sound more authoritative with clothes on."

With a final snarl, Jack tossed the tapestry aside and rose. The queen watched, one eyebrow raised. "You *have* been hiding your light under a bushel."

Beautiful as Selena was, the lascivious sweep of her

gaze left him feeling unclean. With hasty movements, Jack pulled on the clothes the fey had left for him—a tunic and leggings, richly embroidered, with a long leather belt. Next, he hunted through the clothes he had cast off. Lark had been right—he could tell they'd been searched as they slept. But his leather jacket had been buried beneath another of the unlucky tapestries. There he found his phone, wallet and the case containing the vial of Lexie's blood. There was no way to carry the items—the fey didn't seem to go for pockets—so he defiantly slipped the jacket on and turned to face her again. "Better, Your Majesty?"

She smiled at his mocking tone. "An interesting combination of fashion statements."

"They say clothes make the man."

"Then that makes you just as original." Her smile turned feline. "I wanted a word with you alone."

"A word about what?" he asked carefully, slouching against the wall where he could see her every move.

"The little fey. You and I know the Light follow their own counsel. That's always been their way, closing their borders and turning inward, as if no other race was fit to lick their boots."

"Are we having a political discussion?"

"I simply want to know what her agenda is. She's in my house. Of course you want the prisoners back, but what is she doing here?"

"What makes you think Lark has a private objective?"

Selena gave a long, slow blink. "I don't suppose she's ever kept things from you before?"

It was as if Jack felt the knife slipping into him all over again. The memory of white-hot pain roused him from his careless posture. He folded his arms. "Your point, Your Majesty?"

"I'm holding you responsible for her good behavior. As a fey woman myself, I know the power of our allure. Be certain she doesn't lead you down an unfortunate path while you are in my kingdom." Selena gave a pointed look around the room tumbled by their exuberant lovemaking. "I know you're a man of strong will. I trust you will keep your head."

To his disgust, Jack felt himself flush. Lark's acceptance of his dual nature had led him to lower his guard a notch. That was a marvelous gift, but it was a dangerous one. Selena was right about one thing—his demon side could easily develop a taste for freedom. *And every time the demon gains an inch, it is Lark's doing. She started your slide with that knife, but she's kept pushing your limits, hasn't she?*

He wasn't going down that road. "Duly noted, Your Majesty."

Selena was standing in front of him now, the dim light of the room catching the jewels in her elaborate coiffure. They winked like captive stars. "I think you know my concerns are not groundless. You see, I know more about you than you think."

"Oh?"

She put a hand on his chest. Her fingers were long and slim. "You were not made a vampire in the usual way. Your human was half fused with one of the Fallen."

Jack grasped her hand to move it away. "Very few people know that."

She wrapped her fingers around his, her smile playful now. "I paid for that knowledge many, many years ago, but never got the chance to put it to use."

A sensation like cold spider feet scuttled up his spine. "Perhaps you wasted your gold."

She didn't look away. "It always pays to know your friends and your enemies. I haven't decided which you'll turn out to be yet."

"I suppose that depends on whether I help you through the gates." He extracted his hand from hers and took a step back. "I can spare you the suspense. I won't."

"There are worse enemies than me."

"That would be a very short list."

Selena was the most dangerous creature he'd ever met, with the possible exception of Asteriel. The Fallen at least wanted redemption. Jack wasn't sure Selena could spell it.

Her smile was indulgent. "You think you can't be convinced? I can compensate you in ways you can't imagine."

Jack folded his arms again, suddenly feeling the need to protect his vitals. "No. You come in here and cast suspicion on my partner, tell me you know my darkest secrets and then dangle rewards for betraying everything I believe in? Hardly subtle."

"Subtlety is overrated. I prefer the direct approach." She turned away, carelessly strolling through the chaos of the room. She paused to push a cushion out of her path with a dainty slipper. "You want to know if Lark loves you or if she is about to betray you again. You want to know if your demon will win over your conscience. You want to know if you have the strength to remain the pure knight, or if you will transmogrify into a loathsome evil."

Jack was silent, dismay blooming in his chest. The Dark Queen had his number.

"What would you give to know those answers?"

Jack bowed his head. He recognized fear inside himself, and the longing for acceptance. He wanted to believe he was good. He wanted Lark's love. And those were exactly the weapons Selena required to destroy him.

"I would give nothing," he said. His Fallen had been tempted before, and by a far better salesman than her. "I don't believe you could answer those questions or control the outcomes. I'm a great believer in free will."

But she'd seen his hesitation. He might have won the round, but the game was still on. With a slight nod she stepped back, only the corners of her mouth quirking upward with satisfaction. "Fair enough. Now let us go see if you can win your wolf."

At the mention of Kenyon, Jack's temper heated. His demon stirred, raising a prickle of energy along his skin. He followed the queen out of the room, loathing everything about the situation. *It would be simpler to take control and make it right.*

But that would mean letting the demon free, and that meant losing everything.

Chapter 26

"I'll be clear, vampire. I want this dinner because I want a chance to convince you an alliance is in both our interests." Selena cast Jack a sly look. "You are about to tell me that's impossible."

"It crossed my mind."

"But you will listen, Jack. It's no coincidence that you're here. I counted on you coming in person to rescue the princess. I knew you wouldn't trust her to anyone else."

"Manipulation isn't a great selling point for a partnership."

"But you will listen to my offer. Might I remind you that the reward for your attention is the return of your wolf unharmed." Her step was quick, leading them through a maze of rooms and passageways. Her skirts eddied behind her, a flash of blue against the dark stone floors.

In anyone else, Jack would have found such energy exhilarating. In the Dark Queen, it was just alarming. "My willingness aside, I'm curious why you think I'm able to assist you."

"You were there when the spell over the gates was cast."

"I was but one part of the ceremony."

"I have confidence in your resourcefulness. I have Haven. The ring is missing, so your allies must have it. Success is not so far off." She cast him a sidelong glance. "But I have other uses for you besides all that."

"Such as?"

"All in good time. For now, just enjoy the entertainment. I've always believed the best negotiations begin with food, don't you?" Queen Selena cocked her head. "We of the fey courts take our hospitality seriously."

Jack could tell she was eager, blood tinting her pale cheeks. He'd seen the same feverish look on gamblers and those who rose to duel at the first light of dawn. His stomach was a leaden ball of apprehension.

They entered the banquet hall, which was crammed with fey. Conversation was at an almost painful pitch, but there was no evidence of a feast. Suspicion slowed Jack's steps.

Selena caught his look and laughed, a pretty flash of white teeth and dimples. With a flourish, she clapped her hands. The room fell instantly silent. She held the moment, stretching it out as a smile spread across her face. When the tension in the room was about to snap, she raised her slim arms into the air and spun in a circle until her blue skirts swirled. "Bring in the entertainments!"

Cacophony broke out—a whistling, grunting, cheering roar of approval. The lesser fey scattered everywhere, and in a moment they were back, dragging trestle tables and stacks of golden dinnerware. Seating and cloths appeared in record time. Each creature knew its role, and when steaming platters of food began to appear, it was plain they had been waiting for this moment. It took less than a minute to conjure a complete feast.

"Come," said Queen Selena, stopping her pirouette. Her skirts still swirled as she waved to the long table that stretched before the dais. "Come and sit at my right hand."

"Where is Lark?" he asked. "You said she would meet us here."

She grabbed his hand, pulling him to his seat. "So I did. I will send someone to fetch her."

"Now," Jack growled. He wasn't going to be easy until Lark was in sight.

Selena waved a liveried servant to her side and whispered in his pointed ear. With a bow, he hurried off. "Your partner will be here in just a moment."

Forced to be patient, Jack watched what was going on around him. The dinner itself was something out of a nightmare, and he was suddenly glad he was undead and his plate empty. As the silver-domed cover was lifted from one of the dishes, a swarm of beetles skittered out. A trio of pale blue fey snatched them up and dipped the treat in what smelled to Jack like chipotle dressing.

"They need to be fresh to get the proper crunch," the queen commented.

Thankfully, her tastes were more traditional. At least he assumed it was roast chicken on her plate. The gentleman with gills several seats away was pouring butter sauce on something with waving tentacles.

The queen sipped pale wine from her goblet, gesturing toward the room. "Speaking of fresh, who would you like to drink?"

Despite himself, the predator in his soul had already been scanning the room, seeking out the young and beautiful. "Thank you for the offer, but I have no need to dine."

"Yes, you are old and strong and bubbling over with honorable instincts. It's all very charming." She considered the tidbit of meat on her fork. "That doesn't mean you don't want it."

She flicked a finger and a pretty female came and knelt at his feet. The girl looked painfully young, her pale green hair tumbling to her knees. As she bent her head, utterly subservient, Jack saw her eyes were slit like a cat's.

"Exotic," he commented.

"It's good to broaden the palate." The queen tapped the girl lightly on the top of her head. "Not much to her, though. Barely an appetizer."

He could smell the servant's piquant fear, and despite every good and decent instinct he had, his mouth watered. He was a vampire, and the queen was appealing to his basest impulses. The girl held up her wrist and he took it, his fingers easily circling her arm. Now he could see her skin held a pale green cast, visible only where the sun had kissed it.

Slowly he bent and inhaled, relishing the scent of untapped blood. It wouldn't be anything like Lark's—nothing would—but greed prowled through him. He never got to take every drop he wanted, and his appetite clamored. Fey tasted the sweetest, although they went straight to his head—which was a really bad idea when trying to outsmart Selena.

He released the girl's wrist, letting it fall. "Tempting, but I don't drink on the job."

The queen gave a sigh of exasperation. "You're an interesting specimen, my vampire friend. What does shake your puritanical reserve?"

Jack's patience was starting to unravel. "I'm here to listen to your arguments for an alliance. Speak, and be done."

She set down her fork, dabbing her lips with a snowy napkin. "Have you seen the mountain compound?"

"Impressive, although I'm sure you already know working with mercenaries has its risks."

Her mouth quirked. "I do love the way Company men do their homework. Then, you've seen the forces at my beck and call. There is another army ready to defend this castle."

"Against what?"

"There will be a war, and soon. My sorcerers have predicted it, and their future sight is flawless."

"Did they say who was going to win?"

She gave an uneasy laugh. "That has yet to be decided, but I'm willing to play the odds."

"Which means what?" Jack was growing impatient.

Selena's eyelids lowered a moment before she flashed him a brilliant smile. "I'm offering you the winning side if you help me. I will make you my second in command."

"You know that's an offer I will never accept."

"Why not? Think of everything I can give you. Think of everyone you could save just by asking me to spare them. I'm not without gratitude."

Jack sat back in his chair. Selena's lips were parted as if she were already preparing her next argument. She wanted his help badly—apparently so badly she forgot what he knew about her. "I was there at the Vale of Rakkul when you made it rain with the blood of innocents. Whatever you might be promising now, you aren't the merciful type. I will not let you out of this prison."

The queen's head jerked away, breaking their gaze. She took a deep breath that made the jewels at her throat flash. But she did not let her anger touch her voice. "Think on it, Jack. My offer remains open until the end of the night." With that, she rose and swept from the hall.

"It is time you earned my forgiveness," the Dark Queen said when she stormed into the room where Lark was waiting.

Lark's impulse was to bolt, but she was tied to a chair. When the queen came to a stop in front of her, she could feel the brush of Selena's gown against her knees. Fear pebbled her skin.

The queen glared down at her. "I know why you were in Amelie's room. You came to rescue the royal brats. I don't blame you for that—it was an expected move."

She grabbed Lark's chin, tilting it up. "I do blame you for getting your claws into Jack. You have no idea what kind of fire you're playing with."

Lark winced, squirming her way out of the queen's sharp-nailed grasp. "Why do you care?"

"This is not simple jealousy, you idiot girl. I can have my pick of men between the sheets. I want Jacques Armond d'Errondine for his power."

"Who?" Lark asked in confusion.

The queen gave her a withering look. "You don't even

know who he is or why he matters. Let me give you a clue. The Derrondine Pass was named after him."

"Jack?"

"Don't the Light Fey have schools? Jack Anderson is simply what he calls himself now. Immortals change names if they live long enough—which you should also know."

"Of course I know that." Embarrassment heated Lark's cheeks. She was aware Jack had money and connections in Marcari, but not that he owned a mountain or two. But that was Jack, a steel box welded shut.

"You're the only one who can get past his guard."

Not as well as I would like. "What makes you think that?"

Selena made an impatient gesture. "I saw the mess you made of your room. Besides, he looks at you like a hound dog after the last sausage."

The contempt in the queen's words made Lark's skin crawl, but she set her mouth and willed herself to meet Selena's gaze. "So?"

"I'll be blunt. I need him. One fey to another, if you can make him lose control of his Fallen within the borders of my kingdom, the demon will be mine to command. The right spell in the right place will tame even one of the Fallen, but I need you to give me access."

Fury surged up Lark's body, a hot ball of pain that caught in her throat. Her words came out as a rasp. "What makes you think I will help you?"

"You're my prisoner."

"I'm not a betrayer!"

"Oh?" Selena's glance was pure acid. "I'd say otherwise."

That made Lark's head spin. "What do you know?"

"I see the truth spell that still winds through him. It's Light Fey work, and there are only so many ways to put it there. It's a matter of connecting the dots, my little traitor. Has he forgiven you for that?"

The queen bent over the chair, holding Lark's gaze with her own. "No? And what do you think he will say when he learns you used a Dark spell that led Drusella Blackthorn right to the princess's door and your own people straight to oblivion? Because you know it's the Light Fey that I will destroy first."

Lark was pressed as far into the chair as she could go, straining to put distance between herself and the Dark Queen. The queen backed away, leaving Lark dizzy with a storm of emotions she couldn't begin to count. Fright and sadness were there, but shame was clearly at the top.

Selena bent over her, her voice unexpectedly kind. "A pity you ended this way. You've survived the most horrific trials. Swords harden in flame, and you're a magnificent blade. What a waste."

A waste, and about to come to a bad end. Lark steeled herself, raising her gaze to the queen's. She would not die cowering.

But the Dark Queen suddenly changed course. "I can use someone like you, Lark. Don't throw away everything I could give you. For instance, I might give you back your princess. There were rumors she had fey blood, but so far she has shown no trace of it. If she's just a mortal, she's of no use to me. If you give me Jack, I swear on my throne that I will send your princess home."

At that, Lark's heart skipped so hard it hurt.

"Rescuing her would go a long way to restoring your good name."

Lark's pulse pounded, considering the bait, considering what would happen if she was too eager or too slow.

"I haven't got all night," said the queen.

Lark took a breath, held it for a beat and let it out, refusing to speak until she was calm. She could play this game, and she had to believe that she and Jack could still win. She had to believe Jack was right, and the Dark Queen had grown impatient and reckless enough to believe Lark's lie. "Very well, but it won't be easy."

The queen reached forward, running a finger along Lark's cheek. "Good girl. I'll tell you what I want you to do."

Chapter 27

Jack grew increasingly impatient. The queen had been gone long enough for two more courses to arrive before he finally saw her reappear at an arched entrance at the side of the hall, the werewolf at her side. She had a long silken leash tied to Kenyon's silver collar. He padded beside, his head and tail drooping.

The sight wrenched Jack, bringing him to his feet in a surge of anger—and alarm. Lark was not with Selena. Faint blue demonfire crackled over his hands, showing just how far his patience had been pushed. With a curse, he hid them behind his back and fixed a glower on the approaching queen.

"I have brought your friend," she said with a gesture toward the wolf. "The meal is almost over. A little while longer, and your beast will be free to go."

"Where is Lark?" Jack asked in a dangerous voice that made Kenyon whine. Jack couldn't help it. The burden of inaction was building up inside him. He felt about to crack apart in a burst of demonfire.

"She is coming as we speak." The queen subsided into her seat, letting the silk leash drop. "Sit, vampire."

"I will sit when I see Lark."

"Don't be a bore." The queen dug her fingers into the werewolf's ruff. "I prefer it when guests show proper courtesy."

Kenyon gave a sudden yip of pain, a sound Jack had

never heard him make. Without thinking, Jack grabbed the werewolf's silver collar, pulling him free of the queen's grip. Demonstrating how much he cared wasn't a smart move, but he couldn't stand Kenyon's suffering one moment more.

Kenyon didn't resist. In fact, he seemed barely able to stand any longer. Jack ran his hands over the werewolf's long back, feeling tremors of exhaustion shudder through Kenyon's flesh. Fresh outrage surged through Jack. Although the wolf had hardly been in the Dark Fey realm for more than a few days, his fur was dull and matted.

"What have you done to him?" Jack said, forcing his voice to come out evenly.

As his gaze lifted to the queen's face, she flinched slightly—just a tightening of the jaw—but otherwise the beautiful mask of her visage remained calm. "He resisted me. I won't tolerate that."

In the periphery of his vision, Jack saw the other guests looking on with a mix of expressions—fascination, fear, anticipation and even glee. Some faces weren't human enough to read, but this was the kind of crowd that understood power and not much else. The sight snapped him back to reason. Whoever won this battle of wills held a two-edged sword. It might tip the balance of power in the room, but it invited vengeance from the loser. He had to play this the right way.

Kenyon was leaning against him now, a slight vibration still running through him. Fear? Weakness? Jack couldn't tell. He rubbed Kenyon's ears, remembering years ago how the angry youth would barely let himself be touched. Trust had come slowly, and Jack wouldn't let him down now.

The room was entirely silent, broken only by the panting of the wolf. "I've lost patience with this," Jack said in a cold, dead tone. "I've stayed through your banquet. Let him go."

"You've yet to see the entertainment. Banquets must have entertainment."

"If you want me to see them, free Kenyon as we agreed. Let him go home." Any other time, he would have wanted the werewolf guarding his back, but he was too weak. All Jack could think of was getting him to safety.

"You know that's impossible," Selena protested. "I need the ring and the blood and all the other ingredients of the spell."

Jack bared his fangs. "You need all that to escape yourself. But I know you've used Therrien Haven to crack the gates wide enough for the Blackthorns to use raw sorcery to come and go. You must have the power to enable one wolf—a wolf who doesn't truly belong here—to pass."

The queen's look was so mutinous Jack knew he had guessed right. "I agreed to return him to your custody," she snapped. "I did not agree to let him leave my kingdom."

Jack wouldn't budge. "I want him safe in the palace of Marcari, with all the conditions we agreed to in place."

She paled. "It is not as easy as you seem to think. You trapped us well."

"I don't care. You've had plenty of opportunity to rest up. Fix this."

The queen's expression raised the hairs along Jack's neck, but he kept himself still, his fingers loosely buried in Kenyon's fur.

Then her mouth curved. "Do you swear to stay through the rest of the banquet, on pain of forfeiture of your own freedom?"

"Yes," he said instantly—before he could think it through, because not even an idiot would agree to such a condition from one of the fey.

"Good enough," she said, and snapped her fingers.

In that exact moment, Kenyon's silver collar fell away with a clatter. No one moved. And then the werewolf took a staggering step, shaking himself as if shedding every trace of the fey's touch. He turned to Jack, a flash of intelligence returning to the golden eyes.

Then Selena made a sweeping gesture toward the window, and an electric tingling coursed through the air. "The portal is open, but I cannot hold it long. Hesitate and your chance will be lost."

The queen staggered, her hand going to her stomach as if in pain, and she dropped to one knee. Her face went white, twin spots of red flushing her high cheekbones. She hadn't lied when she'd said the spell took power.

"Go. Now," Jack ordered Kenyon, "while you can."

Kenyon didn't need to be asked twice. Gathering his strength, the werewolf sprang forward and bolted past the tables, past the blood fountain and toward the window to the castle yard below. It was plain from the way he moved that he was weakened, but the leap he made showed there was still massive strength in his haunches. For an instant, his gray form arched in the air, and then vanished in a glimmer of light, the afterimage of a wolf fading before Jack's eyes.

Jack fell back a few steps, turning away to hide his relief and satisfaction. One of the knots in his chest released, leaving him almost light-headed. But when he turned back to the queen, he was already lining up his next move. He'd won this round, but Selena was by no means defeated. In fact, he'd been expecting more resistance.

He'd also been expecting the spell to work differently. Selena had opened a portal right there, not in the woods where Jack and Lark had come through the lake. Gates shouldn't move around that way. A sense of warning prickled down his spine, but Jack didn't have time to consider what any of that meant.

"Everything is done as you stipulated. Your werewolf is back among friends." The queen got to her feet, a sheen of perspiration gleaming on her skin. Selena flicked at her skirts and kicked the collar under the banquet table. "I'm rather relieved. He shed all over everything."

It was then Jack noticed that the chairs had been turned to face the front of the hall, turning the space into a stage. She sat and pointed to the chair next to him. "Now you have a promise to keep, unless you wish to wear that collar yourself."

But Jack was still defiant. "For the last time, where is—"

Selena interrupted him with a gesture. "There."

Jack followed the queen's pointing finger to where a tall fey with pale hair and a pear-shaped fiddle stood but a few yards away. The queen's gesture seemed to be the signal to begin, for the musician brought his bow down upon the strings in a perfectly modulated trill of notes.

Jack never saw where Lark came from, but she was suddenly whirling around the fiddler like a leaf on the breeze. The gossamer of her skirts flared, showing a flash of bare thigh. There was a murmur of interest from the tables close enough to watch the show, and Jack felt jealous pride surge through him. One of the lesser fey hooted approval, and Jack could not help but turn and snarl, showing fang. This was his woman.

He had heard tales of the Light Fey's legendary grace, and they were no lie. Lark rose and arched with the melody, undulating as if the notes came from her own bone and sinew. Darting close to the fiddler, she swirled around him and then leaped away, soaring as lightly as her namesake. Every line of her body was strong and filled with spirit, riding the music as if it were a solid fixture in the air.

Jack was transfixed. She was beautiful, her bare limbs graceful as wings. And there was seduction—the costume was as suggestive as her loveliness—but the effect on Jack went far beyond lust. She drew in the soul as well as the senses, making him part of her flight while inviting his embrace.

By contrast, Jack felt the heaviness of his own body,

the bulk of his muscles and the demonfire hot in his veins. If she was insubstantial as mist, he was the volcano beneath. Their afternoon in the bath superimposed itself on his perception, grounding her ethereal dance in a memory of hot, wet sex.

Lark pirouetted closer, the faint brush of her steps barely audible as she moved. Without knowing what he did, Jack stood, and suddenly he was part of the dance. His hands were around her waist, lifting her into the air. She was all but weightless, a creature already in flight, and he couldn't keep her. It wouldn't have been right. She rolled in the air, letting him catch her again—letting him loan his steady strength to return her to earth. Her hands touched his shoulders in a wordless gesture of appreciation, and she was gone again, spinning around him in a circling, sparkling cloud of gossamer skirts.

But Jack wanted more. He'd played enough fey games and wanted his fair turn. With vampire speed, he reached out, grabbing Lark's waist and pulling her close. She melted against him, soft and sweet, her airy dance suddenly languid with desire. There was an intimacy in the move that made Jack's mouth go dry. There was nothing to her costume—a tug would be all he needed to have her naked in his arms. All at once he was aware of desire burning low in his belly. Lark suddenly spun away again, and her loss ripped a growl from his throat.

The Dark Queen rose, her jeweled coiffure sparking in the candlelight. She clapped her hands, and the fiddler wound the music to a final flourish. Lark likewise finished, poised on her toes, with her arms arched into the air.

"You have done well, bringing our banquet to a close," Selena said.

Lark curtsied as the musician faded back into the crowd of tables and diners. When she straightened, she and Jack were alone on the impromptu stage. Jack couldn't take his eyes from her, and neither could the rest of the room. She was as lovely as a single rose.

"The banquet is done," the queen said. "Your promise is fulfilled."

Jack might have calmed, but he knew better. There was a footnote here somewhere. Lark lowered her arms but remained where she was, suddenly awkward with tension.

"We spent some time earlier today stating what we want from one another, and I believe we have come quite some way in establishing mutual trust," said the Dark Queen with a smile as brilliant as it was false. "I have returned your werewolf, as promised. You have attended my banquet, as promised. We should congratulate ourselves on a negotiation successfully accomplished."

"But?" Jack asked.

Selena gave him a hard look. "The banquet is done, but I never let my dinner guests leave without a parting gift."

"A fey gift is a perilous favor," Jack returned.

"Don't worry." The queen's eyes glittered. "This one is freely given, as it is no more than a demonstration of an evident truth. Humanity views the fey as treacherous and beautiful. I think tonight you've seen our beauty exquisitely displayed."

Every eye in the room turned Lark's way. She remained as frozen as a fawn in headlights.

Then Selena made a gesture, as if plucking something from the air. "I now display your partner's treachery."

A flash of light surrounded Lark, and she gave a startled cry. Jack's chest seized, and he started for her, but then the brilliance was gone. And then he saw what the queen had done.

"See how badly she was hurt in that fire, vampire? See how frail all that beauty really is?"

He did. The costume covered little, and he saw all at once how bad Lark's injuries had been. "Lark!" he cried, reaching for her, but she shrank away.

Her face had been spared, but the rest of her was covered with angry red and pink scars. The skin didn't sit properly, but stretched and puckered as if there wasn't quite enough. Shocked silence rang in the room, made worse by the expression on Lark's face as it dawned on her what had just happened. And then her face suffused with physical agony. It was plain that her wounds had left her racked with pain.

Lark made a noise of horror that tore Jack's heart. He wheeled on the queen, the urge to defend Lark boiling inside him. "What in the nine hells are you doing?"

The Dark Queen made another gesture, another flash of light, and just as quickly Lark was whole again, her skin flawless, soft and pale—but she fell to her knees, sobbing. Jack darted to her side, kneeling beside her. He wrapped his arms around her, pulling her close against his chest. She was shuddering as if she'd been drenched in freezing water. "Lark?"

But Lark buried her face in her hands, refusing to answer.

Selena's eyes glittered like chips of ancient ice. "The Queen of the Dark alone retains the power to reverse any Dark Fey spell."

Jack buried his face in Lark's hair, her scent overwhelming him. His senses refused to reconcile what his brain was telling him. "You used Dark Fey magic?" he asked incredulously.

She nodded, desolation in very line of her body. "It was the only way to heal."

Selena broke in. "It was a secret you've kept even from your own people, because Dark spells demand a price."

"What did you pay?" Jack demanded.

Lark said nothing. The Dark Queen answered instead. "Our operatives were able to track your path to the princess and discover her secret. A clever trick, giving her a potion to hide her Light Fey blood, but it wore off shortly after your visit to her room. Your plan to put a royal with Light Fey blood on the throne is undone."

"What—" Jack began, but he couldn't even find words. This was all news to him.

He released Lark, but she barely seemed to notice. She was looking daggers at the queen, her tearstained face gone white with horror. "You said you'd let Amelie go!"

"Only if you delivered Jack."

"No!" Lark cried.

Jack's mind crowded with memories—of the dagger blow that had ended their relationship, of Lark's unexplained reappearance in his life, of sex so wild it was all he could do not to let the demon slip its leash. And then there were the queen's whispers that Lark might be playing a double game. She'd used forbidden spells. She'd involved Amelie, given her a potion. And just now…

He looked down at Lark, grinding the words out. "Delivered me?"

"Apparently the dance wasn't quite good enough to seduce you into my spell." Selena shook her head sadly. "Too bad. I thought she was quite fetching."

Lark's face, already pale, lost the last of its color. He couldn't believe it. She had betrayed him again—or tried to. Jack swayed slightly, not quite able to take that blow without a flinch.

With a cry of shame and fury, Lark surged to her feet and burst through the crowd, pelting out the door. With a casual gesture, Selena picked up her wine cup and took a long, satisfied drink. "Shouldn't you have it out with her, Jack? Surely you want your revenge?"

Chaos caught like fire. Suddenly lesser fey milled everywhere, all gabbling at once. Some of the uneaten dishes took the opportunity to scamper away, trailing sauces in their wake. Jack lunged for the queen, but she slipped out of reach and was lost in the ruckus. He swore and wheeled around.

For once, he agreed with the Dark Queen. Lark owed him the truth.

Chapter 28

Outside, the full moon sailed above the castle's turrets. Jack paused in the yard, looking for any sign of Lark. She could hide herself at will, but instinct said she would flee—probably to the woods. That was where her kind took solace, and no doubt she needed it now.

Jack started toward the drawbridge, his soul churning with unfocused darkness. He was angry, but that was only one element of the storm. He was also hurt, betrayed and ashamed that he had been blinded by Lark's...everything that she was. Of all the people he had met in so many centuries, she had been the one who could unfailingly slip past his guard. He had thought she'd accepted what he was, but there was no way of telling what was truth and what was just fey trickery.

He flew across the meadow, back to the path that had led them from the gates toward the castle. His vampire speed closed the distance faster than a human eye could follow. He entered the gloom, his night vision navigating the indigo darkness. It did not take long before he saw a flutter of gossamer. His instincts about where she'd go had been right.

He paused, still and silent as every sense homed in on Lark. She was huddled on the ground ahead, leaning against a tree. She wept in a noisy, messy way that told him she thought she was alone. Jack's heart softened, but then he remembered Selena's words. *Only if you delivered your partner.* That dance had been a seduction and a trap, designed to set him before Selena like one of the banquet dishes. No wonder the queen had made him watch Lark's performance. It was all part of her game.

Rage surged through him, short-circuiting reason as it went. He launched himself forward. Lark heard his approach and rose, but had no time to do more than stand. Jack caught her by the shoulders, forcing her back against the tree.

Her eyes flew wide with fear. Words stuck in Jack's throat, too many and too painful to get out. He could only manage one. "Why?"

She turned her face away, biting her lip to stop her sobs. Jack growled. He wanted her to see him. The last thing he could forgive was to be shut out. With one hand, he stripped off the long belt from his waist.

"Turn around," he said, demon fury burning in his voice.

She did, wordless and defeated. Jack bound her wrists with the belt but held her there. The slim line of her body radiated warmth in the cool forest. She smelled of heat and blood and he bent close, his nose almost touching the nape of her neck to inhale more of her dizzying sweetness. He could bite her, drain her of life as she had, in a way, done to him. Jack let his lips drift down until they brushed the silk of her skin. She shivered, gooseflesh forming along her bare arms.

Fear. In that moment she became prey. He pushed her against the tree, pressing her close so that he felt the rounded form of her buttocks against his burgeoning erection. Demonfire crackled over his skin. He was losing control. His hand slid through the slash of her skirt, finding her bare hip. There wasn't much beneath the skirt—the merest slip of silk for modesty. His hand crept deeper, finding more warmth and softness. Again, he thought of tearing off the flimsy garment and taking what he wanted. He was Fallen, and wasn't that what demons did? Destroyed everything they loved?

The thought froze Jack long enough that Lark squirmed around to face him. He'd sunk so deep inside his own head that her movement almost startled him. He trapped her, bracing one arm on either side of her head, and then leaned in, catching her mouth with his. It was a brutal kiss—possessive, demanding, bruising. But he had been hurt, the knife twisting deep.

Lark inhaled, arching toward him, her breasts soft and yielding against his chest. The pleasure of her touch was a razor, flaying every nerve. Jack broke away, speechless with pain and loss. He couldn't bear that she'd answered his brutality with gentleness.

"Jack," Lark said softly.

"Don't speak to me," he said, voice rough with too much emotion. He was on the edge, trying to keep control, and the sound of her voice only tempted him.

"Jack, please."

And then his fangs slid out and he struck. The salty, tangy warmth flooded his mouth, and all his hungers focused on this one need. He would take payment for his grief in blood. Now he embraced her, cradling her against him as he drank. Bound, she could do little to stop him. She didn't even try.

The rich fey blood—twice as potent with so much feeling between them—went straight to his head. Demonfire sparked over them both, crackling like something alive. He had no reason left, only desire to have her, whatever it took. If that meant her life coursing through his body...

"Jack, stop!" she pleaded. "You won't solve anything this way."

Some leftover scrap of reason made him release her vein, licking it closed with long, sensuous swipes of his tongue. "You're going to deliver me, are you?" he murmured in her ear, his voice dropping to a growl.

She shuddered. "You're going to deliver yourself."

"What is that supposed to mean?"

"Selena can only control you if you lose control yourself."

Her words hit him like a blast of cold water. The queen had tempted him twice, and he'd escaped her both times. But the scene with Kenyon, then Lark's dance and then her betrayal—that had all but brought him to his knees. Especially Lark's duplicity. He pulled away.

Lark shrank against the tree. "Why else do you think she maneuvered us into a situation guaranteed to make you so angry?"

His mind was on fire. "Explain."

"She played us with her simple, safe dinner invitation. There never was a second round of bargaining, Jack. Selena didn't need one to trip us up. All she required was an opportunity to get you in her power."

"Nine hells," Jack cursed, slamming the flat of his hand into the tree. It shuddered and creaked.

Lark was right, and that was the genius of the fey. Most of the time, victims fell into fairy traps through their own folly. And it hadn't taken long for the Dark Queen to learn that his weakness was Lark.

Except… "You stopped me just now," he said.

She leaned her head back, looking cold and exhausted. "I had no intention of delivering you into Selena's snare."

"Then, why the performance?" he asked, his tone guarded.

"The only way to keep Amelie safe was to play along. I didn't anticipate that Selena would reveal my secret, but I knew the dance wouldn't work to make you lose your head. We've done far more, uh, exotic things than that."

Lark was underestimating her charms. Jack had come close to taking her right in front of the Dark Fey court, but he was too angry to admit it.

"And when the dance didn't work, the queen turned on you. She used you to make me furious." He closed his eyes, drawing in cool forest air. He needed more answers, but he had no appetite for them.

But Lark pushed on. "Lust brings your demon out, but anger is your real trigger. I know you're afraid of losing control then, because that's usually when you tie me up."

A sludge of self-disgust pooled in his gut. "Turn around. I'll unbind your hands."

She obeyed and he loosed the belt, fastening it again around his waist. He was ashamed for behaving like what he was—a demon—but he was still burning with rage. "Dark magic?"

Lark spoke in a dead voice. She looked deflated, her shoulders slumped. "There wasn't enough Light Fey power to heal me. I stole the spell on my way to Marcari. I knew there would be a residue, but not that it would last beyond the point where I could detect it myself."

His tone hardened. "You know there is always a price. You compromised the safety of the royal family."

"I know." She squeezed her eyes shut. "Do you think I haven't cursed myself for that?"

He ground his teeth. "And what is this about Amelie and the Light Fey?"

Lark pressed her clenched fists to her face. "The Light have lived in isolation too long. You're right, our numbers are dwindling. We need the princess on the throne to bind us to the land. She carries our blood through her mother and grandmother."

Jack sucked in a breath. He needed more detail to completely understand the situation, but it was enough to grasp the enormity of the problem. "The Light Court has been planning this for generations. Amelie's mother…"

"She would have been our answer, but she died too soon." She unfolded her fingers, hiding her face altogether. "Now our hopes are on the princess."

Jack folded his arms, wanting to hold her, to feel her soft skin in his hands—but he could no longer trust his instinct to be tender. "Who else knows?"

Lark let her hands fall, but left her head bowed. "Only a

handful of the Light Court. Maybe King Renault. I wasn't briefed until a few months ago, when I was recovering."

"The Company guards the royal family," Jack said in a low, tight voice. His anger wasn't just at Lark anymore, but at the whole fey council. "We protect her. We should have been told."

"This is the survival of a people, Jack. The Light Court trusted no one." She spoke softly. "But I condemned us all when I stole that spell to heal myself."

Jack's chest hurt. She might have made a terrible mistake, but she'd been asked to carry an unfair burden. And yet he wasn't sure understanding was enough—she'd shut him out too many times. As she spoke, his heart slowly froze, as if the truth were sealing his emotions in eternal winter. Light-headedness stole over him, making everything surreal.

"I'll help the Light Court if I can, but my first priority is getting Amelie home safely."

"I'm sorry," Lark said, finally raising her head. She looked devastated.

Jack shifted, forcing himself to face Lark. Rage seared through his icy calm, proving his emotional freeze was temporary. *I loved you.* But she'd wounded him to the quick. Again. "Don't bother apologizing. After everything we've been through, you still didn't see fit to trust me. I can't forgive that."

"Amelie's secrets weren't mine to tell," Lark replied in a voice barely above a whisper.

"With anyone else, I'd agree." Sadness lodged in Jack's throat, roughening his words. "But it's my job to die for the princess. And you should know by now I'd open my veins for you if you merely asked. If you still don't see that, I've no hope of building a real bond with you."

Lark's eyes turned bright with tears. "Jack!"

Her cry went straight to his heart, but any reply he might have made was cut off.

There was a rustle in the bushes. They both spun around. Jack realized they'd been so absorbed in their discussion, neither had been watching for enemies. Jack braced his feet in the soft loam, ready to fight.

But the figure who emerged from the trees was Crown Prince Kyle of Vidon, using a large branch as a walking stick. He looked dirty and disheveled, but very relieved to see them. "Jack," he said. "Ms. Lark. I must say that's quite the outfit."

He stopped, putting his free hand on his hip. He was wearing a cashmere sweater and what once had been an expensive pair of dress slacks, but both were in tatters. His handsome face was smeared with dirt. "I hope you're on a rescue mission. I've been hiking for miles looking for some sign of habitation, but there are *things* in these woods."

The glint in his eye—and several bloody patches on the walking stick—said at least a few of those things had come to a bad end. The prince turned to Jack, his face suddenly grim. "Have you found Amelie?"

"Yes," Jack replied. "She's alive."

Kyle visibly relaxed. "And what were you saying about dying for the princess?"

Jack and Lark exchanged a look. She gave a slight shake of her head. This wasn't a secret the Light Fey wanted to share—especially not with the Kingdom of Vidon, famed for its hatred of the fey.

But Jack had other ideas. "There is no more room for secrets."

Chapter 29

Once they had finished talking, Kyle walked a few yards
down the forest path and stood staring into the forest, his
hands on his hips. Jack had told him everything.

"You've ruined their happiness," Lark said darkly. She
was crumbling in ways she couldn't begin to describe, layers of anger and hurt and a horrible blank abyss shifting
inside her like tectonic plates. As furious as she was, she
wanted Jack's hands on her again, his fangs in her neck
and the rough bark of the tree scraping her back. None of
it was logical, and she seemed trapped in an outward calm
that mirrored his. It was just as well. That calm was the
only thing that made talking possible.

"The bridegroom should not be the last to know his wife
is the anchor for an entire fey kingdom." Jack gave her a
hard look. "Secrets destroy love."

Lark bit her lip so hard she tasted blood.

Kyle turned and walked back toward them. Lark reeled
in her thoughts, forcing herself into the here and now. The
prince leaned on his staff. "The matter of fey heritage in
the royal line of succession is immaterial to me. Despite
what my countrymen might say, I love Amelie, and the fact
that she is not wholly human changes nothing."

Lark felt faint with relief, but the prince turned toward
her with a frown. "Lark," he said, a note of severity making him sound older than his years. "I hold you account-
able for wedging a secret between Amelie and me. You

put a wall there that didn't exist until you created it. We are royals, and trust is hard to come by in our lives. Do not do it again."

She bowed her head. After so much regret, she shouldn't have been capable of more, but still she felt her stomach twist in knots. "I am truly sorry, Your Royal Highness."

Kyle gave a cool nod and turned to stare at the lights of the castle in the distance. "How do we rescue my bride and get out of this benighted place?"

Lark raised her right hand and willed the ring to reappear. As it pushed through her flesh, tears filled her eyes and she ground her teeth against the pain. Then it sat, bright and sparkling in her palm. She held it out. "Gentlemen, the ring and key to the gates."

"Excellent." Jack took it from her hand, the lift in his voice raising her spirits a tiny degree. "We have the ring of binding, the blood of a Haven, a royal for the humans and me for the vampires. All that we lack is a token from the shifters and we can perform the ceremony. Kenyon is gone. All I could think of was getting him away from the queen."

"Was that another of the Dark Queen's tricks?" Kyle asked softly. "Did she mean to deprive us of something we needed?"

A brooding silence followed, which Lark broke with a pleased exclamation. "The werewolf will be present in Lexie's blood. Mark Winspear told me Lexie is pregnant, so Kenyon is represented by the mother of his child. Magically speaking, a blood token does not get much stronger than that."

"The devil!" said Kyle, sounding pleased. "After this ordeal, I am glad our friends have so much to look forward to."

And so they began making plans, or at least Kyle and Jack did. Lark stepped backward, slipping away as only the fey could.

She'd made up her mind. She would trick Jack one last

time, but for the best of reasons. She had a lot to make up
for—all the secrets and half-truths, the betrayal and complicated loyalties. It was her fault the princess was here,
and saving Amelie might be the one apology Jack would
accept. It wouldn't win him back, but Lark hoped it would
make things better.

After Lark got a few steps away from the men, she summoned her glamour and vanished into the night.

"Someone has to mobilize forces to clean out the mountain," Jack said to Prince Kyle. "There's a prisoner there—
Therrien Haven. He's Lexie's father and a brave man."

"I will make it my business to see him safe," Kyle said,
polite but very reluctant. "But why should I be the one to
go? Amelie is still here and in danger. I should be here
for her."

"You have the authority to mobilize an army," Jack
pointed out. "You can ask for aid from other nations in
order to keep the mortal world safe. That's your role and
responsibility as a future sovereign."

Kyle frowned. "I don't like that you're right, but the
princess…" He trailed off. "Jack, what's wrong?"

Dismay pounded in Jack's head, mimicking a pulse.
"Where is Lark?"

Kyle looked around. "She was here a moment ago, but
she's vanished."

"She has a way of doing that," Jack said, holding on to
his temper by a rapidly fraying thread. As angry as he was
with her, worry threatened to derail every other thought.

"Why did she go without saying anything?" Kyle asked.

"We argued." That didn't begin to cover it. Guilt stabbed
at Jack, opening a raw, wounded ache deep inside. "I need
to get you on your way so I can look for her."

*She's a trained agent, and she left of her own accord.
She'll be all right until I find her.* Jack prayed he was right.
And once I find her, I'll strangle her.

A faint growl escaped Jack's chest. He instinctively knew she had gone to find Amelie. He had no time to waste. "Prepare yourself, Your Highness, you're going through that gate. Now."

Kyle caught his expression and went pale. "Whatever Lark's doing, it's no better than a suicide mission, is it?"

The moment she returned to the castle, Lark saw something new was happening. Where the courtyard had been all but empty before, now it was swarming with warriors. There was no rhyme or reason to the company. Some were knights, some foot soldiers carrying spears and swords. Others were wild men who rode strange, lizard-like beasts with spiked tails and flickering tongues. Still more were massive, club-wielding giants who made the drawbridge shudder with their tread. Lark was tempted to linger and find out why the Dark Fey were gathering, but she had a mission to complete.

Lark slid past them all, keeping her distance. This was the type of operation she excelled at, and she was in the zone. When she got inside the castle, she immediately found the stairs and hurried up them, retracing her steps to where she'd seen Amelie last. She was far more careful than before, testing the air for magical wards and the kind of trip wire spells the Dark Fey used. She found a few, but none near Amelie's cell.

It didn't take long to figure out why. When she got to the room, the door stood ajar. Amelie had been moved. Lark slumped, regretting the fact that she no longer had the ring to make a simple tracking spell. She'd have to search the old-fashioned way.

Or not. Selena wasn't trying to bargain with Lark and Jack any longer. There was no reason to put Amelie where Lark could stumble into her cell with ease—and then get caught herself. Lark's pride still stung.

No, now Selena could treat her captive princess according to fey custom. Royal prisoners would be kept in a tower—the highest and most inaccessible one the Dark Queen had. Lark had seen slender spires rising straight up from the castle's center. They were a reasonable place to start looking.

Lark ghosted through the halls and galleries, searching until she found a small arched door that led into the tower stairwell. It was guarded by two enormous figures with bronze helmets and tusks.

Ogres, Lark thought. She'd seen pictures in books, but they hadn't mentioned the smell. However, the books had mentioned such creatures were utterly impervious to Light Fey magic.

Now what? Lark thought in dismay.

Chapter 30

One ogre was posted on either side of the door, at least six feet apart. Still invisible, Lark sidled up to the nearest of the pig-snouted creatures, eyeing his long staff topped with a double-bladed ax. He wore a uniform of burgundy velvet and silver braid, the helmet and breastplate elaborately etched with swirling designs. The finery didn't hide his fearsome looks. Ogres had lumpy, leathery skin like that of an autumn gourd with a fungal disease. Tusks curved from their jaws like hooked blades. Their one weakness was their tiny, wide-set eyes. Lark guessed their vision couldn't be that good.

Silently, Lark moved to the ogre's other side, noting his boot knife, the key ring hooked loosely in his belt and the fact that he had a rather adorable curly tail. She reached out and gave it a tweak.

He jumped about a foot in the air and whirled on his companion. "Whatchu do that for?"

The other started, as if he'd been drowsing with his eyes open. "Huh?"

Ogres obviously weren't that bright. Lark slipped out from between them and went around to the other guard. His tail wasn't as cute, but she gave it a sharp tug anyway.

"Argh!" The second one made a lunge at the first, giving him a mighty shove.

"Your mother roots for acorns, Rog!" cried the shovee, who then rushed at his partner.

"Your father rolls in his own muck!"

Rog dropped his ax and flipped his partner to the floor.
Lark used the opportunity to snatch his boot knife, hiding
it inside her glamour. She got out of the way just in time.
The downed ogre scrambled to his feet, his lips curled
back in a snarl.

"I am Brak of the White Tusk clan. How dare you touch
me?"

"You're nothing but a side of bacon," said Rog, obviously pleased to get in the first throw.

They went down again, this time with Brak on top of
Rog. Lark plucked Brak's keys from his belt with a pick-
pocket's ease. They were starting to throw punches as she
slid the key into the lock and quickly slipped through the
door.

The stairwell was dark and narrow, winding upward in
a tight spiral. Cobwebs clung to the walls and ceiling and
it smelled like rotten eggs. *After all this, I really hope I've
got the right place.*

She had to work quickly. Once someone with any intelligence questioned Brak and Rog, they would figure
out what had happened. With a pounding heart, she began
climbing the stairs, the knife clutched in one hand. Prog-
ress, though, was slow. Her skirts were short enough not
to trip her, but the stairs were crumbling in places and she
had to be careful where she put her feet.

As she got higher, the smell of sulfur worsened despite
the arrow slits piercing the heavy stone walls. It didn't
make climbing any easier so Lark stopped, putting her face
to one of the slits to get a breath of clean air. The ground
looked very far below.

It was at that point she felt a prickle of heat to her left.
Lark spun, nearly slipping on the steps as she did so. It took
a moment to make sense of what she saw. The arrow slits
were letting in pale washes of light, but there was a faint or-

ange glow coming from the steps above. Unfortunately, the curve of the stairwell made it impossible to see the source.

She swallowed, apprehension sending gooseflesh running down her arms. At a snail's pace, she began ascending again, her hand firm around the ogre's blade. Now she could hear something moving above, a sliding, clicking slither. Brick by brick the walls turned to the left, sometimes bright with a flash of illumination, other times dark. Lark kept pushing onward, the heat and smell getting more pronounced until air was barely breathable.

And then she saw the flick of something. Impatient, she took the next few steps quickly to get a better look. What she saw was a scaly orange tail. *By Oberon, it's a dragon!* Lark sagged against the stones, bracing herself from collapse with one hand. Of course a captive princess would be guarded by a dragon. What else?

And that was what the light, heat and stink was all about. Dragons breathed fire. Lark leaned against the wall wrapping her arms around her middle. Fire was not her friend.

You're not a coward. She'd fought plenty of dangerous foes, often on her own. It was the fire she was afraid of. The thought of it alone made her skin hurt, as if her body had stored the memory of pain in every cell. *But the pain isn't real. Don't give in.*

Lark uncoiled herself, taking a better grip on the knife, and rushed up the steps with a cry. Scraping and scratching came from above, clawing at her every nerve. She caught a flash of something bright and she threw herself to the side just as a gust of flame rolled down the stairs, crawling up the opposite wall. Heat scraped along her skin, stinging her eyes and nose. For an instant, she was back in New York, trapped as her body boiled. Tears leaked down her face.

She was only there for a moment, wrestling with her courage, when she heard the scrabbling again. She was instantly on the alert, but froze before she raised her knife.

Two bright green eyes stared down at her, their expression curious.

"Well, hello," she said in the hopeful voice one used with a cranky Rottweiler.

It made a high-pitched noise something between a croak and a cheep, which surprised her. Dragons roared—unless they were just babies. Sudden hope flared, and Lark caught her breath. Come to think of it, a full-grown fire lizard wouldn't fit in this narrow passageway. Very, very slowly Lark crouched, making herself small. "Are you a very little dragon?"

There was a clicking scuttle, like claws on stone, and the curious eyes came closer and blinked. Lark could see the whole head now, with knobby eye ridges and extravagant whiskers. It was scaled, with iridescent patterns of orange shading to gold. Tufted ears stuck up like a cat's. It had the excited, eager look all young creatures shared.

Lark tucked the knife in the sash of her skirt, wanting to show she wasn't a threat. "Hey," she said, holding out a hand. "Come on, little one, let's see you."

She stayed in that position, not daring to startle it. She desperately hoped it wouldn't bite or roast her. The creature slithered down a few more steps, the head swinging from side to side, forked tongue flicking the air. It had short legs and a long body with a snakelike neck and tail, and a collar shone just where the neck flared into shoulders. The scales around the leather band were crusted with blood. Evidently the Dark Queen had a thing about controlling her pets with pain. Lark's teeth clenched with anger.

She judged the creature was little more than a hatchling since the wings folded across its back were too small for flight. Dragons fed their young for at least a few years— this one should be with its mother. Of course, if you wanted to turn a creature into a vicious guard animal, mistreating it as a baby was the quickest way.

It sniffed her tentatively and cheeped again, finally coming close enough to touch. She scratched its eye ridges, looking again at the collar. Who could do that to such a young creature? "Shall we be friends, then?"

She kept at it for a few minutes. Every time she stopped, it bumped her head for more, a strange burbling sound of pleasure emitting from its long throat. Did dragons purr? She paused once, checking the collar for spells and finding none. She quickly unbuckled it, peeling it away from the dragon's hide as gently as she could. The operation must have hurt, because it skittered away with an unhappy chirp. When Lark tossed the collar aside, the dragon flamed it to ash.

Then it crawled back and bumped her knee with its forehead, and the scratching started again. Lark gradually stood, one hand keeping contact with the beast. "Shall we go see the princess?"

The dragon, it seemed, would agree to anything Lark asked as long as it involved affection. She stepped over it, moving quickly up the last few turnings of the stair. It galumphed after her, nails and tail making a racket as it moved.

The door at the top was of an old-fashioned design, locked only by a bar that sat across two brackets—obviously no one expected an intruder to make it past two ogres and a dragon. Lark removed it and pushed the door open.

It was Amelie's room, but Lark's heart plummeted to her feet. The princess lay on a four-poster bed, her dark hair combed over the shoulders of a white satin gown. In the thin moonlight, it was almost hard to distinguish her from the snowy quilt and bed curtains. Amelie's face was pale but for the dark crescents of her lashes and the flush of her lips. She was young and beautiful and as still as death, only the shifting reflection of the gown's beadwork showing she still lived.

The baby dragon made a short-legged shuffle over to the bed, thrusting its snout toward the princess with a curious wheeze. A thin curl of smoke erupted from its nose. Then it turned its huge eyes to Lark. The expression was unmistakably worried.

With good reason. The Dark Queen had put Amelie into a spelled sleep. How was Lark going to rescue the princess now? She ran to the window and looked down, down the sheer tower to the ant-like figures below. Not even a fey secret agent could carry a dead weight down that way. She'd have to have been a superhero of the tights-and-cape variety. And there was no telling what removing Amelie or trying to break the spell by force might do.

Suddenly, the dragon backed away from the bed, chirping in short, tight bursts. It ran to the door, flicked its tongue, and then backed away, ears flattening against its skull. Someone was coming—someone who frightened the little beast.

Lark had a sudden, sinking realization that she had gambled her life and lost. She could have accepted that if Amelie had escaped, but that hadn't happened. Instead, Lark had failed.

Inexorably, her gaze traveled to where the princess slept, lovely and vulnerable and beyond Lark's help. Numb despair crept through Lark, robbing her strength until the knife dangled in useless fingers. She closed her eyes, unable to bear the sight of the princess any longer.

Distantly, she heard approaching steps. The door creaked opened and Drusella and Egon Blackthorn swaggered in, a feral grin curving Drusella's mouth as she pointed her spear at Lark. Egon was silent as usual, his dark eyes in constant motion—checking the bed, the window and finally Lark herself. The dragon scampered away from the pair, wedging itself between Lark and the wall. It was looking to her for safety, poor thing.

For some reason, its misplaced confidence revived Lark's courage. Perhaps she could do for others what she couldn't manage for herself. If there was to be a final hope, a last-ditch effort, this was the time for it. She could hold nothing back.

"Well, well, little bird," said Drusella. "Nice try with the rescue. Sorry it didn't work out."

"Yeah?" Lark held the suddenly blazing dagger aloft and showed them what the Light Fey could do with just a blade.

Chapter 31

"Ready?" Jack asked Kyle.

The prince nodded, his jaw set. Jack had to admire him. As a Vidonese, Kyle had been raised to fear magic like poison. He was far more accepting than most of his countrymen, but the fact that he was voluntarily facing it now showed real courage.

They stood in the forest clearing where Jack had entered the Dark Fey kingdom with Lark at his side. He was no sorcerer, but he knew how to work the gates he had helped to create, and right now he had to get Kyle out. Slowly, he raised his hands and felt the pull of the magic as if it were a magnetic force on his blood.

Jack had borrowed Kyle's slender pocketknife. Working quickly, he scratched a symbol onto a large gray boulder at the center of the clearing. The shape of the mark had some power, but its true use was as a focus for what Jack was about to do. Then he dug in his jacket pockets, profoundly thankful the Dark Fey hadn't gone through them. He took the vial of blood from its case and retraced the symbol in the separating liquid, using it sparingly. He'd added some of Kyle's royal human blood to the mix as the final ingredient for the spell, and the combination of blood types teased his vampire senses. Once he was done, Jack carefully stoppered the vial and put it away. He would need the rest to seal the gates later. Then he withdrew to a safe distance.

Jack had slipped the wedding ring, set with the blood

rubies imbued with the power of the original spell, onto his little finger. Now he made a fist and aimed it at the rock, summoning the power of the Fallen and uttering the Light Fey word commanding it to open. *"Ianja!"*

Power ripped through him, slashing pain through his core. Jack staggered, holding himself upright by will alone. No wonder Selena had balked at sending Kenyon home. She'd used raw power to make it happen. Jack had the advantage of a formal spell, and it still felt as if he was being split open.

A bright light appeared along the strokes of the symbol, growing brighter and brighter, as if the sun itself was contained in the rock. In the next eye blink, the entire clearing blazed pure and bright, filled with potential power. This was the essence of Light Fey magic.

Both Jack and Kyle covered their eyes, stepping back until the flare of brightness subsided to a bearable level. And then they both exclaimed in surprise. Like some photo-editing trick, a perfectly round hole had been punched through the dark woodland. In its place was a sunny expanse of alpine meadow—Jack recognized it as the land below the Derrondine Pass.

"When I came here the gate was underwater," Kyle commented. "Not that I'm complaining, mind you. I wasn't looking forward to the swim."

Jack frowned. Magic gateways weren't supposed to behave like this. Allowing entrance in one place and exit in another was unusual—and it had happened twice in one night. First, Selena had sent Kenyon home through a portal she'd conjured on the spot—and now this passageway was nothing like Jack had anticipated. The original spell imprisoning the Dark Fey was breaking down. That was certainly more than Selena could achieve using the slow leak of Haven's life.

Jack narrowed his eyes, wondering if Selena had meant to show him this when she'd sent Kenyon home. He suspected there was another player here—someone or something Haven had tried to warn them about back in the lab.

But there was no time to think about it right now. He could see the edge of the lake and the meadows beyond and—much to his relief—a fleet of black Company helicopters dotting the sky.

Kyle swore in surprise. "Please tell me that's the cavalry."

"The other Horsemen knew where we were going. They sent help."

But that wasn't the whole story. The earthly armies of the Dark Queen were pouring out of the mountain in helicopters of their own, and in tanks, in personnel carriers and on foot. The cavalry might have arrived, but it was busy.

"They can't help us," said Kyle. "They need help themselves."

Jack pressed his cell phone into Kyle's hand. The phone was in a waterproof case and hopefully had survived the trip through the lake. "Call anyone you can think of to send backup. You're going to be a joint ruler of two kingdoms. Make them pay attention."

Kyle grabbed the phone and started for the portal, but he'd gone barely two steps before he turned. "Promise me you'll save Amelie?"

Jack could see the choice to leave was tearing the prince apart. "Yes, I promise."

With a final nod, Kyle walked through the portal. The distance from one side to the other seemed to jump from one step to the next. Suddenly he was a small figure a good mile away, running as though a demon was at his heels.

Jack breathed easier with him gone. Kyle wasn't exactly safe yet, but getting out of the Dark Fey realm was a good start. He raised the ring again. *"Fialo!"*

Suddenly the clearing looked normal again; the window to the mortal realms vanished. Jack knew better than to think it truly closed—the drapes had merely been drawn for the moment, hiding it from obvious sight. It would have to stay that way until he found Lark and Amelie and made his final escape.

The instant he finished, the sky exploded in another nova of light. Jack flinched, covering his eyes against the brilliance. His first thought was that the gate had reopened, but he quickly saw it came from the top of the highest castle tower. The pure, pitiless brightness made what he'd conjured look like a Christmas tree bulb. He stopped, gaping at the sight around the edges of his upflung arm. He'd only ever seen anything like it once before—when Lark's grandfather had died at the battle of the Star Tower.

That meant Lark was in trouble, and this was her last roll of the dice.

Denial sprang to Jack's lips, but the words died, useless. As he looked again, he saw the light was not pure, white and simple. Just like Lark, the blaze held a complexity of colors and shading, dark and light and a full rainbow of beauty that would take an eternity to catalog with any justice. This was her essence he was seeing spread out like a beacon in the sky.

She was spending her life, and the only reason she would do that was to protect the princess. Faster than the eye could follow, Jack bolted across the meadow. He raced across the drawbridge, leaping past the guards. Some were quick enough to try to intercept him, but he pushed aside the swords and pikes with his bare hands. Nothing was able to touch him.

Inside the castle was mayhem. Lesser fey were collapsed everywhere, felled by Lark's power. Their stronger cousins were either running to escape, or surging toward the tower to stop her. He only had to follow the most foolhardy to know which way to go. Jack pushed forward at a furious pace, soon arriving in a large room. In it was a door. Before the door stood a trio of ogres, and they did not look pleased.

"Get up there and stop this!" roared the biggest to the

others. He had fancier armor than the others, so Jack guessed he was their captain.

"But, sir, we won't survive it," begged the smallest. "It's an invisible being possessed of fearsome magic, and it had fangs and claws and a serpent's tail."

"If it was invisible, how could you tell?" snarled the captain.

"It's me you should be afraid of." Jack stepped forward.

The captain wheeled to face him. The creature's piggy eyes narrowed. "Who, by all the darkness, are you?"

Jack's gaze flicked to the door and back to the ogres. "Get out of my way."

The captain's clawed hand reached for his sword hilt. "I think you need a lesson in manners. Or perhaps you need to learn to count. There are three of us, and one of you."

Jack snarled, baring his fangs. The only thing he cared about was getting up the stairs to Lark. Asteriel's power welled up, blazing along Jack's nerves and muscles like an electric current. The effect was like strong drink, leaving him light-headed. "I said, get out of my way!"

The captain lunged with his sword, proving ogres were more agile than they looked. The point bit into Jack's shoulder with a starburst of searing pain. He twisted aside, whirling close enough to the two guards, that he snatched one of their long-handled axes.

"Still want to give me a lesson?" Jack snarled. His hold on his demon was giving way, like a zipper drawn slowly down tooth by tooth. The relief of it was indescribable.

"You won't make it," said the captain. "Give it up. We'll kill you."

Logic said he was right, but Jack wasn't interested. He could feel Lark's presence now, and it drew him like a magnet. An army of ogres couldn't stop him from going to her side. "Step away."

The captain staggered back at something he saw in Jack's face. Jack raised the ax, ready to press the advantage and then understood. Arcs of blue electricity were dancing over the blade, over his hands, over his whole body. The air around him was glowing an eerie blue. Asteriel was just below his skin, crackling with force.

There was no point in wasting the moment. Jack strode forward, ax poised, and the ogres parted. One of them even opened the door for Jack.

A wise move. Jack could feel himself teetering on the edge of a fine madness, the net that kept the demon contained as flimsy now as a spider's web. He could feel his heart, normally as silent as the night he was murdered, beating in response to the demon's magic. *I'm losing control. I'm losing myself.* This was his greatest fear, the point where he could lose everything down to his very identity. Alarm rendered the world razor sharp, as if every color and sound was amplified. But there was no turning back now. If he did, Lark's gallant sacrifice would be meaningless.

Jack wasn't the first to try climbing the stairs—Dark Fey had rushed that way to stop Lark's spell. They were collapsed, as still as death. Jack ran lightly up the tower, leaping over the bodies as he ascended into the blaze of Lark's power.

The door at the top was open, light pouring into the stairwell from the tower room. To either side of the entrance, Egon and Drusella Blackthorn cowered in the shadows, blinded by Lark's magic. They were the strongest of the Dark Queen's servants and had gotten closest to Lark, but not even they had been able to face the final weapon of the Light. Her essence was simply too bright.

And by their own admission, they had been party to the destruction of the Company, the attack on the palace and kidnapping the royals. Jack barely paused as he put a swift end to them with the ax.

And then he was in the room. Lark stood before the window, a dagger raised in her right hand and a dragon coiled protectively at her feet. She was magnificent and terrible as a goddess, but the blaze was faltering.

He rushed forward, enfolding her in his arms. He could feel the exhaustion in her limbs, but Asteriel knew what to do. The Fallen's energy flared and surged toward her, as elemental as a tide. The moment their powers meshed, his blue light sparked and crackled against her dazzling glow. Gradually, the blaze from her dagger diminished as Jack stemmed the flow of her life force. The room dimmed and she sagged against him with a cry.

"Lark?" He slid his arms around her waist, holding her so that she did not collapse to the floor. Her pulse was as weak and fast as if she suffered a fever. "Lark, can you hear me?"

She braced herself against his chest, bravely trying to stand on legs that wobbled with exhaustion. Then she stilled, bringing her fingertips to his face with a feather-light touch. "Jack, your eyes."

He could see the eyes of the Fallen reflected as bright pinpoints in her own gaze. The sight chilled him to the marrow, bringing a tide of sick fear to the back of his throat. He swallowed it down, steeling his resolve. This was no time to waver. "What happened here?"

"Drusella came."

"No longer a problem," he said flatly.

Lark closed her eyes, "I protected the princess for as long as I could. I don't know if it was enough to save her from—from whatever Serena has done. It's a spell like the one they used on the guards at the Marcari palace, but it's far stronger than anything I've ever seen."

He looked around, for the first time noticing Amelie lying in the four-poster bed. It took him a beat to realize she was alive, and then only when he saw the faintest stirring as she breathed. A dragon no bigger than a collie was scrabbling at the covers as if it wanted to jump up on the bed. It looked at Lark with the soulful gaze of a devoted pet.

"How do we get her out of here?" he murmured, more to himself than her.

"We can't jump out the window again," she said. "There are too many of us for you to carry."

"Let me think a moment," he said, moving to the window. Suddenly, he was transfixed by a sight he didn't quite understand.

At first he thought the woods were on fire, but then he realized the flames weren't flames at all, but riders in golden armor brandishing weapons bright with magic. "By all the hells," he cursed. "The Dark Queen told me her sorcerers had foreseen a war. I didn't know she meant tonight!"

In an instant, Lark was at his side, her hair brushing his skin as she leaned to look out the window. "I saw the Dark Fey armies gathering in the courtyard when I came in."

But Jack wasn't looking at Selena's armies—these were different fey. Banners flew at the head of each group: the black ash and sunburst of the Clan of White Towers, the silver oak of the River Rill folk and, at the head, the black eagle of Harrow. Those were Lark's uncles, their leaf-blade spears blazing in the darkness. Then Jack heard a sound he'd all but forgotten over the long march of centuries: the battle horns of the Light Fey. They rang like the cry of lost souls fading on the breeze.

Jack had veiled the portal, but he'd not closed it. Lark's signal had called through worlds to the forgotten armies of her people. They must have been waiting for their chance.

The Light Fey had returned to the field of battle. His heart leaped until he saw, like a river of nightmares, the Dark Queen's warriors streaming over the parched meadows to meet them.

Chapter 32

"I'd forgotten what a terrible racket those horns make," Queen Selena commented as she materialized in the doorway.

Lark gasped, pulling away from Jack's arms. The dragon dived beneath the bed with a wail. But the queen only had eyes for Jack, who turned slowly from looking out the window.

Lark's heart pounded, as if her body was trying to make up for all the energy she'd spun into light. It wasn't working, and she backed away until she touched the wall. The cool, solid stone steadied her spinning senses. Too much had just happened: the tower, the life-draining spell, Jack showing up glowing with demon power. And now the Dark Fey queen. If all that wasn't bad enough, she witnessed Selena's expression as the queen caught sight of Jack's demon-bright gaze. It was a flash of pure, triumphant greed, because Jack was almost in her clutches. Lark's hackles rose in a wash of terror and protectiveness.

Outside, the sounds of battle rang with distant, savage clarity. To Lark, the tower room felt like the eye of a terrible hurricane.

"Your Majesty," Jack said coolly. "I've been expecting you."

"I didn't have much choice but to come and deal with this intrusion. Evidently, the Blackthorns weren't up to the task." Egon and Drusella were the queen's cousins, but she sounded more irritated than heartbroken.

"They'd demonstrated a history of rude behavior," Jack replied. "I got judgmental."

Her upper lip twitched, as if it couldn't decide whether to sneer or smile. "Well, then. Perhaps they are the cost I must pay in trade."

"For what?"

"It is you I need now, Fallen."

Jack's star-bright eyes grew cold. "And what do you think I will do for you?"

"Everything." Her voice dropped, no longer sweet and silvery but instead rough with desperation. "We need each other, but I don't expect you to understand that yet. Let us start with a simple fact—you aren't the only demon in this picture."

Astonishment energized Lark enough that she stepped away from the wall. *Another demon. Impossible.* "No generation has ever seen two walk the earth at one time!" she exclaimed. *No generation would survive it.*

And yet it made sense: the blast that had wrecked Headquarters, the power it would have taken to build the facility under the mountain—neither were easily achieved within the normal scope of magic.

Selena didn't even glance at Lark. Her attention was fully on Jack. "There is another named Balziel. Not a Fallen, but a true demon of the pit."

Every line of Jack's body had gone sharp with tension. "How did he come to walk the mortal world?"

The queen's chin lifted, her expression brittle. "I summoned Balziel to be my ally."

Lark clutched at the wall for support once more. The Dark Queen was working with a demon! There were historical accounts of such alliances happening before. The sinking of Atlantis had been the most spectacular result.

But that was just the start of Selena's news. "Balziel has proved treacherous."

Jack clenched one fist. "A treacherous demon. Fancy that."

Selena's gray eyes glittered. If Lark didn't know better, she would have thought they were tears. Tears of rage, perhaps—the queen wasn't the weeping kind. "He was stronger than I expected. He bides his time now, but he intends to enslave the Dark Fey the moment we set foot outside the gates. You see, I am putting all my cards on the table. I want your help, Jack. Together, we can defeat him. Apart, he will destroy us both."

Jack seemed speechless for a moment, as if he had expected anything from the Dark Queen but pleading. "You want me to become your new ally?"

"Indeed."

"Why should I?"

"To save your mortal world. Asteriel was once an angel. Maybe the instinct to protect and preserve is still there."

Jack's face twisted. "I'm not your angel or your weapon, Selena. You're certainly not my guide to redemption."

"Don't even consider it, Jack," Lark interjected. "Think about what she's asking you to do. If you set Asteriel free, there will be no turning back." There would be no Jack Anderson, only a Fallen who would have lost his last chance of salvation.

Selena finally deigned to look Lark's way. "Be quiet. The truth spell in your dagger freed Jack's inner Fallen. None of this would have been possible without you." She turned back to Jack. "Only a demon can defeat a demon. Balziel won't spare the mortal world. I doubt he'll bother to spare the supernatural one, either."

"No." Lark grasped Jack's hand, twining her fingers through his. "Don't."

"Oh, come," said Selena. "Balziel has corrupted the spell binding the gates. I still can't leave, but soon he will be able to march his armies into my realm and back out again whenever he likes."

"He would be unstoppable," Lark said in horror. "From here, he can redirect the passageway to attack anywhere he likes. No need to worry about transportation. He can just zap soldiers to where he wants them."

"Exactly," said Selena. "Balziel will have complete mastery of your world. One of the Fallen might vanquish such a power, but no one else can even hope to try."

"I know." Jack turned to Lark, his expression bleak. "You've never seen what a demon can do."

But she had seen the place they called the Dragon's Tooth. She swallowed. Even though she was holding his hand, she could feel Jack slipping away.

The queen shifted her weight, her expression more confident now. "There is another option. Keep your Fallen on a tether and let me go free instead. We could fight Balziel together. You would walk away as you are now, still Jack Anderson—if you let me out of here so I can fight."

Lark stood frozen, barely able to think. The Dark Queen was offering him a chance to live, with everything that meant: love, friendship, a chance to still do good. But that meant releasing Selena into the world. That was a crime that would cancel everything else.

Selfishly, Lark wanted Jack. She closed her eyes, feeling them burn with tears of exhaustion and misery. "Please—"

"No." Jack withdrew his hand from Lark's and turned to face the queen. "Either way I lose. One way, you lose, as well. If that's all I can hope for, I'll take that consolation prize."

"You'll sacrifice your soul before letting me go free?" A nerve in Selena's jawline twitched.

Jack didn't answer. His features settled into a grim mask as he turned to Lark, and the devastation in his eyes left her reeling. It was as if she was hurtling down a slope, about to smash to smithereens.

He cupped her cheek in one hand. "The Light Fey thought my powers held the key to their salvation, and they sent you to me. Maybe I can help you defeat your enemies after all." He smiled, but it was a broken thing.

Lark's lips parted as she desperately tried to frame a reply, but there were no words to unravel the moment. There was no way to go back to a point that made sense and take a different path forward.

Jack kissed her lightly, a brush against the corner of her mouth. "I'm sorry we never found peace together."

And he shoved her toward the wall as Selena swept her arm in a dramatic arc, shouting a word that was immediately drowned out by the cracking of stone. Light flashed, blinding Lark as she fell to her knees and skidded to a thump against the corner of the bed. Through streaming eyes, she saw chunks of granite fly from the wall, spewing into the air as if they weighed no more than pebbles. Suddenly cold wind flooded the room, sending the bed curtains billowing. One side of the tower room was gone.

When Lark blinked her vision clear, Jack was gone. She leaped to her feet, forgetting her own peril. "Jack!" she cried.

Selena stalked to the gaping hole she'd made, screaming in rage. "Demon Asteriel, show yourself!"

Lark was beside herself. "What have you done?" Rage and grief bent the words to little more than a wail of pain.

Selena rounded on her. "Are you still here?"

Eyes flashing with rage, the queen lashed out with another lethal spell, but Lark blocked it out of pure instinct. Selena's eyes widened with surprise, and she struck again. This time Lark went flying, smacking into one of the heavy oak bedposts. Lark's skull banged into the wood and she slumped to the floor, landing on hands and knees. Her vision wobbled and heaved, her stomach lurching along with it.

It was too much for the little dragon. It scuttled out from

under the bed to crouch in front of Lark, tail lashing. Selena laughed incredulously, but the dragon spat flame that came within inches of the Dark Queen's toes.

Selena's eyes widened with rage, but any response was cut short by a furious roar. She wheeled as Jack descended through the opening, sinking down into a feline crouch.

Of course! Lark thought, relief thundering through her. *He can fly.*

"You're back," Selena said to Jack. "And now you're mine. I can see Jack isn't in control any longer."

"Not so fast," he returned, his star-bright eyes wide with mockery. "I'm not stupid like your pit-demon friends. Jack still has just enough hold on me that I can slip through your net."

Lark shuddered as she recognized Asteriel's voice, so like Jack's and yet distinct. The dragon seemed to sense it, too. The beast huddled close. Something moved as the dragon's lashing tail swished beneath the bedclothes. Slowly, without attracting attention, she reached beneath the bed to discover the dagger she'd used earlier. It had fallen from her hand when Jack had broken the spell. She grasped the hilt, feeling better with a weapon in her hand.

"Well, then," the queen said to Jack, her expression cool as ice. "Since you're back, maybe we can come to a compromise. Save my realm from Balziel and I'll give you your princess."

Jack slowly rose to his feet. "The time for bargaining is over."

"Be careful, demon," she said, spinning a coil of light from her fingers. It snapped in the air, rebounding neatly to her hand. "You leave me with nothing to lose."

With that, she cast the coil into the air, snaking it around Jack's wrist. It wrapped around his flesh with a hiss, dragging a shout of pain from him. He bared his fangs, snarling savagely and jerking against the bond. Selena's heels skidded across the floor, but she held on. Blood began to drip from his arm.

Lark sprang from the floor, dagger in hand. Intent on capturing Jack, the Dark Queen couldn't turn in time to deflect the blow. Lark thrust it deep into Selena's back, striking upward between the ribs and aiming for the heart. It took all her strength despite the sharpness of the blade, the scrape of metal on bone and sinew making her shudder.

Lark's aim was true. Selena stiffened, her weight suddenly falling backward against Lark. The magic whip vanished instantly. Jack stumbled to one knee, suddenly off balance as his struggle abruptly ended.

And then, incredibly, the Dark Queen turned in Lark's arms. Lark was still holding the hilt of the blade—somehow, Selena had slid off it. A river of blood was splashing to the floor, but the queen grabbed the blade in one hand, pulling Lark close. Selena's face was a twisted mask of hate. "Wretch!" she spat, and lit the dagger on fire.

Flames sprang up Lark's forearm. She screamed, trying to let go of the searing metal, but it remained fused to her hand. *Fire! Fire!* Burning and the memory of burning shot through her in confused agony. Lark writhed, falling to her knees, and Selena fell with her. Blood soaked Lark's skirts.

And suddenly Jack was there, towering over them both. Selena's eyes flew wide in horror as he grasped her by the hair, jerking her away from Lark. The knife fell from Lark's hand, the flames instantly gone. She rolled away, cradling her arm. Agony lanced through her, but she couldn't take her eyes from the tableau of Jack and the queen. They were both beautiful, her golden beauty and his strong profile, pale as marble. He cupped her head almost lovingly.

"I'm sorry," he said.

Lark closed her eyes, pain rocking her like choppy waves. She heard the click of the queen's spine snapping in two.

* * *

Asteriel looked down at the fair-haired queen, saddened beyond measure. "Rest in peace, sovereign of the Dark."

Sometimes there was no answer but to pluck one life to save the rest. He'd never killed lightly, but he didn't turn away from necessity. Selena had crossed a line by calling Balziel.

And now it was time to step up and set his own journey aside. He'd come as close as a fallen angel could to getting a do-over. In Jack's keeping he'd come a long way, but there were some things that trumped individual needs, and Selena had been right about one thing—this was a big-boy fight.

Asteriel released Selena's limp form, laying her gently on the chamber's stone floor. Lark had passed out, her body overcome by pain and exhaustion. He carried her to the bed, reveling in the softness of her form and the silk of her hair against his cheek.

"You are a miracle," he whispered, "and an utter contradiction."

Lark was the greatest gift Jack had given him. Asteriel's kind loved, but not in the same way as mortals. But with Jack, he'd experienced it all. Earthly love was messy, frustrating, painful and utterly irreplaceable. Asteriel had fallen in love right along with his mortal host, and he'd do anything to keep Lark safe. Maybe even save the world. He might have Fallen, but he still had a few tricks up his sleeve.

He set her on the coverlet next to Amelie, and then noticed the little dragon puffing steam like a traumatized teakettle. It had curled its tail around its feet, making itself as small as possible, and was staring at him with saucer-wide eyes.

"Yes, you can go, too." Asteriel gathered it up and nestled it at the foot of the bed. "We don't have much time."

He regarded the opening Selena had made in the wall, judging its size. *Good enough.* Perhaps he couldn't fly carrying two unconscious women and a baby dragon, but he could certainly carry one object through the portal.

So it was that Asteriel, who had never learned to color within the lines at the best of times, flew a four-poster bed out of fairyland. As he passed through the realm to the gate, he could see the devastation the sudden war had brought with it. Below him raged the terrible clash between Dark and Light Fey—the Dark far more numerous, but the Light far more skilled. Fairy horses screamed and spears flashed. Swords crashed on armor and claws and teeth tore flesh. *This has to stop*, he thought with a pang of grief, *or there will be no fey left*.

Things were just as bad outside the gate, where human armies fought the nonhuman soldiers of the mountain on foot and in the air. Asteriel recognized the black helicopters of the Company and knew these were the raw recruits Sam Ralston had been training when the blast had hit their headquarters. They were brave, but too green for this battle. *This has to stop, and I have to stop it.*

Asteriel set the bed down in the safest place he could find, and flew to the highest point to survey the scene. It didn't take long to find Balziel. All he had to do was follow the rush of black flame flowing down the mountainside like a drop of Armageddon. Wherever the flame had touched, everything lay twisted, wasted, choked of life. As Asteriel watched, an entire swath of forest died and nothing but ash and the shattered bones of bird and beast remained. It was hell come to Earth. *That would be my cue.*

Asteriel flew into the air, manifesting huge, black wings to better ride the air currents. Such things mattered in a fight, and the hum of the air through feathers brought back days of glory he'd all but forgotten. He rolled in the air, sporting between the helicopters that wheeled frantically above the destruction.

"Hey, sulfurhead!" Asteriel roared at the demon. One

couldn't spend centuries among humans without adopting some of their irreverence. "Listen up!"

Balziel reacted predictably. The black flames coalesced into a giant of flickering shadow that gave a mocking bow. "Asteriel," it said, speaking mind to mind. "I heard rumors that you had cast your lot with lesser beings."

He thought of Lark, protecting the helpless princess with the light of her own spirit. "Fragile, but certainly not less."

"Strange words, coming from a Fallen."

Asteriel's first instinct was to deny that, but he knew better. His kind had always been quick to discount any creature less powerful than themselves. Even his grand scheme to do good in the world had been all about him. But the daily grind of life—even undead life—was a school-room second to none. The so-called lesser beings knew much of humility. They learned how to look outside themselves, and through that they learned mercy, caring and the infinite manifestations of beauty. Love, too, if they were lucky—and it really didn't matter in what form love found them, as long as it did. He owed Jack a lot for sharing his life.

"Here is something even stranger, hellspawn. I've fallen all over again," Asteriel said. "A magnificent woman needs my help, and I mean to give it to her."

Balziel wasn't impressed. "What do you want?"

Asteriel kept it simple and literal. "I want you to go to hell."

In reply, Balziel reached a claw into the sky and plucked one of the helicopters from the air. Then the demon opened its maw, where flames licked in shades of orange and ash and smoldering bloodred. It tossed the chopper down its throat, swallowing in a single gulp. Balziel laughed, a sound more horrible than any shriek of pain. "Just like that I shall devour your pitiful world, Asteriel, and leave nothing behind."

"Please don't spare the melodrama."

Sarcasm seemed to fly past Balziel's radar without leaving a blip. Instead, he bulged and flickered with anticipation. "Think hard about who you love most, and I will begin there."

Which of course meant that Lark sprang immediately into Asteriel's mind. Balziel plucked her image from the air with no effort at all. With a shriek of anticipation, the demon unfurled into a lake of flame and slithered down the mountainside, leaving a trail of smoking wasteland behind.

Asteriel shot into the sky, avoiding the sudden rush of heat from below. He had to protect Lark, and would spare nothing to do it. He could be destroyed in this body, and he probably would be. Fear and doubt circled him, but his determination held firm. If he'd learned anything from Jack, it was how to be stubborn.

And how to care. The spreading devastation sickened him. He feared for the lives of those he loved, and for those he'd never met.

Balziel was headed in a straight line for the humans. Right in his path, Prince Kyle was coordinating with his commanders. Reinforcements from the far-flung branches of the Company were arriving to save what lives they could. And, most precious of all, a four-poster bed nestled among the trees, holding the life Asteriel and Jack held dear.

Asteriel's second chance had run out. Only an unfettered Fallen with his tainted, soiled soul could stop this evil. *It's up to us, Jack, old friend*, Asteriel thought, filled with love and regret. *At least we'll go out fighting.*

After nine hundred years of battling for his soul, Jack surrendered utterly to his demon.

Chapter 33

Lark gradually regained consciousness. It took her some time to identify the roaring, rattling noise as chopper blades. That meant they were no longer in Selena's realm—but that was as far as her logic would go. Disorientation threatened to engulf her as her eyes flickered open. She was outdoors, but she was stretched out on the four-poster bed that belonged in the castle tower.

An orange, scaly head poked into her field of vision. The creature made a questioning noise, snuffling under her chin. Lark reached up with her good hand, stroking its neck. The dragon was pumping heat like an electric blanket.

As she turned her head, she saw Amelie was there, too. The princess was still asleep, but something had changed. A healthy color was returning to her cheeks, as if leaving the fey realm had weakened the sleeping spell. Gradually, Lark sat up. The change in position brought the pain from her burn to new life and she groaned. She needed help. A doctor. Maybe a stiff drink. She looked around and realized the bed was on a rise of land with a spectacular view. She searched for Jack, but instead saw that a battle raged in the valley below.

Lark scrambled to her knees, rising up for a better look. Her heart began thumping wildly as she put the facts together. One of the armies looked a lot like the mercenaries from the mountain.

And that was when she saw the portal in the distance. It was a little way up the slope of the mountain, like a bright movie screen floating in space. Lark shifted to get a better view, drawing a complaint from the dragon.

A vast number of fey were spilling from the portal, both the Light Fey in their golden armor and the bizarre rabble of lesser fey. A little distance apart, a cluster of Dark Fey nobles huddled together within a ring of Light Fey guards. Lark couldn't see the prisoners' faces, but their slumped posture looked defeated and bewildered. That was small wonder. The Dark Fey realm beyond the portal door was in flames, collapsing even as Lark watched. She strained to see the castle, and could just make out a shard of stone in the distance, as if it had exploded from within.

She was still staring at the portal when a movement to her left caught her attention. It was a black shape in the far distance, but it seemed to be hurtling toward her at a breathtaking pace. A moment later the dragon, which had been pressed up against her, leaped from her side and scrambled into the brush. Alarmed, Lark rolled off the bed and to her feet, ignoring the wave of pain that surged up her injured arm.

"Stop! Come back!" she called after the dragon, but she was immediately distracted as the black shape fell out of the sky and rolled toward her. It looked no bigger than a golf ball, which made no sense. She was sure she'd seen it in the distance, but this was far too small to be visible at any great range.

The dark sphere radiated a magnetic presence, as if it meant to suck her in. Defying gravity, it rolled uphill toward her. Lark was in no mood. With a swift, disgusted swipe of her foot, she kicked the object back down the hill and sent it skittering and bouncing toward the lake.

It struck the ground three times before it exploded. Lark ducked, expecting a blast. Instead, it unfurled into a monster made of sooty flames. The thing stank like sulfur, as if every rotten egg in the world had been crammed into one noxious cloud. Heat shimmered around the thing in waves, stabbing through her burn with razor intensity.

Lark gave an involuntary cry, backing up so that she was between the creature and the bed where the unconscious princess lay. And then it came to her with the certainty of solid fact. This was the demon Balziel.

Lark's chest ached with terror, as if she breathed it in along with the foul air. Nevertheless, she braced her feet and locked her trembling knees, determined to stand her ground.

"What do you want?" she demanded. *I think I am about to die. If I'm lucky.*

The flaming figure bent as if to peer down at her, though it had cavernous pits where its eyes might have been. It didn't speak, but it laughed. The forest shook with the sound, the trees quaking until branches fell with a cascade of crashes.

At that moment, something fell from the sky. No, not fell—it struck, like a stooping hawk, blade quick and nimble. Lark had an impression of something bright and dark at once, like a scrap of starlight hurtling her way. And then it stopped, suspended motionless in the air—and time seemed to freeze along with it.

The winged figure was the Fallen, Asteriel, swathed in blue arcs of light that crackled and snapped along his skin. He wore Jack's face and Jack's clothes, but there was nothing human about him now. The black wings were enormous, broad and curved like an eagle's. He turned to regard Lark, both desolation and determination in his bright gaze, and in that moment she understood Jack had given everything to stop Balziel.

For an instant, nothing moved save the wind stirring Asteriel's feathers. It was like a painting by an old master, an image of primal forces doing battle when the world was young. But this was now, and it was Lark's life, and this was all that remained of the man she cared for.

I love you, she thought, but her lips would not move to say the words. She was stupefied by the beings in front of her, in terror of them both and yet desperate for Asteriel's safety.

"Be careful," she managed to croak out, and wished she hadn't. Was there a more ridiculous thing to say to a fallen angel?

She caught a flash of amusement, as if Asteriel had read her thought. But then he grabbed for Balziel in an impossibly quick movement. A snarl bared his vampire fangs, Balziel howled a protest and...

Suddenly both figures were gone. Only the hum of wind in feathers remained in Lark's perception, as if an arrow had flown past. Lark staggered back to sit on the bed. What had just happened?

Physical weariness slammed through her. Lark suddenly gave way, weeping for the look she'd seen in the Fallen's eyes—the understanding of the sacrifice he'd made, and of the love she'd seen there. There was no way out, but he'd done it anyway because it was the right thing to do.

Sobs wrenched from deep in her exhausted soul. They weren't the elegant tears of a Light Fey, but as soggy and messy as any human's. She didn't care about the fate of the world right then. She wanted to snatch Jack back from the brink and hold him close while everything else crumbled to ash. She wiped her face with her hands, then her sleeve, unable to stop the flood of crying.

Something nudged at her foot. Lark wiped the tears from her cheeks one last time and looked down to see the dragon had returned from the forest. It put its chin on her knee, a sympathetic look in its eyes and a faint plume of steam curling from its nostrils. Lark's heart squeezed and she reached down to reassure it, but it jerked its head up at the last instant, trilling with alarm. Lark looked up, following its gaze.

And gasped. Two figures were tumbling through the air, end over end, leaving a trail of sparks and smoke in the sky. Whatever battle raged between the Fallen and Balziel was nearing its end. Asteriel's wings blazed with black fire, and he was losing altitude fast. Lark leaped from the bed, straining her eyes to see. Suddenly, their tumbling forms changed direction and they streaked across the battlefield.

The helicopters parted, making way for the airborne combatants. Below, the gunfire had stopped, as if both sides knew any battle but the one in the sky was irrelevant. There was barely room to fight anyway. Fey now covered the valley, Dark and Light crowding the field along with humans and the mercenaries from the mountain. It was as if every creature had fled from the Dark Fey realm and they were all milling before the gate.

The Fallen dragged Balziel before the portal, hovering high in the air. Even at a distance, Lark could tell both opponents were exhausted—they were slowing, movements jerky even if their blows were still powerful beyond mortal comprehension. Balziel seemed to engulf the Fallen in darkness, strangling him in dark flames. For a terrible instant, the blue light that surrounded Asteriel winked out. Lark dragged in a horrified breath, but in the next beat the Fallen was free again, tossing Balziel toward the portal. The demon flew, a ball of black, ragged flame.

The moment Balziel hit the portal's mouth, it set off every ward in the spell that bound the gates. Ancient fey magic sprang into action. He passed through, but the air began to thrum with warning. Then Asteriel threw something that flashed gold, and a word of power roared over the scene. *"Fialo!"*

The wedding ring, Lark thought. *Haven's spell to imprison the Dark Fey.* Except now it was going to do more than close the gates. Lightning forked from the lip of the portal, smashing into the earth. A brilliant ruby light sparked, flooding the portal with a bloody glow that seemed to harden to a transparent shield. Through it, the collapsing world was visible. Trees heaved, toppling, rotting, sprouting and toppling again in the space between one breath and the next. The meadow of dead grass sucked down into the earth, and the mud folded in on itself, seeming to accordion out of existence. What was left of the castle tumbled, then dissolved beneath a melting sky.

The red haze grew brighter and brighter, blotting out Lark's sight of the Dark Fey realm. The ground began to tremble, drawing cries of fear from the watching crowd. The dragon wrapped its tail around Lark's ankle.

And then Balziel made his bid for escape from the collapsing realm. The portal bulged toward them as his ragged black form pressed against it, straining against the magic shield. White streaks of fire began to flare, as if splits were forming where Balziel pushed the hardest. Lark heard herself chanting, "No, no, no," beneath her breath, as if words alone could bolster the ancient spells.

Asteriel raised his hand again, the fierce power of the Fallen pouring into the gates. She felt the magic begin to build, like the pressure before a sneeze. It wasn't enough. The cracks in the shield grew wider, and one paw of black flames poked through. The Fallen dived, bracing the shield with pure physical force to keep the demon in.

And then the pressure in Lark's ears popped as a blast of white split the sky in a final explosion of magic. Shrieks of pain and joy rang through the valley in echoing waves. Lark grabbed the bedpost, needing an anchor to cling to.

The portal was gone. Balziel was gone. The Dark Queen's prison realm was no more.

Neither was her fallen angel.

Chapter 34

It was not long after the portal collapsed that Prince Kyle found them. He was disheveled and had a rifle slung across his back, as if he'd been fighting. His gaze first went to Amelie, who sighed in her sleep, then to the dragon, and then to Lark. Kyle blinked once, swallowing. "You look hurt."

Lark cradled her arm. Any movement seemed to be a very bad idea, and she was barely keeping the agony at bay. "I'll live," she said, not entirely convinced. The physical pain was the least of her wounds, and she was too numb to say anything about Jack. Not yet. If she spoke of him, she would shatter to pieces.

"Are you all right?" she asked instead.

Kyle wiped a hand across his forehead. "I'm the lucky one in all this. I might have been in charge of a war, but once the queen died, the Dark Fey realm started collapsing. Nothing changes the game like whole acres of forest suddenly winking out of existence. The Light Fey have been rounding up the survivors on both sides and riding like the devil to get them to this side of the gates. We think everyone escaped before the portal collapsed."

Kyle's last words trailed off, as if the prince in him was fading and the lover taking the helm. He knelt by the bedside, stroking Amelie's dark hair. "Why is she asleep?"

"The princess is under the effects of a spell."

He blinked quickly. "How do we break it?"

Lark didn't want to give him false hope. Sleeping spells were tricky at the best of times, and who knew what twisted version Selena had used. But if there was a time and place for the traditional cures, this was it.

"You could try kissing her," she suggested. "You are a prince after all."

Kyle looked dubious. "Does that really work?"

"I'll tell you what. If it does, I'll be your child's fairy godmother."

One corner of his mouth twitched up, but he didn't take time to reply. Instead, Kyle cupped Amelie's cheek and put his lips to hers.

The kiss was tender, right on the border between chaste and seductive. It reminded Lark too much of Jack and everything she'd just lost, and she tried to look away. Her throat ached with all the pain she couldn't afford to feel yet. Not yet. Not until she could be alone.

Still, she couldn't stop herself from snatching a peek from beneath her lashes. Kyle had been a playboy for many years, but Amelie had inspired a deep and lasting love. The kiss told that story, and promised a whole library of tales to come.

The dragon cooed approval as Kyle sat back on his heels. Love and worry stamped the prince's handsome face, but he remained silent and simply watched for any sign of change. Nothing happened. Lark's heart went out to him—his disappointment was almost a touchable thing.

She was just gathering words of solace when Amelie finally stirred. There was a quick breath and the princess's violet eyes flew open, apprehension furrowing her brow.

Kyle clasped her hand. "Hush, I'm here."

Amelie blinked, looking around in bewilderment. "What happened?"

"I kissed you."

"What?"

"You were enchanted." He laughed suddenly, the release

of tension plain in his flushed cheeks and dancing eyes. "Right out of a fairy tale! My kiss broke the spell."

Amelie put a hand to her mouth. "Please tell me I wasn't a frog!"

Days later, Lark found herself back at the Marcari palace.

She entered the council room to find it exactly as she had seen it last, with tapestries and ancient shields hung on the wall—but this time Jack wasn't there. Tears filled her eyes and she blinked them away, desperate not to break down during a gathering of Company agents. It wasn't easy. The harder she tried to banish Jack's face from her memory, the more fixed it became.

The ancient table stretched the room's length. However, only a few dozen seats were filled at one end. She directed her steps that way, examining the other agents. Many were familiar, but there were some who'd flown in from other countries. Perhaps a third were new to her.

This was the last of a string of encounters that day. She'd forced down her grief long enough to see her former design assistant, Bree, and rejoice in the young woman's happiness over her career and son and loving bond with Mark Winspear. Before that, Lark had seen Haven reunited with his daughter Lexie. It would be a long time before the fey would be well again, but he would live. Those had been happy occasions. This gathering promised to be harder.

The remaining Horsemen were already there, clustered near the head of the table. The largest chair, almost a throne, remained empty. That was where the Company's commander usually sat—but he was confirmed dead. *What piece of information prompted you to call Jack that night?* she wondered. Although they all knew where the story ended, some pieces would always remain a mystery.

Lark took her seat, cradling her bandaged arm. Across from her sat Sam Ralston and Mark Winspear, both of whom were fully recovered. Faran Kenyon was back in human form but still looked exhausted. An ugly scar ringed his neck from the silver collar. There was another figure at the table—one that made Lark look twice. "Uncle Soran?"

"Niece." His dark eyes, so like hers, held her in a gaze filled with pride. "I am glad to see you are well. I am here on behalf of the Light Court." And for once—for the first time—he awarded her the same satisfied smile he gave to his warrior sons.

"Welcome to you all," Sam Ralston said, breaking into her thoughts. "In the absence of any other authority, I'll start this meeting by saying the handoff from the Marcari police to our own people is complete. We owe Captain Valois a debt of gratitude for his expert work on the investigation into the destruction of the Company headquarters. Needless to say, there is still much to be done, but we are much closer to a formal identification of all the victims."

Absolute silence fell in the room, as if no one wanted to break the solemn mood. Lark closed her eyes, overwhelmed with the need to be anywhere else, anywhere there was a little less grief.

Ralston cleared his throat. "However, I have word regarding the mountain stronghold. Thanks to Prince Kyle's efforts, and especially his personal leadership, the mercenaries are in custody. An examination of the stronghold will be conducted prior to dismantling the facility. A preliminary report should be ready by the end of the week."

Winspear sat forward next, folding his hands on the table. "With regard to seizing the stronghold and the battle in general, naturally there were casualties on both sides. However, it could have been much, much worse. The real concern is dealing with the fate of the remaining Dark Fey. They are, in effect, refugees."

"I can speak to that," said Soran. "They are leaderless now that the Dark Queen and the Blackthorns are dead. Most are so grateful to be free of the gates and of their former masters, they will agree to any terms."

"Can we trust them?" Ralston asked.

"Their oaths are binding," Lark put in. "It is always the wording that counts."

Soran sat back, folding his arms. "Quite correct. Any among them who will not swear solemn fealty to the prince and princess can take their chances with my knights. I do not blame Selena's subjects for following their queen, but I recommend the nobles be watched with great care."

The room fell silent. "Do we have enough resources for long-term peacekeeping?" Winspear asked at last. "We lost a lot of agents when Headquarters was destroyed."

"The Light Fey will send recruits to the Company," Soran said at once. "It's time we rejoin the rest of the world. We have been too isolated these past years."

Lark was astonished. "When was that decided?"

Soran gave her a sidelong gaze. "At the same council that decided your lack of obedience is deplorable."

Lark felt a flush creep up her cheeks. So the Light Court had heard about the Dark Fey healing spell.

"However," her uncle continued, "your courage is an example our warriors demand to follow. Many are demanding permission to join the Company. They claim that working with other races has made you a superior fey."

It was impossible to know how to answer. Lark had always wanted her uncle's approval, but she'd had no practice in accepting his praise. Her throat ached with everything she yearned to say to her uncle—about pride and friendship and heartbreak and what it meant to be part of the wider world. She didn't know where to begin.

It would have to wait. Soran looked around the table, measuring every agent with a considering gaze. "Events have given the Light Court a second chance. It's up to us to see that it lasts."

Lark swallowed. Amelie would be queen and the Light Fey had ended their isolation. At last, her people were out of danger. All her life, Lark had been dedicated to their cause, and now she felt that responsibility slipping from her like a huge weight. Maybe she could finally find a life of her own.

"There is one other thing," said Ralston. "Not that I'm big on administration, but we need to put some command structure in place until we can hold an election to replace the leadership of the Company."

Kenyon dropped his gaze to the table and said what they all were thinking. "Not yet. Not today. The next commander should have been Jack."

Ice squeezed around Lark's heart. *I could find a life of my own, but it won't be the one I dreamed of.*

After that, no one had the heart to go on. Kenyon's words haunted Lark as the meeting broke up, and she returned to the rooms Prince Kyle had assigned her close to the royal apartments. She kicked off her shoes at the door and began fumbling with her suit jacket. Her arm was still too sore for even the most ordinary tasks—though she had no plans to try another Dark Fey spell to speed recovery.

Hands slid over her shoulders and eased the jacket off her arms. Lark froze, pulse suddenly racing with surprise and disbelief. She spun to see Jack neatly folding the garment over the back of a chair. Her mind skidded, unable to find traction.

"Hello, Lark," he said.

"You did it again!" she cried. "You let us think you were dead. That's a *horrible* thing to do." And then she clapped a hand over her mouth. "I'm sorry."

He looked as though he'd been to hell and back. The wings were gone and he was wearing clean clothes, but his face was haggard. He sank down onto the couch, his hands dangling loosely between his knees. "I did not have the strength to face the others just yet. I became disoriented when the portal was destroyed. It took me some time to get back."

She wasn't sure where he was getting back from, and she

was afraid to ask. "You're here," she whispered. "Thank the fates, I dared not hope for so much."

"I am," he said, although he didn't sound completely convinced of the fact.

Now that the first shock had passed, Lark studied him more closely. His eyes were the same icy blue she'd always known, but starlight lurked just beneath the surface. "Who am I speaking to," she asked, "Asteriel or Jack?"

He rose and paced, prowling as gracefully as a tiger. "Both. Neither. The magic that closed the gates and destroyed Balziel changed everything."

"What does that mean?"

"There's no split between us anymore." He stopped, his hand clenching. "I am a vampire, easily destroyed, and I have no force that compels me to redemption except my own conscience."

Lark very nearly laughed. "That's how most of us live."

He wheeled on her, eyes flashing with sudden temper that faded almost at once. "But I am one of the Fallen. I… I still have much to learn."

"And you saved us all," she said gently. Lark approached him slowly, silent until she stood close enough to reach up and smooth his collar. His body was warmer than she was used to, almost human hot. Perhaps Jack was still physically a vampire, but that wasn't all he was. "You're afraid of being taken over by evil, but you're the best man I know. Trust yourself."

"How can I?" His head bowed, his brilliant eyes shadowed by sadness. "When I came back from the Crusades, I had Asteriel's fortune to do good works. The task seemed so simple, until I was killed and my brothers went to war over the treasure. Think of the hundreds of years of feuding and death visited on Marcari and Vidon because I brought that treasure home. If I had died in the Holy Land, none of this, not even the kidnapping, would have happened."

She shook her head slowly, drawing him down to the couch. "You didn't murder yourself. You can't be responsible for your brothers' actions."

He sat, but he didn't relax. Every muscle seemed coiled with painful tension. "But that's what being Fallen means. Everything I touch is corrupted. I became a demon."

Lark understood what he was saying, but he was wrong. "Maybe that was true once, but not now. I saw you face Balziel. You were every bit an avenging angel."

His mouth quirked in a bitter smile. "I'm no angel, Lark. I haven't been for a very, very long time."

"But you saved us. You fought for us out of love."

"Yes." He closed his eyes. "Jack knew how to protect. He taught me much."

Lark saw her words had struck home, and she seized on it. "You learned those lessons. Demons don't sacrifice for the greater good. Demons don't risk their lives for their captive friends. Demons don't save delinquent werewolves from a life of crime. Demons don't care."

She took his hands, squeezing them until he looked up at her. His eyes were wild with a flicker of hope. *There has to be hope, especially for someone like him.* She couldn't live in this world any other way.

"I know you, Jack. You're the one who has everyone's back, plain and simple."

"I want to believe that."

"Know it. When I raised that knife in the tower and set it alight, I knew you would come. I gambled my life on you, and you saved me."

Her words were magic far beyond any spell. He relaxed, the tension leaving his shoulders. All at once he seemed lighter—steadier and more solid—though he had not so much as moved a muscle.

Lark didn't move, not wanting to break the unfamiliar peace. But finally, his hands moved to clasp hers. In another moment, they were standing again, his body so close they touched.

"You're wise in ways not even a long life can grant. You see with your heart." He cupped her face in his hands and kissed her, drinking her in as surely as if he had pierced her vein. She arched into him, rising up on her toes to get the best angle. When he broke the kiss, releasing her, neither of them moved for the longest moment. His mood had shifted, a fresh intensity taking over. And it was focused on her. Lark could feel they were standing on the precipice of a new partnership, and she felt suddenly painfully shy.

"I don't want to be without you again," she said, and then turned away, stepping out of the circle of his arms. Her face was hot and she needed a moment to hide. It was ridiculous—they had been together many times before, but it had never been quite like this. Maybe it was because Jack was different now, but suddenly the future felt weighted and serious, with their tomorrows hanging in the balance. All at once, she was afraid.

"It's late and I'm tired," she said, even though neither was true.

"Shall we go to bed?"

She jumped. He'd slipped up behind her, vampire quiet. Now he reached around her middle, his fingers deftly undoing the buttons of her blouse, one by one. The tiny disks of pearl betrayed her, giving way to him in an instant. Then he slid the silk from her shoulders, tossing it to the side. With a rumble of triumph, he planted a kiss on one shoulder.

With that casual touch of his lips, she was lost.

Clothes fell, a piece at a time, with unhurried ritual. Just days ago, Lark had hidden in his bathrobe, reluctant to share so much as a glimpse of skin, but now it was different. She had no more secrets. He was no longer split in two. There was a chance for trust between them again. All at once, with so much less of her energy spent guarding herself, she had the leisure to discover him anew.

She took his hand in hers, pressing a kiss to his palm. Jack's hands were always calloused—she guessed it had been from holding a sword when he had been alive, and the rough skin had never quite faded. Responding to her kiss, his fingers curled around hers, gentle despite his incredible strength. He pulled her against him, her back to his chest, and cupped his hands around her breasts. It was a gesture of simple possession, of celebration.

But now his fingers grew clever with the delicacy of a safecracker. Lark closed her eyes, shivering as he played and squeezed. She sucked in her breath, trying to steady herself so he would not end the game too soon. As her pulse quickened, the throbbing of her blood made her burned forearm ache beneath its bandages, but the pain only danced with her pleasure, making both more deliciously acute.

He turned her around, wringing a protest from her until he took a nipple in his mouth, bringing one, then the other, to perfect peaks. Lark pulled away, taking his hand and drawing him to the bed. It was almost a dance move, both moving with one mind. She fell backward onto the soft mattress, crooking a knee up as he hitched himself forward to join her.

Their bodies brushed, skin to skin, and anticipation brought gooseflesh trickling down her limbs. His hand traveled up her calf, as slowly as if he was memorizing the curve of it. Lark closed her eyes, finding it almost impossible that his touch there, cupping her ankle, could feel erotic, but it did. His lips brushed her knee, then those amazing fingers worked their way up her inner thigh with a feather-light touch, teasing, but never quite promising. Lark closed her eyes, pressing her head back into the mattress, loving and hating how immortals took their time.

And then his mouth was there, too, fangs and tongue sliding against her most intimate parts. Gasping, Lark froze, pressure building inside her—but she dared not move. Not with razor-sharp teeth right *there*. And yet the urge to squirm and buck was rising as Jack delivered everything she wanted in a mind-blowing way. "Let me move," she begged. "Please."

His response made her fingers dig into the coverlet as she shuddered, muscles straining, and she cursed his delectable torture. He kissed and sucked, proving centuries of practice made pretty damned perfect. When he finally rose, sliding his body up hers until their lips met, she could taste herself on his mouth. Then his fingers slid to exactly the right spot, and she came again, finally able to grind and rub where it felt so good.

After that, he slid easily between her thighs, filling her to the edge of discomfort before he withdrew again slowly. Lark moved under him, admiring the curves and valleys of his torso. Shadows played across the muscular ridges as he worked, a living sculpture bent to the task of her pleasure. Her palms braced against the heavy bulk of his shoulders, demonfire crackling between her fingers and the silk of his skin. The glowing, brilliant creature from the tower was there in her arms—tender and protective, a guardian of the night. He cradled her against him as if she were the one thing in the universe he cherished.

He loved. Demons didn't love.

She wanted to speak, to say something, but words slipped away as the rhythm changed between them, hitting a new stride of urgency. Suddenly all thoughts were lost beneath a wave of need as he grasped her hips, holding her still, stroke after deep, thorough stroke.

Lark dissolved, helpless and gasping, giving herself to the wildness of desire—and then so did Jack. Light flared from him, enfolding them both in a corona of energy so powerful, Lark squeezed her eyes shut. Jack, a vampire, blazed like the sun. She had wanted him to give up his iron control—and now he had. As she trusted him, at last he trusted her.

And what he revealed was magnificent. Heat kissed her face, and she turned to it as instinctively as a flower, knowing it was life and joy and blessing.

Chapter 35

"Let me get this straight," said Kenyon the next day. "You're a Crusader and a fallen angel blenderized into a supervampire who can sprout wings and wrestle demons from the pit?"

"Pretty much," Jack replied.

"Cool. Is there an action figure?"

The Horsemen sat in the tiny living room of Jack's secret apartment in the castle. With four large men, it was very crowded, but nobody cared. It was the first time they'd sat down together since Jack's supposed death in a fiery car crash.

"Does that mean you won't stake me?" Jack said, just a tiny bit worried. "Technically, I'm some kind of demon."

"Stake you?" Winspear shrugged, his face solemn as the grave. "Worse. You get to be the new commander."

The mood slipped a moment. They had come from a teleconference with the heads of the branches of the Company—Los Angeles, London, Mumbai and Tokyo, among others. All agreed the Company should be restored in Marcari, but newer divisions wanted more freedom to run their own affairs. If Jack became commander, he would be ushering in a new age for *La Compagnie des Morts*. And in the meantime, there was a funeral to plan for all those who had been lost.

Ralston slapped Jack on the back, bringing him back to the present. "I've kinda let the paperwork slide. You'll catch up eventually."

Paperwork. Ugh. "If you're threatening me with key performance indicator reports, I think the bromance is dead."

Kenyon crossed his ankles and cracked a beer. "Seriously, dude. We need you."

Jack smiled, but there was a cold feeling in his chest. He felt the bonds of love and friendship among the Horsemen and their mates. They had accepted him back, even knowing what he was. He wanted to reach for that warmth with both hands, but something held him back. *I'm a demon. They deserve better.*

"I'll think about it," he said lightly. "First, we've got a bridal apocalypse to get through."

It was Valentine's Day. Jack sat in the cathedral, every nerve on high alert, because today was the royal wedding. Two kingdoms would be united, a war ended, a new era begun. After so much bloodshed and drama, even Jack was a little amazed that it was finally going to happen.

But it was happening because, bloody and battered, the *La Compagnie des Morts* and its allies had risen to the occasion. So had the prince and princess and the humans who loved them, the fey and their magic and even one very small dragon who was now everyone's favorite pet. The power of love worked in mysterious ways.

The Horsemen were scattered through the pews. Kenyon was on the other side of the aisle, looking as keyed up as Jack felt. Winspear and Ralston were keeping an eye on the royal couple. Company security had arrived from around the globe and, along with the Light Fey, had the route between the palace and the marriage altar locked down tight.

The crowds were even thicker than anyone had anticipated. After the battle at the gate, the proverbial cat was out of the bag about the supernatural. Amelie was the ideal fairy princess bride, complete with her own prince and a wicked queen to boot. The press was experiencing a paparazzigasm and a handful of old-school Vidonese were sure it was the end of days.

Lark slid into the seat beside Jack. She was wearing one of her own designs, a discreetly sparkly gown in flesh tones that made Jack's mouth water. Like all the women in the cathedral, she wore a hat, though hers was elegantly simple compared to most.

"How's it going?" Jack asked.

Lark gave a smirk. "Your niece has everything well in hand. I think Chloe is about to become the most famous wedding planner in history. Sam Ralston is marrying a woman who would make a competent general in a pinch."

Jack couldn't stifle a grin. His reunion with Chloe had been one of the highlights since his return. "I knew I raised her right."

"You did," Lark replied. "And she's got Bree and Lexie to help. We don't need to worry about the wedding itself. It's going to be exquisite. Of course Kyle had to find a new ring after you tossed the first one into the gaping maw of a collapsing dimension."

"I'm sure he found something in the treasury."

"He went to a proper jeweler. You can't blame him for wanting something without magical baggage."

"Kids these days," Jack muttered. "No stomach for a little curse here and there."

They stopped talking as Crown Prince Kyle and his groomsmen approached the altar. Kyle was wearing the uniform of Vidon, gold and silver glittering against the dark green of his coat. He looked a trifle pale, as if the enormity of the day was hitting home.

And then there was a commotion and every head turned. Princess Amelie was there on King Renault's arm, wearing the magnificent diamond-spangled dress that had nearly cost both Lark and Jack their lives. For an instant, Jack remembered Lark taking the gown from her armoire in New York and making him promise to get it safely out of her studio. This moment made everything worth the trouble.

Jack was no dressmaker, but he understood female beauty. The gown fit tight to Amelie's knees and then flared out in a froth of lace, as if the princess were actually Venus rising from the ocean on a cushion of sea foam. But the princess herself, with her violet eyes and long, loose dark hair, was what everyone saw. A hushed murmur ran through the crowd.

Jack glanced at Kyle. He looked poleaxed, as if he was indeed about to wed a goddess. Perhaps he was. After all, every woman had a spark of the divine, didn't she?

The choir in the galleries rose with a rustle of robes, and suddenly there was music.

"There is magic in a wedding, especially a royal one. Every fey in the room felt it, both Light and Dark," said Lark, long after the last guest had gone home. "It was everything we'd hoped for."

"I'm glad," said Jack, deciding she looked spectacular with the sunrise behind her. Larks were morning birds after all.

They were on one of the upper balconies of the palace, enjoying a breath of salt air off the Mediterranean. The reception room behind them was deserted, most of the dishes and leftover food cleared away. It had been a long day and a longer ceremony, and nobody had relaxed until the future king and queen had been safely packed off to their undisclosed honeymoon location, which Jack knew was a ski holiday in the Colorado Rockies.

And while all that was wonderful, Jack was much more fascinated by the woman before him. The dress was clinging in all the right places, and he was thinking a successful mission deserved a reward—preferably one they could share. He eased closer, dispensing with some of the unnecessary space between them.

"Are you listening, Jack?"

"Sure." He mentally groped for something to add. "Even the humans made a fuss about it being Valentine's Day."

"And they're not wrong. All those hearts and doves are symbolic. If everyone thinks they're a good omen, they are."

He made an agreeable noise as he slid his arms around her, careful of her bandaged arm. He could tell that after a long day, it was bothering her. "Are you going to get Winspear to check that tomorrow?"

"Yes. He said it will leave a scar."

"And?"

"I'm going to let it." She gave an elegant shrug of one shoulder. "Speaking of symbolism, I want a memento of that particular trial by fire. I'd like to think of it as a rite of passage."

"It was a triumph."

"And also a perfect reminder about secrets and their consequences." She smoothed his lapels. "And speaking of responsibilities—"

"I thought we were speaking of symbolism."

She turned her large, dark eyes up at his. "You really need to take that job as commander of the Company. You know you can do an amazing job. Headquarters has been through a lot, and the men need a hero right now."

Her expression was perfectly serious. Jack felt a surge of confidence. *I'm a demon, and maybe they do deserve better, but you make me think I can do this anyway.* "Maybe. On one condition."

She waited, her hands still resting on his chest. She looked delicate, but he didn't let that fool him. She was strong in all the ways that mattered. "Which is?"

"I want you with me."

Her eyebrow crooked. "This is your condition?"

"It's a request. Consider it a plea."

"Are you thinking side-by-side offices or…?" She trailed off, a teasing note slipping into her voice.

He pulled her close enough he heard the whisper of her dress against his suit. "Side by side sounds as if there's a wall in between. No walls. Never again."

Her arms draped around his neck, the gesture casual but with a hint of implicit seduction. "I hope I at least get a desk, or I'll have to sit in your lap. And *that* could interfere with paperwork."

Paperwork. Ugh. "Say yes."

"To being your personal assistant?"

"Don't be ridiculous. You're an agent."

"Then, what am I agreeing to?"

He didn't answer, but she seemed to understand because her arms slipped around his waist, returning the embrace. Jack buried his face in her hair, smelling the sweet, wild perfume that was Lark's own scent. He kissed her temple, and then took her mouth when she tilted her face up to his. Something shifted in his heart, and a honeyed warmth sprang up, as if something precious had come to life at the seat of his soul.

"I love you," he said.

They were the most important words he had said in nearly a thousand years, and it was the first time he had said them with his whole being. He felt the shift again, a pain so sharp, so exquisite, that it wasn't true pain at all, but ecstasy. And he knew he would do anything at all for this brilliant, beautiful creature.

And with that emotion, he knew everything had changed forever.

Demons didn't love, but he did. All of him. He wasn't a human, or a Fallen, or an angel anymore, but a whole being made up of dark and light—fallible, vulnerable and blessed with his share of happiness. Humility and sacrifice had played a large part in his redemption, but so had learning simple human affection.

"I love you," he said again, putting all his soul into his words.

It wouldn't be the last time he said it, not to this woman. Everything of worth in all the universes began with love. Perhaps a bit of paradise had been returned to him.

Lark began to weep, but her eyes were bright with joy. "I love you, Jack."

They kissed again—what else could they do?—and he felt it down to his toes. He worked his lips along her jawline, seeking out the soft spot just under her ear. She was fey and powerful, but oh-so-fragile at the same time. He wanted to wrap her inside his jacket and keep her next to his heart for safekeeping.

"Be my wife." He grinned, but his stomach tightened with trepidation. "My everything."

"Jack!" Her eyes had gone wide with surprise.

Please say yes!

She considered him for a long moment. Jack started to sweat. Even after nine centuries, he didn't know vampires could do that. "But you never forgave me," she said, suddenly solemn.

Jack closed his eyes, as close to trembling as a being like him could get. "First, I had to forgive myself for being what I am. On some level I believed I deserved to be betrayed."

"Oh, Jack."

"You hurt me, and sometimes I was less than kind to you," he said. "But what changed everything was that you never stopped caring for me. Eventually, I learned to forgive myself because you always forgave me first. In return, I could step back and understand the terrible position you were in. That left the door open for change. As long as we still cared, we could make things better."

He opened his eyes, holding her rich, brown gaze as he went on. "Of course I forgive you. And I thank you for teaching me what it means to love."

Tears clung to her dark lashes. "Then, yes, I would be pleased to marry you."

A breathless pause followed while Jack absorbed her words. *Married. After so long, I'm going to have someone to call my own.*

Then Lark winked, her fey sense of mischief chasing solemnity away. "After all, War, Plague and Famine all found true love. I can't leave Death loitering about in want of a wife. The only thing is, I'd kind of like a flashy code name, too. It doesn't seem fair not to get one."

With a burst of joy, he reached down, sweeping her up in his arms. She squeaked in surprise, and he laughed. He couldn't help it. He was ridiculously, enormously happy. He jumped up on the stone railing of the balcony, balancing with her in his arms.

"What are you doing?" she protested.

"I have a very nice castle in the district of Derrondine," he said. "I think it's time to pay it a visit. Then maybe that B and B with the rose garden in Connecticut. It's time we went back."

Lark glanced down, her face going a little green. "Tell me you're not going to fly all the way to the mountains."

"I have a vintage Alfa Romeo," Jack said drily. "This is the shortcut to the parking lot."

Lark's smile was relieved. "Then, take me home," she said in a voice just short of a purr.

But Jack paused on the rail a moment longer, his blue eyes for once as soft as April skies. "You want a name. There's one from the myth of Pandora that would suit you. After all the evils had been let loose, there was a spirit who remained to keep beauty in the beleaguered world."

She frowned. "Who was that?"

"Hope," he said, without any hesitation. "You are Hope."
And with that, he leaped into the dawn.

* * * * *

REQUEST YOUR FREE BOOKS!
2 FREE NOVELS PLUS 2 FREE GIFTS!

H HARLEQUIN®

I N T R I G U E

BREATHTAKING ROMANTIC SUSPENSE

YES! Please send me 2 FREE Harlequin® Intrigue novels and my 2 FREE gifts (gifts are worth about $10). After receiving them, if I don't wish to receive any more books, I can return the shipping statement marked "cancel." If I don't cancel, I will receive 6 brand-new novels every month and be billed just $4.74 per book in the U.S. or $5.49 per book in Canada. That's a savings of at least 12% off the cover price! It's quite a bargain! Shipping and handling is just 50¢ per book in the U.S. and 75¢ per book in Canada.* I understand that accepting the 2 free books and gifts places me under no obligation to buy anything. I can always return a shipment and cancel at any time. Even if I never buy another book, the two free books and gifts are mine to keep forever.

182/382 HDN GH3D

Name	(PLEASE PRINT)	

Address		Apt. #

City	State/Prov.	Zip/Postal Code

Signature (if under 18, a parent or guardian must sign)

Mail to the **Reader Service:**
IN U.S.A.: P.O. Box 1867, Buffalo, NY 14240-1867
IN CANADA: P.O. Box 609, Fort Erie, Ontario L2A 5X3
**Are you a subscriber to Harlequin® Intrigue books
and want to receive the larger-print edition?
Call 1-800-873-8635 or visit www.ReaderService.com.**

* Terms and prices subject to change without notice. Prices do not include applicable taxes. Sales tax applicable in N.Y. Canadian residents will be charged applicable taxes. Offer not valid in Quebec. This offer is limited to one order per household. Not valid for current subscribers to Harlequin Intrigue books. All orders subject to credit approval. Credit or debit balances in a customer's account(s) may be offset by any other outstanding balance owed by or to the customer. Please allow 4 to 6 weeks for delivery. Offer available while quantities last.

Your Privacy—The Reader Service is committed to protecting your privacy. Our Privacy Policy is available online at www.ReaderService.com or upon request from the Reader Service.

We make a portion of our mailing list available to reputable third parties that offer products we believe may interest you. If you prefer that we not exchange your name with third parties, or if you wish to clarify or modify your communication preferences, please visit us at www.ReaderService.com/consumerschoice or write to us at Reader Service Preference Service, P.O. Box 9062, Buffalo, NY 14240-9062. Include your complete name and address.

HI15

REQUEST YOUR FREE BOOKS!
2 FREE NOVELS PLUS 2 FREE GIFTS!

ROMANTIC suspense

Sparked by danger, fueled by passion

YES! Please send me 2 FREE Harlequin® Romantic Suspense novels and my 2 FREE gifts (gifts are worth about \$10). After receiving them, if I don't wish to receive any more books, I can return the shipping statement marked "cancel." If I don't cancel, I will receive 4 brand-new novels every month and be billed just \$4.74 per book in the U.S. or \$5.49 per book in Canada. That's a savings of at least 12% off the cover price! It's quite a bargain! Shipping and handling is just 50¢ per book in the U.S. and 75¢ per book in Canada.* I understand that accepting the 2 free books and gifts places me under no obligation to buy anything. I can always return a shipment and cancel at any time. Even if I never buy another book, the two free books and gifts are mine to keep forever.

240/340 HDN GH3P

Name	(PLEASE PRINT)	
Address		Apt. #
City	State/Prov.	Zip/Postal Code

Signature (if under 18, a parent or guardian must sign)

Mail to the **Reader Service:**
IN U.S.A.: P.O. Box 1867, Buffalo, NY 14240-1867
IN CANADA: P.O. Box 609, Fort Erie, Ontario L2A 5X3

Want to try two free books from another line?
Call 1-800-873-8635 or visit www.ReaderService.com.

* Terms and prices subject to change without notice. Prices do not include applicable taxes. Sales tax applicable in N.Y. Canadian residents will be charged applicable taxes. Offer not valid in Quebec. This offer is limited to one order per household. Not valid for current subscribers to Harlequin Romantic Suspense books. All orders subject to credit approval. Credit or debit balances in a customer's account(s) may be offset by any other outstanding balance owed by or to the customer. Please allow 4 to 6 weeks for delivery. Offer available while quantities last.

Your Privacy—The Reader Service is committed to protecting your privacy. Our Privacy Policy is available online at www.ReaderService.com or upon request from the Reader Service.

We make a portion of our mailing list available to reputable third parties that offer products we believe may interest you. If you prefer that we not exchange your name with third parties, or if you wish to clarify or modify your communication preferences, please visit us at www.ReaderService.com/consumerschoice or write to us at Reader Service Preference Service, P.O. Box 9062, Buffalo, NY 14240-9062. Include your complete name and address.

HRS15

REQUEST YOUR FREE BOOKS!

2 FREE NOVELS
FROM THE SUSPENSE COLLECTION
PLUS 2 FREE GIFTS!

YES! Please send me 2 FREE novels from the Suspense Collection and my 2 FREE gifts (gifts are worth about $10). After receiving them, if I don't wish to receive any more books, I can return the shipping statement marked "cancel." If I don't cancel, I will receive 4 brand-new novels every month and be billed just $6.49 per book in the U.S. or $6.99 per book in Canada. That's a savings of at least 19% off the cover price. It's quite a bargain! Shipping and handling is just 50¢ per book in the U.S. and 75¢ per book in Canada.* I understand that accepting the 2 free books and gifts places me under no obligation to buy anything. I can always return a shipment and cancel at any time. Even if I never buy another book, the two free books and gifts are mine to keep forever.

191/391 MDN GH4Z

Name   (PLEASE PRINT)

Address   Apt. #

City   State/Prov.   Zip/Postal Code

Signature (if under 18, a parent or guardian must sign)

Mail to the Reader Service:
IN U.S.A.: P.O. Box 1867, Buffalo, NY 14240-1867
IN CANADA: P.O. Box 609, Fort Erie, Ontario L2A 5X3

Want to try two free books from another line?
Call 1-800-873-8635 or visit www.ReaderService.com.

* Terms and prices subject to change without notice. Prices do not include applicable taxes. Sales tax applicable in N.Y. Canadian residents will be charged applicable taxes. Offer not valid in Quebec. This offer is limited to one order per household. Not valid for current subscribers to the Suspense Collection or the Romance/Suspense Collection. All orders subject to credit approval. Credit or debit balances in a customer's account(s) may be offset by any other outstanding balance owed by or to the customer. Please allow 4 to 6 weeks for delivery. Offer available while quantities last.

Your Privacy—The Reader Service is committed to protecting your privacy. Our Privacy Policy is available online at www.ReaderService.com or upon request from the Reader Service.

We make a portion of our mailing list available to reputable third parties that offer products we believe may interest you. If you prefer that we not exchange your name with third parties, or if you wish to clarify or modify your communication preferences, please visit us at www.ReaderService.com/consumerchoice or write to us at Reader Service Preference Service, P.O. Box 9062, Buffalo, NY 14240-9062. Include your complete name and address.

SUS15